Saving Abel

Rocker Series

Gina Whitney

This is a work of fiction. Names, characters, places, and incidents either are the product of the author's imagination or are used fictitiously, and any resemblance to actual persons, living or dead, business establishments, events, or locales is entirely coincidental.

Saving Abel — Gina Whitney

Text copyright © 2014 Gina Whitney

Edited by: Elizabeth Llewellyn

Formatting: E-BookBuilders

Books by Gina

Blood Ties

Beautiful Lies

Saving Abel

Forgiving Gia

Avenging Us

Luca

The Power of A Woman

Contents

You can close your eyes to what you don't want to see, but you can't close your eyes to the things you don't want to feel.

—*Unknown*

Abel's Dungeon

Dream

On ecru initialed paper, the understanding was brutally clear … You're to be *blindfolded* and waiting on your *knees* for your master. I reread it a couple of times, my hands shaking with both fear of the unknown and the excitement of being delivered to the brink of aching pleasure. Man, I was fucked!

I folded the note in half, perfectly seaming the edges while I wondered if I had bitten off more than I could chew. The thoughts swirled cyclonically in my head, causing a fluttering in my stomach to mount to vomit worthy levels, as I picked up the Hermes scarf. I gently ran it along my cheek before breathing in his alpha scent. *Him.* My eyes closed on their own accord, heart beating in concert with my pussy. My clit charged and already primed with wetness. My inner *demon-ess* was scratching the surface of my psyche, relentlessly thrashing against its confinement.

Twirling around in a sexual dreamlike state, my eyes took in floor-to-ceiling windows, the lush, red velvet drapes pulled back. Gasping heavily, I held my hand over my heart to keep the fucker in there. Was he planning to take me in the open—voyeur delight? I wasn't sure how I felt about that. Then again, this was about surrendering. A place my control had no say. On the left was a free-standing bar, his guitar leaning against it. Chrystal decanters lined the top. Amber colored courage called out to my parched throat, begging, needing something to quell the tremors that plagued my body. I couldn't. Could I? Or was that breaking the rules? I couldn't afford to piss him off, nor did I want to. I wanted to please him, to hand over the keys to my soul for him to take up occupancy. I needed to take purchase of the prime piece of real-estate—his heart. Old demons plagued my thoughts with their clever mind tricks, fighting their way to the surface—sneering that I would lose the man I'd come to love because of my deceitful heart. The mother of all motherfucking Karma was going to bite my ass—hard. I needed to lock these incessant, nauseating thoughts where they belonged—behind a door that had no moral key and slam it shut.

Looking to the left, I saw that a fire raged stunningly in a pastoral styled fireplace. Above, an erotic portrait of Abel. It was done in simple black and white. In one hand, he held a set of handcuffs. In the other, a red scarf—the exact red scarf I now held in my hand. Crackling embers radiated warmth to nurture my chilled body. Perfect spot! Unbuttoning my pants and blouse, I let them both pool at my feet. I then took off my bra and panties. Flames licked my skin, helping gentle the goose bumps that stepped forward across my body. Double-knotting the scarf around my head, I lowered to my knees, thankful for the plush carpet. I sent a silent thanks upward. God had no place here today. Today, I would be rejoicing, reveling, and partaking in rituals practiced by heathens. Tempering my breathing … *Namaste.* A shiver redirected my attention to the door as I searched my mind to identify its source. The squeak of the door knob stopped all thought process—all thinking. His innate maleness seeped into my pores, cocooning my skin in his alpha scent—marking my heart as *his.* Instantly, my body recognized him. An unwilling groan escaped, making my nether region clench in anticipation. He chuckled.

"Very good. I see you followed my directions flawlessly. I see that beautiful pussy is shaved bare for me. This pleases me, Gia. And you will see how much very shortly. But, are you ready for your master? If I part your folds will you be slick and hot for me?" His warm breath tickled my ear.

My mouth opened and closed a few times like a fish out of water, until I finally croaked out, "Um, yes. I, um. I believe so, Abel." Christ, why am I reduced to a stuttering adolescent? He's fucking dangerous and hot, that's why! Steeling myself, I needed to woman the fuck up and show him who I am.

Palming my chin, he spoke gruffly, "Love, when we're in this setting, I am your God, bringer of pleasure and pain." He released me, clearly awaiting a response of praise.

"Yes, Sir. I understand perfectly," I affirmed. My body chilled, knowing the moment he stepped away. The ring of the crystal decanter signaled loudly in the air. Rolling shudders had me clenching—hard. Moments ticked by at a snail's pace and I wanted to rip my hair out. My frustration grew as he took his time, leaving me in a vulnerable position. He swallowed his drink. Padding back over in my direction, he brought that delicious signature scent of his my way. It smelled of musk and something wild I couldn't put my finger on.

"I'm going to taste you now," he quantified. *What? Christ on a motherfuckin' cross!* Two thick fingers teased my clit, round and round, spreading my silky juices along my seam, preparing me for his invasion. I held my breath. What else could I do?

"You smell like you want to be fucked." He smiled appreciatively. "Breathe, Gia. Your God would like to sample you. I want to commit your taste to memory. Savor you on my tongue. Swallow your goodness," he rasped, leaning into my ear. I wanted to scream *just do it already*. His scruffy beard ran along my face, leaving his mouth against my ear. Every breath, every heartbeat, every swallow was mine. I had a front row seat to an erotic movie that I starred in.

Holding my shoulders firmly with his left hand, he roughly entered my opening. *One breath in, one long breath out.* With precision, he inserted two fingers inside me, keeping his thumb on my trigger. I ground against his palm.

"You will not come. Yet. Stay still or I'll stop," he affirmed. Well, that did it! I needed release and I needed it now. *Fuck.* Squeezing my eyes tightly, I was thankful for the blindfold. He had to see how challenging this was for me. With a final, stretching thrust, he vacated my pussy. The scent of my juices permeated the air, releasing another gush of wetness. His sucking sound ended with a loud pop, followed by a growl of approval.

"Taste." He fisted my hair, driving his fingers into my open mouth.

"Taste how sweet your pussy is?" he queried. I had the perfect opportunity to bring him to his knees. My tongue languidly snaked its way around his fingers, sucking greedily any remaining ambrosia—with my own kickass resounding pop. *Umm…* I purred my contentment.

A seismic roar rumbled its way free from his alpha chest. Oh, he was affected. Breaking dominate control momentarily, he lunged forward and fisted my hair, his tongue forcing my mouth open. Damn this *Dom!* My lungs fought for air. My hands braced against his muscled chest, alive with the vibrations from the beast tethered within—Abel. Dizziness threatened to take me under. Pulling air into my nose, I took a breath. Consuming me from the inside out, he didn't let up. Apparently, my survival was to be damned. My brain had only registered oxygen. Now I needed to return his kiss. My hands found their way up his neck into his thick hair. Grabbing a fistful of it, I pulled. He answered my call with his masterful tongue and gnashing teeth. Needing his cock in my pussy now, I reached for it, feeling its thick steeliness through his jeans. He gently removed my hands. Disappointed, I lowered my head, taking the opportunity to nourish my blood with oxygen. He forced my hands behind my back. I adjusted my position on the floor with the balls of my feet to steady myself.

"You have to earn that, babe. You haven't earned my cock yet. And he has a bigger ego than I do." He chuckled as he stood up, leaving me again. *Was he serious? His dick had an ego?*

The sound of drawers opening and closing to my left had me turning my head in that direction. My legs tingled with anticipation and lack of activity. I hoped I wasn't going to be on my knees too much longer. The snap of something caught my immediate attention. Licking my dry lips, swallowing the golf ball sized knot, I readied myself. Sweet-smelling leather assailed my senses.

"Do you know what the cat o'nine tails is, Gia?" he asked. I did some Googling before this night, so I wouldn't be ignorant to basic BDSM—knots, whips, and positions 101. I schooled myself quickly.

"Yes, Sir. A traditionally favored whip with nine separate tails," I qualified. Quirking a smile, I awaited his answer. He answered by running the tails along my breasts … down to my pussy … snapping my clit to attention. Over and over again, my body became acquainted with this new form of torture. Legs shaking, I thrust myself to an upright position, hoping this little exercise would stop this embarrassing bodily display of minor earthquakes. No such luck. My body wanted to surrender to its master. My breathing ratcheted to panic-attack levels. An explosion of epic proportions was near. *Whack!*—across my behind. *Ow!* "Fuck me!"

"Not nearly yet, sweetheart. That nice shade of red on your ass is making me hard as fuck, though," he countered. Well, that's not how I really meant it, but that's exactly what I wanted—right the fuck now. He was turned on. And that turned me on. If his lash marks on my skin do it for him, I think, then so be it.

"I want to taste you, master. It's only fair." I was practically whining: throw me a fucking bone. This BDSM shit was killing me. I'm not a patient person by nature. So I deserved a reward for the restraint I had shown. The sound of his zipper lowering caught my attention. The lava started to trickle down my legs again.

"Is this what you want, pretty girl?" He stepped up, smearing his pre-cum on my lips. I moaned embarrassingly loud.

"Yes! More!" I demanded. He presented his cock to my tongue. It stroked something unfamiliar. Was it a piercing? Bracing myself on his thick thighs, I fished for the object. Yep, he was pierced. *Fuck me.*

I expertly lavished it with my tongue, paying homage to this rock god. Maybe his cock deserved its own zip code? This was a locale I wanted to move to—like, *now*. Pushing forward, I sought his engorged bell. Licking, flickering, and tonguing at break-neck speed to the best of my ability, I made him roar. He ripped the scarf off, freeing my eyes from their prison. Sight was returned—though I couldn't see a fucking thing. Squinting, I looked up toward his beautiful face; it was twisted in agony. He needed release. His eyes sparking with warning, he looked as if his thread-like hold on reality was virtually nonexistent. A sardonic smile pulled on his lips as he continued stroking his cock. Up. Down. Up. Twist. Down. Release. Up. Twist. Down. Release. His left hand squeezed his tightened sack roughly, his eyes glistening. His tongue snaked out to wet his plump lips. His sooty-lashed eyes closed for a moment as he blew out a long breath, battling for control. I gulped—hard. Something sparkly caught my upturned eyes, bringing my gaze back to his sack.

"Like what you see, babe?" He smiled proudly. It was then I noticed his tatted dick. Whoa. His cock was a kaleidoscope of vivid colors. The body of the dragon was done in green with the underside in orange scales, running the entire length of his cock, ending with the dragon's head on his dick-head. His Apadravya shined brightly against the dragon's head, looking like it was coming out of its mouth. His *Mons* provided the backdrop for the wings. I didn't have enough

Dedication

To all my badass bitches. We don't chase
em'. We replace em'.

time at the moment to quell my fascination. He was a work of art that I intended to worship fully. I was over-stimulated visually, tilting my head awkwardly left, then right. What was *that*? I wasn't naïve. I knew there were guys who pierced the head of their dick. Shit. One was right in front of me. But all along the dragon's scaled underside were generous loops. Can't say I ever saw that or even heard of that before.

"It's called frenum loops, or Jacob's ladder, babe. The one through my head is an Apadravya. You'll be thanking me soon for it." His toothy smile made me blush at my naïveté. He took my lip-licking as a signal for further instruction in How to Suck Abel's Cock 101.

"Relax. Open real wide. Get it nice and wet," he instructed. Relaxing my gag reflex, I readied my throat for his invasion. Not only did I have to worry about his girth, but his hardware as well. My mouth was desert-dry, so I pursed my lips to conjure up enough saliva to get the job done. The wide tip of his cock made its way past my lips, netting a groan from me of appreciation for this male. I lavished the small beads of pre-come on my tongue, relishing his heady taste. *God damn.* His hooded eyes caught mine as I acquiesced. I closed my eyes and sucked his head hard with a quick swirl around his Apadravya. I spit into my palm, pumping his cock once. Twice. A throaty groan made my clit swell. I loved his male sounds. I knew I was doing this right. I wanted more. More of him. More of *that* noise. Widening my mouth even further, I took his cock deeply. Paying close attention to his Jacob's ladder with my tongue. The jingling within my mouth had me shuddering. Up. Down. Twist. Suck. Tongue. Up. Down. Twist. Suck. Gag. Up. Down. Twist. Suck. Gag. His fingers found their home deeply embedded in my scalp, the pain making my eyes mist. Licking from base to tip, I was on repeat. His eyes bore into me, watching me intently, appreciatively.

Though I didn't see him watching me, I knew he was. One final, swirling suck. I let my lips pop loudly. Making jerking sounds of wetness, I tried the impossible: to swallow *him*. Breathing through my nose, I watched. He watched. I swallowed. The thickness of his cock swelling was all the indication I needed. He was ready to blow—hard. My throat relaxed and opened to accommodate his girth further. Abel hissed his thankfulness by thrusting deeply. Once. Twice. Three times. He growled loudly, face-fucking me into oblivion. Surprising even myself, I swallowed his gift of spicy goodness, humming my appreciation to this deity. Swallowing it down and suck-tonguing his Apadravya, I inwardly smiled as I milked every last drop of elixir.

With a final groan I fell back and let the fibers of the rug absorb my fatigue. Mentally and physically, I was *wiped out.* I rubbed my fingers through the filaments, trying desperately to soothe my restless soul. At the moment, I didn't care where his was or what he was doing. His gentle fingers caressed my cheek. I closed my eyes, savoring his touch.

"Oh, babe, we're not done. Come, I'll carry you to my bedroom." He bent and scooped me up. Swaddled in his arms, I caught the look in his hooded eyes. A few long strides, and we were in his bedroom. He gently laid me on his king size bed, then stepped back.

"I'm gonna take a quick shower. Care to join?" He motioned his hand to the bathroom in invitation.

"Nah, I'm good here for now. You go. If I change my mind, I'll find you." I smiled sleepily.

He nodded and left through the en-suite. Raising myself up to my forearms, I took in his room. *So this is his room here.* Monochromatic black and white made up a majority of his palate choice, aside from his poppy-red, silk shantung comforter. Everything was simple, yet elegant. It was clear to me that Abel sought home comforts and swathed the hotel room with his possessions. I guess a life on the road was a lonely one. Cocooning myself in the lush bedding, I concluded there was no better place. And no better thing than *his* scent. Lord above, if I could bottle his essence, I'd be a wealthy chick. Grabbing his pillow, I brought it to my nose, inhaling his heady alpha scent. A groan escaped me, and my clit was beyond engorged, it needed release. *I needed to steal this pillow.*

"Enjoying yourself?" he asked, his smile reaching his eyes. I cursed inwardly. *Busted.* He abruptly reached for my legs and pulled me across the bed. *Holy shit.* His eyes were alit with mischief. He pulled until my bottom was at the end of the bed. I laid there naked and started to feel self-conscious. I turned to grab the edge of the comforter.

"Don't hide your body from me, Gia. Spread your legs for me. I want to see what's mine. I want to taste your nectar," he commands and I obey, spreading my legs. When he doesn't respond, I get anxious. There's a mirror on the wall next to the bed and I can see my reflection. What a turn on. Me watching him—us—as his eyes devoured my pussy. He removed his towel from his waist and turned to see me watching tentatively through the mirror. He grabbed hold of his thick cock, stroking and smiling as he watched me for a good long-ass minute. It was one big mind fuck—and I could barely hold my own. My blood boiled while I watched his erotic exhibition. Boy, was he a showman. He knelt down and seized both my thighs, pulling them back into a V across my chest. The image of us in the mirror is suggestive. He pressed his nose along my pussy, inhaling deeply.

"You've got such a pretty pussy, Gia. I'm a man starved for this pussy. When I'm done, I'm going to fuck you like the devil. My cock will be everything you've wished for, babe!" He winked. *Cocky motherfucker.* Holding my legs in place, he dove face-first into my pussy, pushing his tongue deep inside me—growling, devouring. The sounds of him sucking, licking, and nipping my pussy had my muscles locking up. I reached for his hair. I needed to touch him. I wanted to hold his head to my pussy until I was good and ready to let go.

"Gia, put your damn hands above your head or I will tie you to the bed," he growled. I acquiesced. I would fucking die or kill someone if he stopped. *Oh God, don't stop.*

"God has no place here, babe." His voice was demonic. Did I just say that aloud? Never lifting his face from his meal, he pushed my knees almost flush against my chest, lathering his face in my juice. *Oh, God.* His growling, biting, and sucking were sounds I would never forget. He was feral. Possessed. Using two fingers, he started finger fucked me as he sucked my clit. My legs were shaking with deep vibrations and I started to rock my hips. Twisting the comforter in my hands, I started to scream my release. He didn't stop. I barely registered the rumbling from his chest as I floated back down to earth. My eyes opened to a savage beast, leaning over to bite my inner thing. I yelped in surprise. He stood tall and proud, stoking his long, thick, massive cock; his face still glistening with my cum. Nothing registered to this alpha. He had one thing on his mind and that was sinking his gorgeous cock into my soaked pussy.

"You want this cock now, babe?" he asked through gritted teeth. Still stroking his cock, he spit in his hand. *Fucking hell.*

"Please, Abel. I want you now," I begged. I needed him now.

"Need to hear you say it, babe. Tell me you want me to sink my cock deep into you." His voice was barely audible.

The grit in his tone had me wanting to grab his dick and fuck myself with it. He was watching me closely, his control threadbare.

"Abel, fuck me with that big gorgeous cock of yours. Grind that piercing over my clit," I hissed. That did it! He couldn't wait another minute—neither could I. He teased the entrance with the head of his cock. Going agonizingly slow, he paid special attention to my clit with his Apadravya; back and forth, round and round. The pressure mounted. I couldn't handle another second of the exquisite torture. I leaned forward and grabbed his cock—hard.

"Stop fucking with me, fucker, and fuck me already," I pleaded. He answered by feeding me his cock—one motherfucking inch at a time.

"I have to loosen you up a bit. I can't go balls deep yet. Let me work myself in there. Love my girls greedy for my cock. Gets me harder than fucking stone," he growled breathlessly. Leaning over me, his eyes hooded, he fed me his delicious, scorching cock. He leaned down over my face, arms positioned on either side of my head. His warm breath hummed in my ear as his hand reached down to stroke my clit.

"Come on, babe. Open for me," he rumbled. His thrusting became a bit harder and quicker, and I felt my body opening up for this mythical creature. My eyes closed tightly and I tried to wrap my legs around his waist to lock him in place.

"Not yet, babe. I haven't worked in my rings yet. I'll tell you when you need to hang on." He nipped my ear. I sighed. Fuck, I thought he was all the way in. Christ, I'm not built for this kind of torment. I reached down to his butt cheeks and clamped down with my hands, pulling him deeper into me. He corkscrewed his ass over and over. I screamed my pleasure.

"That's it, mama. Scream for me. You'll be doing a lot more of that," he exclaimed. Biting my lip to stay present and not float away, I took a mental screenshot of this moment. I felt so full. My walls stretched to accommodate his girth. With each thrust, he sank deeper. And I fell a little harder. Yeah, I was fucked. Literally. The sound of my blood pumping through my veins roared in my ears. I couldn't tell if it was my breathing or his that echoed around me. It was a hodgepodge of ecstasy. He placed his hands over mine, pinning them above my head.

"Arch your back for me, babe, and spread those pretty legs nice and wide. I'm going to own this pussy right the fuck now," he hissed. I did as he asked, completely submitting. After all, this was what he asked for: complete and utter submission.

"That's it, babe. Offer me that sweet cunt," he whispered. How did he make my least favorite word sound like a fucking sonnet? I felt so incredible—so alive, our bodies in tune with one another, rutting rhythmically in a crescendo of lust. His frenum rings hitting spots I've never sensed before, he manipulated my body with expert precision. I regarded his handsome face, relishing this beautiful man on top of me. His eyes bore into me with stealth precision. Looking directly into my soul, he smiled wickedly, then kissed me deeply. *Arrogant prick.* Yeah, he knew he was the best ride in town. *Fuck me.*

Grinding my heels into the mattress to get better leverage, I met him thrust for thrust. He moved his fingers from my clit. With his other hand still pinning my arms above my head, he pushed my right thigh up from under my knee. Just then, he hit a whole new angle and I lost it. Screaming his name, I clenched my pussy, squeezing his cock. As he jack-hammered me, I felt his head swell further. He released my hands, rushing to his knees. After a few long strokes of his dick, his hot, thick ropes of cum painted my tits and stomach. Yeah, he was an artist, all right. His eyes were closed, his mouth parted. His breathing was hurried, his body still. He looked like a fucking god—absolutely stunning. I will never get this image out of my head.

He finally opened his eyes—to see his handiwork, watching me closely. I smiled in post-coital bliss. I was blissed the fuck out. He leaned over and on top of me, kissing me with his full lips, coaxing my mouth open with his talented, wicked tongue, and not caring that his cum was smeared all over his body. Most men would mind. But he *wasn't* most men. I accepted with a moan.

He kissed me for a long while until sleep drew me under. I slept without dreams, with just the sensation floating behind my eyes of colorful, pastel swirls. I barely had a conscious thought; it felt much akin to Alice and the rabbit hole. My body was enveloped in his scent, marking me right down to the bone. I would forever be his—whether he knew it or not. His to control. His to do with as he wished. His to consume, to eat away at my very soul. I was in that deep. My veins ran with his essence, the fuel, the nourishment that my body craved. His melodic gritty voice carried me to the surface of consciousness. It was faint, but spoke to my heart—awakening me. I opened my eyes, seeking him out. He was singing an acappella version of …? What song was that? I knew it wasn't one of Lethal Abel's. I listened keenly, searching for any frame of reference. Oh, I knew what it was! It was his cover of "Dark Horse." His had an edge to it. Nonetheless, it was beautiful. And more importantly, it was quintessential Abel. He mastered everything he did. It was always on his terms.

Make me your cupid—
Make me your one and only
But don't make me your enemy, your enemy, your enemy
So you wanna play with magic
Girl, you should know what you're falling for
Baby, do you dare to do this?
'Cause I'm coming at you like a dark horse
Are you ready for a perfect storm, a perfect storm?
'Cause once you're mine, there's no going back …

Oh, God. His version of reality was quickly becoming mine. I laid back down and let his voice pull me back under again, swathing me in his gravelly tones—carrying me to him.

[Listen to OLN's version of "Dark Horse"
here: http://www.youtube.com/watch?v=cKVknRFEhpc.]

:

Chapter One

Gia

Getting a job at Gunner ESQ was a dream come true—or the beginning of *my* dreams coming true. The brick fascia building loomed in comparison to the other buildings. Its cold, detached stature gave a feeling of wealth and privilege. Large, bay-front windows gave its occupants a spectacular view of Colorado's snow-peaked mountain tops.

I acquired this job with the assumption that I would run into Mr. Timothy Gunner's gorgeous, rock-star son, Abel. This scion's son was a dreamy tatted-sleeved god that had my girly parts thick with cream and clenching. Thank God for my roommate, and sister from another mister, Cindy. I owed her everything. After all, it was all *her* doing that I had a desk in this salacious world of moneyed elitists, aiding me in my quest to get tall, dark, and dangerous into my clutches, and then appropriately in my bed. We had a bet going that I couldn't succeed in bedding this enigma. Hands down, I stepped up and accepted the challenge. Fuck, yeah! I'm no pussy to challenges. I wear that shit like a badge of honor. Besides, I need to get out of this Podunk town and in to his Beverley Hills estate.

All I needed was to lay on copious amounts of tease and sex while he was here on one of his impromptu visits with his dad. It seems this bad-boy got himself in a jam with one of his conquests. I snuck a peek at a confidential file in Mr. Gunner's office. Yeah, I could lose my job *if* I were caught—but I was all ninja and shit.

"Incoming," Cindy blurted manically as she rounded the corner of my desk walking to hers. Cindy was a tall, waify blonde with the grace of a runway model, the mouth of a dock worker, and in addition, she was on the official Karma police street team. Her blue-grey eyes, long legs that went on for days, and lengthy, thick blond tendrils reached the middle of her behind. Cindy loved the law, loved having that conversant edge over people. Not enough to practice it, but enough that being a law secretary was *her* only option.

"Incoming?" I asked. What was she getting at this early I wondered?

"Incoming. Hello. As in: the eagle has landed, chick," she huffed with her signature eye roll.

"Speak fucking English, will you!" I snapped. Christ almighty, it was 9am and I already wanted to pound her face in—hard.

"Abel—you fucking retard!" she spoke through gritted teeth as she sat at her desk, clearly frustrated with my lack of understanding. The *fuck*. I quickly reached under my desk for my makeup bag, rummaging through it blindly till I landed on my favorite lip gloss. I wanted my lips glistening to the point of obscenity. I left nothing to chance. Chance was the fist-fucker of all fist-fuckers—and I left nothing to it. I had enough squandered opportunities in my life to know this intimately. One breath in. One long breath out.

A foreboding shadow hung in the doorway. *Christ almighty.* I swallowed, allowing my eyes to take in fucking perfection at its finest. My eyes found their way, climbing ever so slowly, to his beautiful face. I gasped audibly. One breath in. One long breath out. A bolt of white-hot energy ran from my nipples to my clit. Weirdly, my thoughts drifted to Ben-fucking-Franklin. My eyes closed on their own accord, as I mentally collected myself, refocusing on the task at hand.

"Good morning, Mr. Gunner." I smiled congenially, and then he turned to Cindy.

"Morning Cin," he warmly greeted *her*. My heart squeezed for a moment at his playfulness and familiarity. He readjusted his eyes, bringing my face back into focus.

"Call me Abel." A slow smile played on his *perfect* lips. Yeah, my eyes were *there*. God, they were luscious lips. Mmm. Probably tasted yummy, too. Speaking of tasting … My eyes paid his body another visit. Quickly jerking my eyes upward, I met his enigmatic eyes: perfect brows framed his face, and his strong jaw line accentuated his perfect cupid dimple, making him incredibly handsome—mouthwatering.

"Okay, Abel it is," I replied, licking my own lips. *Mine, mine, mine,* my lascivious mind chanted. My body was battling an internal war that was quickly spiraling out of this galaxy.

"Can I get you some coffee, tea, or water?" I offered.

"Nope." He gestured to his venti Starbucks cup. Duh. Man, he was an addict just like me. This was *perfect*. He leaned in, bracing himself with his hands on my desk, scanning the top of it. I leaned back with wide eyes. He grabbed my name plate, gesturing to it.

"Gia Mastro." His raspy voice was velvet to my ears. He arched his picture-perfect brow.

"*Ms.* Gia Mastro." I accentuated the *Ms.* so there was *no* misunderstanding that I was available—unattached.

"That's a beautiful name, Gia." He fingered his front pocket for a piece of gum, then put it in his mouth.

Cindy and I watched in intense fascination as he chewed, his Adam's apple riding up and down his throat like an elevator. Damn. What woman doesn't find a man's Adam's apple sexy? As he stared to and fro, between Cindy and me, I took the opportunity to lean forward to better access his wears. He wore a closely fitted, *consider yourself saved* tee-shirt that clung to every ripple of his muscled chest. Dark-washed, black denim enveloped his thick, long legs, leaving that all-important V to peek out, winking at me. Oh, what do we have here? A hint of a colorful tattoo came dangerously close to his happy trail and disappeared into his pants. Going lower still, my eyes zeroed in on his maleness. Oh *my*. Was he turned on? Gesù Cristo. *Jesus Christ.* Gulp. Eyes up! Eyes up! I willed my mouth to speak, as I was quite positive I had just gotten busted for checking out his dick.

"Ah, thank you. Abel's also very beautiful." Ugh! "I mean, it's different. But it suits you." I tilted my tongue-tied head, awaiting his response. His eyes flashed a warning: heat, and a glint of danger—all of which sent a flood right down to my basement.

"Yeah, it's cool. Anyway, I'm out. Nice meeting you, Gia. Enjoy the day, ladies." He turned and was gone in three strides.

Still in a fog, I stood up from my solid cherrywood desk, pushed back my rolling leather chair, and was hit from behind with the force of an NFL fullback. I lost my balance, catching myself awkwardly on my file cabinet. I steadied myself and whirled around to give Cindy a what-the-fuck-for look.

"You've got to be fuckin' shittin' me?" Grabbing my arm mightily, she nearly yanked it free from the socket.

"We need to talk. Bathroom. Now!" she huffed. I acknowledged her by ripping my arm back.

"Pipe down, you twat. Just wait a goddamn minute and stop making a fucking scene, jackass."

I rolled my eyes hard while massaging my injured arm. What the fuck. Apparently we were still practicing grade-school etiquette when it came to boys.

"What the fuck ever, G. Let's go now, before Mr. I'm-gonna-hump-you-where-you-stand comes back." She grabbed my arm—*again*. But this time, I went with her theatrics. I needed to break this shit down, second by second, to see if we came up with the same plausible possibilities. He *wanted* me. Sure as fuck: he *wanted* me. I was 100% clear on that shit. Unless it was my deluded mind again, seeing what it wanted. My mind had that shit down-pat: it fed my sickness, and shoveled mental acid to this day-tripper. Damn. I didn't know what the fuck just happened.

"Christ, Cindy. What the fuck, chick!" I pushed the heavy, massive bathroom door, stepping into something out of Versailles. I huffed, ejecting my arm from her clutches—again.

"You're playing a very dangerous game, babe." She raised her designer brow, nodding.

"And? Your point being?" I turned around, squatting to see if all the stalls were empty. This place employed some nosey fuckers.

"Hello? Am I addressing the living?" She clucked her tongue, then turned to the mirror to blot her lipstick. Sheesh. The bathroom had a décor rich in deep ebony and cream with flecks of gold immersed within the marble. An elaborate chandelier suspended from the ceiling gave well-off clients a little bit of home. The extravagant mirrors with intricate woodwork adorned the walls artfully, continuing the main theme of exclusivity—belonging.

"Well, I snuck a quick peek of your rocker's personal file. And it seems an old flame or conquest is threatening to expose his sexual preferences to the public. Which I don't have to be a public relations expert to tell you this will be very damaging to Abel, his family, and of course, the band. Total nightmare. Why do you think he's here at 9 a.m. on a Friday morning taking a meeting with his dad and manager?" All this she said in one long breath. Yeah, I already knew that.

My lips curved into a big, toothy smile and I nodded knowingly.

"What kind of sexual preferences? My sexual preference is often." I laughed. I felt her give pause. Oh, here comes the motherfucking karma police. Even though Cindy's sexual prowess preceded *her* at times, she suffered from some kind of trauma in her past that she flat-out refused to speak of. She didn't like overly dominant men—at all. Yeah, she talked the talk, but walked closer to vanilla then her lascivious mouth.

On the other hand, I was fearless ... at least that's what I projected. I got down with all that alpha male shit. I had never experienced a true BDSM Dom. I had a couple of jealous boyfriends, but I mistook their insecurities and possessiveness as love. I had even gone as far as letting a dude tie me up. Nothing on a Mr. Grey level—but was there really even a Mr. Grey? Or was that just the fabrication of a horny homemaker with a nonexistent sex life? Lord, just talking about being bound had me all—*tied up.* A thousand tiny fires broke out across my skin, causing a heated sweat.

"Snap out of it!" She snapped her nimble fingers across my eyes. I blinked rapidly, dispelling another daydream.

"Okay, relax. We don't even know if he wants to go out with me—yet."

I excused myself to pee. I turned and headed for the handicapped stall. I needed to think for a minute in a stall that was a little bigger—more spacious. Quite a few people had a real problem with a non-disabled person using those facilities. Fuck em'. I had a handicapped grandmother with polio and the way I figured it, I had just as much right to be in there as a handicapped person. Christ, she was a pain in my ass. Talk about giving someone a Cinderella complex. Well, fuck—I owned Cinderella. Dislodging my belt, I lowered my pants and sat down, relishing the moment of silence. As I extended my hearing range wider, I could still hear Cindy barking and growling about *isn't it obvious this, and moth to a flame that.* Shaking my head, I let my mind drift until I got to my floaty, peaceful place. Letting out a sigh of relief, I wondered how I got to this state. Was I really going to duplicitously latch onto a guy to further my station?

Chapter Two

Abel

My father always had great taste in women. He married a beauty—my mother. And he hires exquisite looking help with rockin' bodies. I wondered if the old man had hit Gia up yet. Fucker! Nevertheless, I needed to play my love life close to the vest. Morgana, my ex, was trying to fuck me, and fuck me good and hard. She pulled some pretty fucked-up shit, trying to turn the vanilla media and public against me. They wouldn't understand my need to bind, dominate, and fuck women within an inch of their lives. I had something broken in me. A need, a want that I had little control over. I loved brutal sex. Liked it real rough. Bringing a chick pain with a side of pleasure was on the daily specials for Abel's appetite menu. And I had a very healthy appetite. The more they screamed, the harder my dick got—and the harder I came.

Some would say that I'm a sexual deviant. I say, why label people? Oh yeah, and mind your own fuckin' business. This was how I was born—how I chose to live. How my parents made me. It was in my DNA to be dominant. Spanking a chick till her ass came up a pretty shade of red made me wanna blow my load all over her ass—*mark* her. But, people and their opinions? Did I really care?

That was a loaded question. And the answer was both yes and no. As a rule, I was a private dude. But because I was in the public eye as a performer, I had signed away all rights to privacy. And prying eyes wanted to know what went down behind *my* bedroom door. The cold, hard facts were: my family and band would *pay* for my preferences and indiscretions if they were to be put on blast. Could it ruin my career, because I preferred to tie up women? I mean, they loved it. Came back for more and shit, screamed my name at the top of their lungs. That had to mean something, right? We were all consenting adults. Most chicks praised our heavenly father for the multiple orgasms I gave them.

Speaking of coming. I needed to get that little vixen Gia firmly under me. My cock was twitching hard while I was speaking to her earlier. Fuck. I was as hard as stone just thinking of her. I could *go* for working some of my kink on her. My dick throbbed and was fighting my zipper MMA style. Poor guy wanted out in the worst way.

"Sweet Agony," one of our most downloaded songs, was written as homage to my love of BDSM. Its heavy bass laced with my throaty lyrics set it apart from anything those Top 40 lovin' DJ's were playing on the radio. It was erotic as fuck, and every time we preformed it, my balls pulled up north, relishing the phantom sensations of past fuckings. Man, I loved to fuck. I needed to get laid. I'm not one to rub one out. Don't get me wrong, if it was absolutely necessary, I would. But I preferred a female's firm fist on my cock. A nice squeeze and a twist on the upstroke. I loved seeing their faces when they got an eyeful of my hardware and tatted dick. Most were awestruck, some hesitant—no matter how they tried to play it off. Their eyes always gave it away … followed by their mouths forming a perfect O. As in: O shit, I'm in trouble with this badass. Some chicks were concerned about hurting me. They didn't know their way around my hardware. Didn't understand that if they were blowing me they needed to use some serious spit to work my loops properly. But, there were those few fan-girls who wanted to permanently face-plant themselves there, too.

Yeah, my dick had his own groupies—got fan letters and shit. I caught shit from the guys. Fuck it. What did I care? I had a nice, wide fatty. Fuck, yeah. It was all part of the scene. Rock and Roll and babes. I was never going to settle down. Well, actually, come to think of it, I settled down every night. Ha! Yep, I loved my life.

Christ, where was my father? Why was I always on the back burner? My manager Dave was sitting across from me, playing with his fucking new phone. I needed to pace. Being here had me anxious as shit. Between the chick out front and my father's disapproving eyes, my day was gonna be hell. I walked over to the water cooler to quench my thirst. Standing there daydreaming about the festival this weekend, I saw Gia's smoking reflection. Oh, yeah, it's playtime for Abel. I turned and had a nice view of her ass, as she practically ate the file cabinet while falling over. She quickly recovered, making sure no one saw her epic fail, but she didn't count on me being at the water cooler. I laughed. Chicks didn't find that shit funny—got embarrassed. Whatever. I could hear her and Cindy scuffling out there. I was going to check out what the problem was, but by the time I got there, they were gone. I decided I'd catch up with Cindy later. I wanted to ask her what the deal was with Gia.

The elevator door opened and my prick of a father exited in a huff. I turned ass to have a seat. I sat in the white Queen Ann's chair next to Dave which was across from Dad's desk. His daunting, solid mahogany desk fit his persona perfectly. He was an arrogant, wealthy elitist who grew up with the preverbal silver spoon up his ass. His sense of entitlement was epic. He surrounded himself with like-minded people. His friends, most of which also came from old money, were successful and full of themselves. A cross between a Viking and a piranha, my father was revered as a counselor. His skill in the courtroom was legendary. And I was grateful he was on my side. Morgana wasn't too bright going up against me. My father might not agree with my lifestyle, but I was his son, and we were family. Family was everything to my father. At least, that's the perception he gave. He could be a selfish prick. I'm pretty positive he felt the same way about me—especially with this Morgana crap going on.

Oh, and my mother, Deirdre Gunner; what a piece of work there. She insisted I call her Deirdre as soon as I spoke my first word. Hated the word mom. My parents were the same age. Same pedigree. Same everything. They just didn't share the same bed or anything intimate. It was all a show. They are loving, pleasant, and nauseatingly smitten in public. Image was everything. Unity was everything. The shame was, I was just a pawn between the two. There was no love lost between any of us. No love period. I grew up a bratty, rich, spoiled kid with day help shaping me. Yes, I did go to the finest school. I received the finest of everything. If money could attain it, I had it. It was the other stuff that I craved. It was nurturing, security, and warmth that I needed. Fuck it. That was a lifetime ago. I made my amends with it. They had to live with themselves—which they did very well every day, perfectly fine. What time was it, anyway? I looked at my watch; it was 9:18. The boys were late, and at any moment, my dad was going to chime in. Three, two, one...

"And the rest of the boys are?" he asked snidely, looking at his estate Breitling watch. As if he needed to check the time. He knew exactly what time it was. And the fact that they were late. This was his typical condescending behavior.

A ruckus in the hallway told me they were finally here. My band members were the best of friends—brothers. Woody, our drummer, was an exchange student from Ireland. He never exchanged. Once he was in America, he never even thought about going back. People loved to fuck with him and piss him off. Once his mouth started going, he was unstoppable. We barely understood anything he said. With careful listening, we came to understand him over time. He had that nickname since the tenth grade. He's never *not* had his sticks in hand, always workin' beats. His blond, blue eyed, all-American look had the ladies swooning. His look didn't fit our vibe. But he was a badass drummer. And he joked and cursed incessantly. Life was definitely interesting on the road with him, being such a practical joker. Of course, he tells babes he got his nick-name because of the tree-sized wood between his legs. What did I know? I never looked at the dude's dick. Whatever.

Jake, who's on bass, had hair as dark as midnight, and eyes that were pools of sapphire. I thought they were strange, so blue they didn't look real. We all loved to bust his balls about them being contacts. And this usually ended with a wrestling match. He wasn't what I would call a good sport about it. He also co-wrote some of the songs on the album. He can be lyrically brilliant when he's not cranky.

Last, but not least, was our lead guitarist, Surrender; we called him Ender. He was a gamer at heart, and was also our resident Latin dude. His dark brown hair, green eyes, and olive skin had girls creaming in their panties. A true Lothario, he had a mouth on him. He could curse in almost every language—and did. He loved pussy about as much as I did. That's saying a lot, because I did love me some pussy. We were all close. There was no jealousy between us. We appreciated one another's talents. And most importantly, we loved and supported each other— would kill for one another.

"Puta, besame el culo!" Ender called out to me, meaning, "Bitch, kiss my ass!" Yeah, he was in a mood. Can't blame him there. I didn't want to be out of my bed this early, either. We rehearsed until 2am the night before in order to be ready for the Telluride Blues and Brews Festival that weekend, Colorado's biggest, most epic, four-day festival.

"Fuck you, Ender!" I spat back. He flipped me off and walked over to sit next to Jake.

"Enough! Sit, gentlemen—or should I say children? I have other clients today. *Paying* clients!" my father tersely stated. Woody took the seat to my left.

"How you holding up?" he whispered, leaning over. I nodded. I had no words. What would I say? *I'm sorry the cunt everybody hated and warned me about was now affecting them?* I shook my head in disbelief. They warned me about her at least a hundred times. "She's a conniving cunt, Abel." "All she wants is your dick and your money, dude." "She'd let you do anything, be anything, so long as you keep funding her shopping habits." Man, was I an asshole. Thought she was really into me. She was the only chick I was close enough with to maybe call my girlfriend. And even that was a stretch. But she was cool, and loved to fuck. And she let me take her with no hesitation—ever.

"Extortion is the crime of obtaining money or property by threat to a victim's property or loved ones, intimidation, or false claim of a right," my father stated. Christ, the counselor was in. Goddamn blowhard.

"Speak plainly! I think we all have an idea of what's going on. Enough with the legal vomit," I said contemptuously. I looked around at the guys. Their eyebrows were raised disapprovingly. I guess they thought *I* was being a dick. Whatever. Woody patted my leg again.

"Dude, chill," he whispered. Nodding yeah, I was fucking stressed. I didn't want to be there. I wanted to be practicing or getting my dick wet. I needed to chill the fuck out.

"Cabron!" Ender murmured, looking toward the window. This was his way of calling me a "dumbass." What a dick he was. Jake, who played peacemaker at times, shook his head at Ender in warning. Taking a long deep breath, I tried to hold my shit together.

"As I was saying. Extortion can take place either over the phone, by mail, email, text, or any other wireless communication. Nevertheless, it is a federal crime. She has engaged Abel by text and voicemail. I could also make the case for defamation of character, slander, and bribery. Now, this is how we're going to handle Morgana," my father instructed us. He picked up the receiver and barked out an order. A minute later there was a knock.

"Here's the file, Mr. Gunner. I was just going to file it away." Gia sashayed around his desk and handed it to him. She waited a beat, looking at the boys. Finally, her eyes landed on me. I winked. She blushed. Ender, being closest to her, popped out of his seat to greet her. *Of course.*

"Hey, I'm Surrender, but you can call me Ender." He shook her hand.

"Hi. I'm Gia. Nice to meet you, Ender," she said, smiling softly. With that, the rest of the band introduced themselves, causing a minor disruption. I knew this would make my old man twitch.

"That will be all, Gia," my father snapped, dismissing her. She nodded. A rosy hue colored her cheeks. I found her self-consciousness endearing. My dad didn't do subtle. He must fancy her—otherwise, there would've been a shit-storm. Time was money. And money was *his* god.

Ender jumped out of his seat. "Gia, if you don't have plans the weekend of May 30th, I have two extra tickets to the festival. We happen to be gigging at the Telluride Blues and Brews that weekend. If you're interested—that is." He winked at her. *Son of a bitch.* He turned to me, smirking.

"That would be awesome, Ender. You're totally sweet. Thank you!" She smiled happily, then turned and left. I knew what he was thinking, because I was thinking the same thing a few minutes ago.

"Got a problem, Putu?" he asked. I loved him, but he had some big balls. What the fuck did I care, anyway? I had enough women to go around. Don't need another bitch on my ass. We had a little healthy competition between the two of us. With the understanding, of course, that if we were 'feeling' someone, the other would back off. No questions asked. Gia was hot, but as I said, I had enough on my plate at the moment. Let Ender have a go at it. And just like that, I rationalized it, and I was ok.

"No problem, dude." I shrugged, basically saying whatever. We nodded—man-talk for "It's on, motherfucker. Good luck." I leaned back and swung one leg over the other, trying to give the impression I really didn't give a fuck. But my old man was giving me the stink eye. Nothing got past him. After all, he was my maker. We were alike in some ways. One of those ways was women. He was better at the discretion part than I was. With photogs following me everywhere, it was nearly impossible not to end up in a tabloid, no matter how careful I tried to be.

"As I was saying, gentlemen. It's my understanding that Morgana Jennings has certain elements of her past she'd like to keep there. I'm not at liberty to discuss the details with you, but I will say it does look very good for our case against her. Nevertheless, you will *all* refrain from any contact. And if contact is unavoidable, have security politely escort her away. And for the love of God, please use what He gave you—your better judgment. That's all, men. Are we clear?"

He ended his rant by looking each and every one of us in the eye for a beat before moving on to the next. I was the final nod. I rolled my eyes. Obviously, I didn't need to be told to stay away from that twat. I was done. Getting ready to leave for his next meeting, my father grabbed his briefcase and some files. I wondered what he was getting at by telling "all" of us to refrain from contact. It was certainly ominous. And as far as I knew, no one from the band ever spoke to her. Huh. Everybody hung back for a heartbeat. No one said a word until we heard the ding of the elevator, enclosing my father within it.

"Well, boys, its 10:00. Why don't we get some grub and head to the studio? We can get a few hours of time in," Dave proposed, pulling his e-cigarette out for a quick toke while looking around.

"I need a nap," Jake said, yawning and covering his mouth with his hand. Ender gave him the thumbs-up. They were out. I looked at Woody, who looked indifferent. I stood up, grabbed my phone, and started toward the door.

"Why don't we hook up at 2:00?" I counter-proposed. "Meet at the studio. I could use some eats though. Dave? You in?" I threw my chin at him, waiting for his reply. He was a typical redneck—always up for food and beer. Thank God Colorado didn't have a demand for boiled peanuts. Garlic or hot sauce were his two favorite flavors. And that shit stunk up the place. We kicked him off the tour bus two months ago; made him ride with the roadies. We were all gagging at the noxious smell those peanuts gave off.

"I already said I wanted to eat. So, obviously I'm in," Dave answered, then went back to texting. He was addicted to our Facebook fan page. In fact, he answered a majority of the questions fans asked when we were gigging or rehearsing. He was our official social media stalker.

"Ok, I'm out. Later." I walked past them, readying the elevator for exodus. As I waited, I made sure my eyes made contact with Gia's. I didn't need words. What I needed didn't need verbal justification, my eyes conveyed my message. For a few heartbeats, our eyes danced seductively, hinting at erotic things to come. My posture was pensive. I was suddenly fighting a hard-on again. I wanted to spank that sweet, tight ass of hers for doing that to me. She had the nerve to wink at me. Oh, this chick was going to get a nice spanking in the future. And I'll enjoy watching my handprint blossoming on her ass …

My attention was derailed as the boys approached raucously. Ender grabbed Woody in a headlock. The elevator came. We all stepped in. I hit lower level. Ender blew Gia a kiss, and then the donkey kicked me after.

"What the fuck, man?" I pushed him against the elevator wall. Woody and Jake got between us before fists started flying. We loved each other completely. But we also frequently got on each other's nerves. That led to a whole lot of punching and posturing.

"Bollo," Ender spat, trying to break free.

"Go fuck yourself, esse," I cursed back.

"Puto, I'm not Mexican, asshole. I'm from Spain," he corrected.

"You've been an asshole all morning. What's your deal?" I asked. Oh, I knew this was just his alpha macho shit. Everything with him was a competition. Who had more allure? What the fuck ever, already. Get over yourself. I needed to count to motherfuckin' ten or he was going to eat my fist. One of my many therapists over the years suggested this technique for managing my anger issues. I disagreed that I had issues. I was just surrounded by assholes.

"Lads, I'll break your faces if ye no' stop acting the cunting maggot. You little fuckin' arsehole cunts," Woody shouted. This wasn't a rare comment for Woody. In Ireland, they called everyone cunts. It's almost a term of endearment. But we all loved hearing it, and so we cracked up laughing. And that's how most of our arguments always ended—in laughter. We needed this reprieve—even if it only lasted a few minutes. It lightened up the vibe considerably.

The elevator door opened and everybody took off except for Dave and me. We hoofed it over to the diner to fill our bellies and talk of our impending festival dates later in the month. While he talked, I fantasized about Gia. There was something about her. Something that made me itchy. It annoyed me. Either way, I needed to scratch that itch. I would soon find out I should have left that itch alone—should never have scratched it, should have just fucking ignored it. But there was no leaving her alone. I had the feeling she and I would always have unfinished business. We were made to be broken. I've since come to realize this, but I still can't accept it. Over the next few weeks, despite my denials, I made a habit of grabbing an extra non-fat latte with two extra shots of espresso for a certain someone every morning. My old man was in trial over the next few weeks. So, that meant he wasn't in the office most mornings. That lined up perfectly for our sunrise dates. I never woke up early for any chick—ever. Gia was magnetic—dangerously so. That was the only word to describe her. She drew me in with her essence, coiling around my core with enough torque to destroy me on a molecular level. That was some fucked-up deep shit—the type of shit you can't even explain to a dude. Not unless I wanted said dude to commit me to a mental hospital. A man knew these things. Men knew when they were done for. I knew as soon as I tasted her pussy, there would be no going back.

Gia wasn't your usual stateside fan-girl. We all had those in every state. She was the type of girl you wanted to be *your* girl. She tried to act like a badass chick. But she wasn't. She was pure. Pure to the acts I wanted to involve her in. To the world I'd ask her to be a part of. That pureness fed the beast. The beast didn't want to court anyone. Didn't want to go slow. He wanted her bound and screaming. Normally, I didn't do *Lilly White* chicks. Hated them, in fact. Didn't take on new subs. I never had to. Never wanted to. She made me want to. I wanted to spend the time it would take to do so. However, I was conflicted about that, too. Being someone's first—of anything—was an emotional suicide. There's no getting around that. Especially with chicks. First kisses, first loves, and first fucks were all complications. I didn't do complications. Bottom line: Gia was bad news—trouble. But her smile did me the fuck in. Her smile lit up my shit brighter than Aurora Borealis. It did things to me. Had me thinking fucked-up romantic shit. On the other hand, I was writing the best music I had written in a real long time. I'd found my muse, my sub, my soul.

Chapter Three

Gia

I was feeling electrified, stimulated, and alive for the first time since I could remember. I had purpose. A goal. And God willing, I would achieve it with open arms. Especially if those arms were Abel Gunner's. Abel had been bringing me coffee every morning, which had me swooning big time. My body pulsed with excitement, so much so, I could barely sleep at night.

I watched him move to the elevator, as he departed his father's office. He looked into my eyes, and in his, I saw deep desire with a hint of menace. I wanted to sign up for it ASAP. Damn, that boy was some fine, grade-A man candy. His probing gaze never faltered. My insistent eyes were up for the challenge. I wasn't going to blink first. I let my eyes peruse his body slowly, thoroughly … I smiled and winked before his band mates found their way to the elevator. Then our moment was gone. As they stepped inside, Ender's voice rang out as he shouted his goodbye, sealed with an air-kiss. I responded with a smile and a wave, not wanting the sound of my voice to linger on Abel's ears. I wanted to leave the words unspoken between us. I was looking forward to the weekend's festival, mainly because I would be running into him. Abel would be front and center for my private concert dwelling within my subconscious. This attraction was undeniable, and most definitely unavoidable. And I wanted to take nasty to a whole new level. Game on!

"Damn, Gia. That was some serious eye fucking right there, babe," Cindy observed, inching her chair closer to mine. She had a cautious smile on her face. She loved a gorgeous man just as much as the next woman, but as my best friend, she wasn't supportive of my plans concerning Abel. Since Mama Lioness was in the house, I decided I wouldn't be as forthcoming as I normally was. She would be on a need-to-know basis in regards to any of my future endeavors concerning Abel. Her unwanted opinions would drive a wedge when there was no need for one.

"Yep, he has been properly eye-fucked by yours truly. There will be no confusion as to what I want," I said confidently, smiling in amusement. She leaned in awkwardly, giving me a one-handed hug.

"Babe, you know I just want the best for you, right? I'm protective of you. And I'm especially protective of your heart. That boy there is dangerous, Gia. Please just promise me you'll be careful." I wrapped my arms around her and nodded in the affirmative. Her heart was in the right place. But I was driven by certain needs—and it wasn't my heart I was worried about.

"Of course, chick, I know. And I appreciate your concern—more than you know." I kissed her cheek and gave her a final squeeze before disengaging from our embrace.

The day went by without incident. It was quite boring after the interesting morning I'd had. I got my paycheck, headed to the bank, then home. Eager to file the day away, I moved to the next task at hand: to plot the next four days' worth of vixen couture. My attire needed to be both thought- and boner-provoking. The floor of my room quickly became a mess of clothes and shoes. I needed something jaw-dropping that would get me past eye-fuckery and into the paint. Yeah, I'd go hard in the paint for this man. I fell asleep amongst the piles of fuck-no's, eh-maybe's and hell-yeses. Cindy's gentle voice brought me back to the land of the living.

"You ok? You slept on the floor all night? WTF?" she shot at me. I attempted to stretch. Damn, I had slept through a dreamless night. I hate when I don't dream, or when I can't remember them.

"Apparently so! I guess I was more exhausted than I thought." I sat up, groaning. I wanted to go back to sleep, but it was Friday morning, and that meant a few hours of work followed by a weekend of getting down and dirty—with any luck.

"Cin, bring some coffee, please. I need a swig before I can even shower. I'm still *that* tired, dude. Please?" I begged. I had zero energy—not to mention, my neck was stiff. Hopefully a hot shower would remedy that. I had to be kink-free for this weekend. Walking around with a stiff neck is *not* a good look. The last thing I needed was to look like C-3PO.

"No prob, baby girl. Get your ass in the bathroom and into the shower. I'll bring it in there. You don't have all morning to lay around. Got to get ready. I want to start this day already. I'm pretty psyched for tonight, myself."

She smiled widely, extending her hand to help me from the floor. Thankful for her help, I slowly found my way into the bathroom, then put the shower stream on full-blast. Cin returned with my coffee. I took it in the shower with me. Yes, I drink coffee in the shower. I also drink wine in the shower. It relaxes me. And I use my favorite woodsy, male body wash—another defect in me. I loved men, loved their scent. So much so, I bathed and deodorized in it. I relished the scent caressing my body, while it provided some much-needed aroma therapy throughout the day. It didn't take very long to be in a vivid and hot daydream. That morning's was a real doozy, even for me. But, daydreams were a part of my life. They were how I worked things out.

Often times, I found peace and happiness there. Who would begrudge me that?

Ok, back to *him*. His hands found their way to my ass, roughly lifting me off the floor. I wrapped my legs around his trim waist to balance myself. He leaned into the wall for leverage, gripping my cheeks and spreading me for entry. He pushed me against the shower wall to open my legs wider while spreading my ass cheeks with his hands, prying them open. He positioned his hard dick at my opening. I rolled my hips in invitation. He licked his lips, turned on by my gesture. He entered my channel in one rough thrust until his balls were flush against my ass. He allowed me a moment of adjustment before starting the endless waves of deep, rolling thrusts.

"My cock belongs in you—longs, aches for you, my balls kissing your ass, my piercing kissing your cervix. I'm home with you," he sang his filthy words into my ear in the sing-song way that was undeniably Abel. The filthier he was, the wetter I became. He rubbed my nub like he was playing his favorite song. A song he wrote especially for me. A song only he knew the words to. He was an expert in all things Gia. And when it came to my body, he knew it better than I did.

"Gonna get rough, babe. Lock your ankles together and hold the fuck on. I'm not stopping for anything." His gruff voice had me at "rough"; my brain was mush. Whatever the fuck he said was of no consequence, just as long as he continued his brutal assault. I had no words. I couldn't formulate anything articulate. Thoughts swirled around the empty space inside my cranium. I couldn't latch on to a single one. I shook my head, desperately trying to free up a notion. Anything. I was officially lost in this man.

"Gonna come deep in this pretty cunt of yours. Leave you with something of mine. I want to see it drip down your legs." His decadently sexy voice spoke words of possession in my ear. He pushed his weight into me, leaning me against the wall. With his freed-up hand, he wrapped it around my throat, applying pressure. He loved it when I screamed his name. But the air was barely making its way into my mouth. My voice wouldn't sing his praises. Instead, he got something more valuable—my complete submission. My clit throbbed as my pussy fisted his cock. Blackness softened around the edges of my vision. My legs started to quake. He removed his head from the crook of my neck to look me dead in the eyes. Tearing up, I quirked a smirk. His eyes glazed over. He knew I was ok. It was our signal. I couldn't be a wiseass if he was being too rough.

"Oh fuck! Uh … Gia. What the fuck are you doing to me?" He rode out his orgasm, long and hard, as I whimpered mine. *Christ, what was I doing to him?* This beast of a man kissed me ardently, grabbing my face with both hands while pinning me to the wall with his chest. I accepted his delectable tongue, opening fully for him to explore, our tongues doing an erotic dance of passion, his teeth gnashing against mine. We were both fighting to hold on to the moment a little longer. I could feel him getting wickedly hard again. I wiggled. He smirked, gently putting me down.

He grabbed the soap to wash me—another act of adulation. It gave him great pleasure to bathe me, shampoo me, and dry me off. Taking care of me was his first concern. He was grateful for my submission. His gratitude squeezed my heart. I wanted to submit all over again.

"Gia, there will be no hot water left. What the fuck?" Cindy yelled through the door. That was the best daydream yet of him. With my hands braced against the shower wall and my head leaning on the cool tiles, I needed the feel of something tied to this earth—something real. The ghost of Abel was already haunting me, seducing my mind, squeezing my heart.

"Yep, just getting out, babe. Give me a minute. I'll be right out." I bit my lip, needing the sting of pain to feel alive. My feet firmly on the ground, I got ready quickly and headed to work.

Cindy and I shared a light lunch. We felt much like little kids, bursting with joy and excitement. It was a relatively quiet day— thankfully. My head was not into work. I was flying with the clouds, my feet never touching the ground. I was high on Abel. By the time five o'clock rolled around, we were punch-drunk and laughing hysterically. I begged Cindy to stop at Starbucks for a quad of espresso. She passed on the coffee, opting for a smart water instead. I needed caffeine.

We pulled into the lot of our building. We lived in a nice part of town. The rent was a little more than we could afford separately. So, rooming together was a no-brainer. It was your standard two-bedroom. Nothing to write home about. It was respectable and I was proud to call it home. The furnishings came compliments of Ikea. We picked out modern art, deco-style pieces to show our unique taste. The walls were painted a rich rust and went perfectly with the artwork I had selected.

None of it was to my mother's taste, and since she absolutely hated leaving her gated community, there was little chance she would be visiting—which suited me just fine. By no stretch was there any love lost between us. For the most part, we were at each other's throats. People assumed because of her alluring smile and natural beauty, she was a warm, caring mother. But there was nothing natural about her. It was all an act. A very public act. Behind closed doors, she was an abusive, manipulative, controlling, demonic Jezebel. My greatest fear was stepping into her shoes without thinking—becoming her …

They say you're a product of your environment. My environment was tolerable, only because I escaped it inside my head by turning my pain into laughter and sarcasm. Only another fucked-up person would be able to see through my veil—my mask. And those people were few and far between. My days consisted of pushing the pain and ugliness behind the closed doors of my mind, sweeping them into neat little piles and shoving them inside, locking them away. If I got lucky, they would never surface again. But my past told me that I would never, ever, get *that* lucky.

Cindy came out of the bathroom dressed to kill. She was wearing a black leather mini-skirt paired with a silver, backless, lamé top. Her black five-inch heels finished her look epically.

"Damn, you look kick-ass, chica." I let out a low whistle. She blushed, but smiled brightly. She had bought this outfit for last New Year's Eve, but never got the chance to wear it. She got the flu instead.

"Ooh ooh, I want you to wear my Cartier bracelets. The silver and gold will be a nice contrast," I called out over my shoulder as I walked into my room. They were my mother's. She had begrudgingly given them to me, because she couldn't stand the gold-plated bangles I loved. *Bitch*.

"Thank you, Gia. I would've never thought to ask," she said, playing with them on her wrist.

"Ok, my makeup's done. Give me a minute to get dressed." I went to get my clothes hanging perfectly on the hanger. Stripping my tank top and shorts off, I put on a nude lycra/spandex, thigh-high mini dress. The front and back were cut very low. The nude color gave the illusion I was wasn't wearing anything. This dress was entirely too much for this venue. I was overdressed, but ask me if I cared. I needed to close the deal tonight with Abel. And sure as fuck, this dress would seal it. I bent over the mirror to apply one final coat of gloss. *Perfect*. Grabbing my bag, I left my bedroom for the big reveal, not caring what Cindy might think about my choice of clothing. Life was about decisions. And I was deciding to look jaw-dropping, mouth-watering, boner-inducing, drop-dead gorgeous.

"Christ on the cross!" She patted her heart, fanning herself obnoxiously. "Hun, I think I have a lady-boner." We both laughed at her theatrics. "Seriously G, I need a panty-liner if I'm going to be next to you all night in *that*." She motioned her index finger up and down.

"Deal with it, babe." I laughed. "All kidding aside, let's hit it. We still have to get our tickets from the 'will call' window." I grabbed my keys and proceeded to the door. Luckily for her, she was right behind me, because I would've left her ass. She had a nasty habit of walking slow. But I had a quick gait, so she was always ten steps behind me. We would end up fighting. I was always walking too fast. However, if you asked me, she was always walking too slow.

We hit traffic closer to the venue, adding to my anxiety. When I was nervous, I cursed. Well, actually, I normally cursed in any given situation.

"Move it or lose it, fucker!" I screamed, rolling down my window. The driver had the nerve to glare at me. "Yeah, that was me calling you a motherfucker. Pretty girls curse, too." I stepped on the gas, but not before saluting him with my finger.

Yeah, it was that kind of day. I had no patience for hot-girl rubberneckers. We had to wait in line to get into the parking lot. The parking attendants wore jeans and "fly me to the moon saloon" tee-shirts advertising a local bar and co-sponsor for the event. Cin yelled out her window at one of the guys as we pulled in. I slowed to a crawl, pulling up next to him.

"Hey, hun, do we have to park in the grass?" She touched his chest, dragging her finger down slowly. "My heels will get all dirty."

Cin then proceeded to stick her five-inch heel out the window, turning her foot this way and that way. *Oh, dear lord.* I rolled my eyes at her antics. This was a classic signature move. She hated to walk—anywhere. Period. End of story. She did what she had to do to get what she wanted, no matter how abhorrent. She came off at times as a ditsy bimbo. But this was an act. She was Mensa smart. Which was scary as fuck, because she played an entirely different role in front of people. Most people who were gifted had a habit of making you feel inadequate. Not Cindy. She went out of her way to hide her intelligence, as if she were embarrassed by it. She was a chameleon, like me. It was all kinds of fucked-up. But, hello pot, meet kettle. Who was I to say what was right and what was wrong. The cutie pointed in the direction where we were to park.

"You ladies go right through there. Tell Steve I said you can park in the handicapped section." He moved the wooden barricade so we could drive through, and then stepped aside.

"Handicapped?" she shouted. He looked surprised by her outburst. I hoped she wasn't one of those—the people who sneered and leered at folks like me who took liberties with handicapped parking.

"Stick a cork in it!" I retorted. "My grandmother was handicapped. Hello? Remember? I'm handicapped by association, remember? It's in my breed. I told you!" She rolled her eyes while shaking her head. That was my cue to hit the gas, park, and get the hell out of that freaking car before she could have another outburst. I reached for the door handle to exit the car—but her hand stopped me before I could. I turned in question.

"Yes, now what?" I waited for her answer.

"*Breed?* Did you just say *breed?* It's in your *breed?*" she asked incredulously.

"Yep, that's what I said. Now, move your ass, sister." I made a bee-line for the entrance. I didn't even want to look back for fear she would ramble on about how wacked I was. *Breed* was a perfect way to describe what I was meaning to say.

"Slow your gait, please. I can't walk so fast in these heels. Shit. The balls of my feet are already starting to hurt. You know what that means, right?" She pulled on my arm, slowing me down.

"I'll bite. What does it mean?" I asked, scratching my arm. It was getting buggy out. I hate bugs. Her eyes zeroed in on my newly-scratched arm. Then she started scratching, too—both of her arms simultaneously.

"It means, I'll have to figure out a way to keep my feet up—preferably while I'm on my back." She smiled with a snort. She was a funny chick. And that right there was why I loved her, through and through.

"You're a genius. I don't even belong in your presence. In fact, you should have a court. I will request an audience with you," I said, grabbing her hand. We laughed. Both of us were Royalty nerds: we loved and watched anything having to do with Monarchy.

Chapter Four

Abel

A pair of sexy, milk-chocolate eyes haunted me. Not in a scary way, but in an "I'm never going to let you rest until you've tasted me" type of way. It was fucking with my head—hard.

Unfortunately, the eyes looking up at me were blue. Not the brown ones I've been fantasying about. But, I needed this—needed release. I took a deep breath, relaxed, and closed my eyes, trying to focus on the sounds of her sucking me off. Yeah, that was much better. I widened my legs, giving her ample access to my balls and hoping she'd take the hint. It pissed me off when I had to school a girl in how to suck cock properly. The chick on her knees was a brunette. She was yanking my dick so hard, she had broken a sweat. This was getting ridiculous and fuckin' annoying. The sounds of some girl's laughter in the hallway distracted me. Girls weren't allowed to troll around backstage. So who the fuck was that?

Before I could get the chick off my dick, a knock sounded, followed by the door opening. *Fuck me,* those same milk-chocolate eyes connected with mine—then focused on the back of the head of the blue-eyed chick bobbing up and down on my dick.

"Shit. I'm so sorry, Abel. Um, Ender told us he'd meet us in here. Fuck, I'm sorry," Cindy exclaimed while hustling back out of the room.

Gia, however, said not a word—but in her eyes I saw possessiveness. She turned and slammed the door behind her so hard it echoed in my ears for a minute. I hardened. Blue-eyes never took her eyes off the prize. She continued lavishing my cock with her tongue, without even looking up. Gia was feisty. I liked that. And that right there made me lose my shit in Blue-eyes' mouth. What was it with this Gia girl? Would my appetite for her be sated when I finally got her?

I just stood there, buttoning my pants, and then I turned and left the room without a word. I had some questions for Ender.

Notes of a Latin melody drifted off stage. He was tuning his guitar. This was his usual routine before we gigged. His sultry vibe had a calming effect on the beast within him. I knew exactly what he meant. Dealt with the beast myself. However, I needed to talk to him. He was fucking my shit up with Gia. And it was pissing me the fuck off.

"Dude, why in the fuck would you tell Cindy and Gia to come into my dressing room?" I asked, folding my arms. He never looked up, but just smiled and continued playing.

"Yo, motherfucker, I'm talking to you. What you did wasn't appreciated." I kicked the side of his chair with my boot. This time he opened his eyes, placed his guitar in the holder, and gave me his undivided attention.

"What I told them is meet me in *our* dressing room. Now, if they interrupted your pre-performance get-down with a chick—that's on you, *bollo [cunt]*." He stood up, stepping into my personal comfort zone, smirking. *Fucker knew he was fucking with me.*

"Newsflash, *esse [spic]*. I was getting head, asshole. I don't need two chicks fucking my shit up. They work for my old man. It's a respect thing." I turned and started to walk away. But, he wasn't going to let this go. Fucking pain in my ass.

"Let me get this straight, Abel," he huffed incredulously. "You're worried about coming off as disrespectful, because of your dad? Not for any other reason like, maybe a brown-eyed reason you've managed to bring coffee to every morning? Afraid what she might think of you now?"

I knew then I needed to walk off some of this tension that was still coiled within my body. I didn't need this. What I did need was to be loose and ready for this performance. Performing got me off just as much as a tight pussy. The pulsing energy from the crowd fed my beast, nurturing my soul in the most visceral way. I felt invincible—complete. But afterward, I needed to release my darkness. The demon in me needed to be fed, to relish in someone else's pain, agony, and pleasure. It was my cross and I would bear that cross as long as I lived. I needed it as much as I needed oxygen. That night, I would be laying down some pipe. Who the lucky girl was … I had no clue.

When I reached the green room backstage I could hear her melodic laughter. Her sensual lure drove me to the brink of a C4 explosion. I needed to be around her. Possessiveness rode me hard. I wanted to be the one to make her laugh—and the one to hold her when she cried. My mind was already breaking it down for me: one hand around her throat, the other twisted firmly in her hair, as I simultaneously pushed my way inside her. The caveman in me wanted to rear his face with Gia. I was always forceful and dominant. It's who I was. I had accepted my alpha tendencies years ago. But there was something unique about Gia. And it spoke directly to the Master in me. This girl was playing with my fucking mind. I craved her being across my knee like no other.

"Ten minutes," I said, grabbing a water. Woody nodded and then continued with his sticks tapping out beats on his knee. Jake gave me the thumbs-up. And Ender was making the girls cocktails. *How very hospitable of him.*

Cindy turned toward me with a knowing smile. *Hmm, what was that about? Was I being obvious?* I needed to get into my zone. Not wanting to engage in conversation, I put my ear-buds in, cued up our new album, and reclined in my favorite chair. Ender led the girls to the couch to sit down. He sat between them. He was in full peacocking, Lothario mode. The atmosphere was relaxing, but the sexual tension was knife-cuttingly thick. It wasn't until Ender leaned back, wrapping the girls up in his muscled arms, that my eyebrows cocked questioningly. My jaw was tight with pressure; my hands closed around my iPhone, cracking the screen in one squeeze. *Fuck.* Gia leaned forward, away from his touch. That pleased me. She licked her lips, eye-fucking me. Now, that right there would get her on her back and under me real fucking quick. My cock sprang to life. We needed to take the stage. I jumped up, hard-on and all. I had no shame.

"Let's hit it, boys!" I grabbed my guitar and got the fuck out of there. I could feel her heated eyes on me. I didn't need to look. My body knew they were on me. I burned for her. My cock was hard for her. However, at the moment, I was going to rock the fuck out. That was what my fans came to see—and I was going to give them what they came for. And Gia would experience it from backstage. That should get real fucking interesting …

Chapter Five

Gia

It was just my luck he was getting a blowjob when I walked in. Life was so unfair. It couldn't be me, right? It had to be some unworthy hole. My body completely locked up. I had no words, only thoughts of one very dead skank. His eyes found mine. He knew. My eyes always gave me away. I never could hide shit from anyone. And right then, I was one nauseous girl. I needed a goddamned drink and quick, before I lost it.

Catching myself in my momentary psychosis, I high-tailed it out of there, thinking I'd have to bleach my fucking eyeballs after seeing that shit. I slammed the door harder than I should've. Cindy threaded her fingers through mine, giving me a frown. Yeah, having to watch him getting blown by another bitch sucked. I knew he was a whore. Hell, they all were. They were rock stars. But damn, that had me aching. It turned me into a zombie. Cindy pulled me along, opening the doors as we continued looking for the guys.

"Thank *fuck*," she said, walking into the room where Jake and Woody were. They looked up curiously. I just shrugged as I tried to come out of my stupefied state. I needed to move past it real quick. Who needed something like that to ruin their night? Not me! My obsessive-compulsive mind had that vile image tethered to it. *Just great!*

"Hey guys," I called out, waving. "Ender said for us to come hang. I'm assuming he'll join us shortly. Said something about tuning his guitar," I rambled on. I needed a drink, stat, or I'd be a blatantly obvious mess. I didn't want to tip my hand where Abel was concerned. That needed to be slow and steady.

"Ender likes to tune his own gear. We usually let the roadies handle that shit. That's what they get paid for, anyway," Jake explained. "Did you happen to see Abel?" He seemed puzzled.

Cindy and I just looked at each other, not wanting to bring up that mishap. I just wanted to forget about it.

"Let's just say we accidently walked into his room and he may or may not have been getting a blowjob." Cindy waved it off nonchalantly. Woody, who normally seemed to be in his own world, laughed his ass off while pounding the table he was sitting at—which oddly brought a smile to my face. Damn, there wasn't an ugly guy in the bunch, each one hotter than the next. He was quiet. It was amusing to see that side of him. Jake joined in the laughter.

"Fuck, I wish I were a fly on that wall." Knowingly, he smiled at Woody. Maybe it was a private joke? I felt the need to explain further.

"He actually frowned. I think he was upset. It was an honest mistake. Someone should tell him to lock the door next time. Simple solution," I said.

"Yeah, I bet he frowned… that had to be priceless. By the way, you two just made my day. Thanks for coming, girls." he chuckled, grabbing a beer.

"Who needs a drink?" Ender entered the room, slamming the door behind him. He threw an old pair of guitar strings in the garbage.

"I do! What do you have?' I chimed in, joining him at the bar. Cindy was still watching Woody with fascination. He looked up from the TV and winked at her. She blushed. *Well, lookie here.*

Standing next to Ender, I could smell his natural scent. It was musky and spicy. Cindy bumped my elbow. I rolled my eyes. I wasn't interested in Ender—just curious.

"Dealer's choice, Ender." Cindy smiled warmly.

"You got it, babe." He walked behind the bar, grabbing a shaker. Whoa, he was getting all professional on us, twirling that shaker in his hand. *Cute.* A chill ran up my spine and the door opened abruptly. *Abel.* Instantly, I concentrated on the walls: they were forest-green—dark, yet calming. The forest was always peaceful to me. I loved nature. I was an earthy person, though most people didn't know it. Ender handed us our drinks. Some kind of delish, pink, fruity concoction. I thanked him.

"Ten minutes," Abel blurted, then walked over to the chair with his iPhone. Wow, was he going to be rude and not talk to anyone? He still looked pissed. I couldn't help but bristle.

"Let's have a seat ladies," Ender offered, motioning toward the couch. Then he squeezed himself between us, wrapping his thick biceps around our shoulders and pulling us closer to his insanely hot body. He sported a big toothy smile and winked at me. I moved forward, not wanting him to get the wrong idea. I was here for Abel and no one else.

However, Abel was watching me closely, too. My lips suddenly dry. I focused on his mouth while licking mine. What kind of pleasure could that mouth bring me? Lord, my lady bits were getting wet already. I took a sip of my cold cocktail, needing to do *something* with my mouth. Completely and utterly enraptured, I was his for the taking. I was so wrapped up in his smoking hotness, I could've fucking slapped myself. *That was not good.* There was no playing it cool with this bad boy. I tried, but his face did shit to me. Made me stupid. I hadn't realized I was zoning in on his face, mentally raping him, until he said something and abruptly exited the room. *Damn, what did he even say?*

Stunned, I watched the band dutifully file out behind their leader. Cindy was glaring at me again.

"What?" I gritted through my teeth.

"Way to be cool, chick. Do you have any self-control where he's concerned? Gia, you're gonna fuck this up, kid. Reel it in!" She hugged me, then turned tail to follow the band out as well, with me in tow. I hung on tightly. She was my life-line. God only knew what ridiculousness I would get myself into that night. I needed to keep my big mouth shut and my emotions switched off so I could enjoy the rest of the evening—while hopefully not making a fool of myself.

Before moving to his kit, Woody came over to ask Cindy if she needed anything. It didn't escape my notice that he was also subtly warning her to "stay put where he could see her." Yeah, something was up with that. But at that point I didn't have the wherewithal to even ask. I was just happy for her.

He commanded the stage with the ease of a seasoned performer. To say I was pathologically obsessed would be putting it mildly. My eyes never left him; entranced, they watched as his muscles flexed with his every move. However, I did notice Woody's gaze intermittently meet Cindy's. There was fire there—not on par with what Abel and I had, but fire, nevertheless.

Fan girls savored his deep throaty lyrics like syrup-soaked pancakes. And yet, it was bittersweet and it made my heart squeeze painfully. Normally, I wasn't the jealous type; until now, I had never cared enough to be. But with Abel, I couldn't help myself; those fan girls made my temper flare with possession. I wanted his attention, his smiles, and the taste of his lips all to myself. Standing to the left of the band backstage, I felt thankful for the dim lighting, allowing me to gawk at him all I wanted without everyone seeing.

With his guitar strapped across his body, Abel looked to my side of the stage, his eyes meeting mine. His sparked with something akin to danger. A slow smile graced his beautiful face as he winked at me. Blindly, I grabbed my neck to thwart the fire that moved across it to my face. I was glad there was no one paying attention to this blatant display of heat. Anyone with eyes could see how viscerally he affected me. Grabbing the mic, he leaned forward, his eyes slowly taking in his legions of worshipers. The audience quilted the countryside and seemed to go on for miles. However, he had a way of making you feel as if you were the only person in the room. His gaze had the ability to penetrate your deepest, darkest thoughts, leaving you naked. Bared. Stripped of all dignity…

The melody for "Forever" started. The crowd went crazy with screams. I felt the same way. It was one of my favorite songs, and I was excited to see him perform it live.

Cindy was, too. "Wow, they rock. Holy shit, look at him up on that stage. He's a god, right?" she screamed over the music.

"Yep, he certainly is! You see the looks he just gave me? The wink?" I yelled in her ear.

"Um, I'm not blind, chick. Of course I saw. The sexual tension between you two is killing everyone around you. I say just get it over with already. You're killing me Smalls!" she half-laughed in sympathy, then turned back to the performance.

"How ya doin' tonight, Colorado?" he asked the crowd. The cheers reached ear-shattering levels. The event was sold out all four days. It was a beautiful night to be at an outdoor festival. A girl in the front row threw her black, lace bra at him. Of course, he caught it, inspected it, and then scrunched it into his back pocket—but not before turning to smile at me. I wanted to slap his face, set fire to that bra, and kick the chick who had tossed it in her teeth. My possessiveness hit a homicidal pitch. I went to DEFCON 1, cocking an imaginary pistol in my mind. One of the roadies accidently bumped into me on his way over to Abel with a chair.

"Excuse you!" I screamed. The fuck! I was ready to throw down. How in the world did I ever think I'd be able to handle Abel? How would I ever deal with his personality, his man-whoring, or the hordes of slutty fan girls?

The lights dimmed as a single, muted spotlight illuminated him in all his epic glory while he took a seat.

"Feel free to join in the lyrics, loves," he urged the crowd, strumming his guitar in concert with the band, their instruments blending beautifully for the start of the ballad.

The memories of you and me
Haunting me every minute of
Every day. One more breath.
One more taste of my dirty girl.
You are my heroin. My addiction.
I want to mainline your love
until the reaper pulls me under.
Forever. Forever. Forever…
Cold and empty is what remains.
A life without you
I wanna get high on you
It's all right to pray to
your God because I'm coming
for you.
Forever. Forever, Forever …

I was fantasizing about taming the bad boy. I wanted to be the one he was singing to—singing *about*. I wanted those words to define what we had. The hairs on my arms stood stock-straight. My skin felt feverish, and my panties were dripping wet. The tears I was holding at bay caused my throat to squeeze tightly. His words both pissed me off and had me deeply affected. The pain in his voice hit a nerve with everyone. He had that kind of disturbing effect on women. However, I needed to keep my eyes on the prize. He was my way out. I deserved it. I deserved him. I would stop at nothing, risk it all—my reputation, my sanity, and my heart. Feeling overcome with angst and passion, I turned to Cindy.

"Chick, I, um … I could really use a drink," I muttered. I was praying I would not tip my hand. Otherwise, she would see how in over my head I already was for this rock-god. I needed something to take the edge off, to calm my nerves and make me numb—*and* turn off the water-works in my panties. Just then, someone tapped me on the shoulder.

"Looking for some of this, kid?" Dave asked as he leaned into my space. Long live Dave. He was the band's manager. And as far as I was concerned, he needed a raise right the fuck then. Hell, yeah.

"Shit, you're a lifesaver. I'm parched," I said, smiling as I took the flask.

"Sure you are." Nodding knowingly, he moved back to his dark corner. *Whatever.*

Now that I had some much-needed alcohol in hand, in a matter of minutes, I hoped to be in happy-land.

The crowd was screaming their praises to the band. They did put on a ridiculously good show. But it was Ender and Abel's unplugged rendition of "Sunrise" that brought down the house. Women climbed on top of their boyfriends' shoulders, dudes lit up their lighters and held them up, and the crowd swayed as one. This was a beautiful tribute to people who were bullied. They were lecturing their audience in song—and the message was one everybody identified with. Everybody's been bullied at some point. I knew I had, and it sucked. It was the band's way of saying to those of us who had been bullied, "We stand behind you, with you, and for you. You're somebody—and you're everything to us. Let us be your pillar, your strength."

And that song got me to thinking. When I set out on my mission to get myself a self-made man, namely Abel, I had no idea how complex and deep he truly was. But standing there on the same side of the stage, watching him sing his ballad against bullying, I had a brief moment of clarity. He was a good man. I could see that clearly. And once I knew that, I started to wonder if I could really play him the way I had planned … I brought the flask to my lips in consternation. Yes, I could, and I was going to. End of story.

Dropping my head back, I downed the drink, needing the warming numbness of the alcohol. I had never been at a concert where a crowd was literally wrapped around the singer's finger. It was breathtaking—powerful. All in all, the first night of the festival was epic. How much better would the rest of the weekend be? I was pumped for the lineup, but *he* was the real reason I was there.

Abel bellowed out to the crowd, "Thank you, and goodnight. See you tomorrow night. Enjoy Dire Straits up next." He bowed gracefully. The band waved and departed the stage. I moved aside to let them pass, hoping to get a moment, a second, alone with him. Grabbing the heavy draped curtain for support, I waited. The band filed past me, Abel included. His gait hurried and deliberate, he did not even stop to acknowledge me. Did he have somewhere to go? Did I do something to warrant his disapproval? Or was he bipolar, maybe? Cindy hip-bumped me into the present.

"Let's party!" She practically ran after the band down the narrow hallway. A tented, outdoor venue was the site for the after-party. It was a perfect night for it. It was set up in the back of the festival to drown out the screams from the concert, enabling us to talk and party while the next band performed.

The party guest list was made up of lottery-picked fans, media, photogs, and us. I had a funny feeling about it. Cindy would hear none of my drama; she had her *Fourth of July* juju for Woody displayed proudly. If aura had a color, hers would be blinding. Not even I could spoil the night for her, at least not knowingly. If Abel pissed me off, or worse, *hurt* me, I'd retaliate. That was my go-to defense. I would fuck him before he fucked me. It might not be right, but it was who I was. It defined a part of me—the part that was vindictive.

Chapter Six

Abel

During our set, I flirted with Gia. What can I say? I was drawn to her. I felt a magnetic pull, a yearning from somewhere inside my soul. It was more than getting my cock wet. I knew that feeling all too well. And it wasn't that. It was something else— something I didn't like, something that made me feel weak, like a pussy. And I *ate* pussy; I wasn't one.

No, it was fucked-up. Above all, I had to resist giving in to that particular need. Because if I started, I would never get enough—and fuck that. My life was a rollercoaster of fucking, gigging, partying, and more fucking. I didn't need to be tethered to some chick who would constantly be yanking my chain. And what the fuck was going on with her and Ender? I didn't like how I felt about that, either. Fuck it all to hell. I'm out! We were celebrating. I was not getting pussy-whipped by some chick who was flirting with my mate.

Dave offered me a much-appreciated beer. I loved my scotch, but that night wasn't a scotch night. Beers and shots were our usual celebratory libations. But still, I was on edge. *Big Abe* desired some attention. And who was I to deny my cock anything?

The tent was a bit of a mob scene, with photogs snapping away, their close-range cameras clicking. However, it was getting on my nerves.

"Get that light out of my fucking face dude or lose it." I stepped up to the cameraman. I wasn't in the mood for it. I was wishing I had brought my bike like Woody and Ender had done. They had the right idea. Problem was, the last time I took a ride post-gig, the fucking cretin paps almost ran me and my bike into a ravine. *Motherfuckers.* And I was very protective as all get-out of my Custom Chip Foose Harley; one scratch on it, and the motherfucking apocalypse would descend. After that incident, I called in a favor and Chip delivered. Chip Foose normally didn't fuck with bikes. He was a muscle-car gear-head. Muscle cars were my other addiction. Give me a hemi and I'll give you a taste of what Hell's like. *Fuck, yeah.* A Harley between my legs, purring like a kitten, was the best sound ever. I would slow my breathing and heart rate to become one with my Slut. Yeah, that's what I called my girl—Slut. My Slut. When I downshift, it's like putting my fingers in a slut's pussy in search of her G-spot. I would hit that sweet spot—and open her wide. Take her for a good long ride. My Slut felt nice, vibrating with power under my dominant body. Fuck, just thinking about it got my dick hard …

And then, as if on cue, Cindy entered the tent with Gia, both of them looking lost until Ender greeted them with a tray of Patrón shots. He was up to something, likely looking to get Gia fucked up and take her home. It would be interesting to see how she played it. I didn't normally obsess over girls, but fuck if this girl wasn't under my skin like an annoying splinter. Dave's hard hand slapped my back, bringing me out of my reverie.

"Dude, let's hit the bar," Dave said. "Shots?" He smiled and I nodded knowingly. The bar was nicely set up with all the top-shelf liquors. There were a few of Puff's Ciroc girls passing around shots. They wore leather get-ups with five inches of fucking glory on their feet. How in the world they managed to walk was another story. I needed to get one of those babes wrapped around my waist.

"What are we toasting to?" Dave asked, raising the shot glass to his parched lips.

"Here's to suckin' and fuckin', and not catchin' nothin'!" I crowed, downing my drink. Dave nearly choked to death.

"Went down the wrong pipe," he sputtered, coughing his brains out. I patted his back.

"There, there, candy-ass," I cajoled. He turned red, and that only made me laugh harder. Maybe this night wouldn't suck after all …

But then Ender joined our party of two, making it a party of five.

"What's up, Holmes? Abel, you up for going to club Blue tonight?" he asked. "I called Bobby, got us a booth." He laid his accent on a little thicker than usual—which meant one of two things: either he was extremely comfortable and relaxed, or he was showing off his pussy-tease cadence. I wasn't digging option two.

"I'm up for any place but here," I said, meeting Gia's gaze. Immediately, she lowered her eyes to the floor. Good girl. At least she knew her place. And that pleased me more than it should, making me smile. Cindy stepped forward, putting herself between me and the bar. Looking up through her thick lashes, she asked, "Wanna do shots with us? I'm in need of some liquor, and the faster the better." She smiled up at me, then turned toward the rest of the gang.

"I'm up for shots, darlin'. Name it." I motioned for the bartender to take our order. He was busy eye-fucking Gia. I slammed my fist down hard on the portable, wooden bar, nearly splitting it in two.

"Fucker, I'm talking to you!" I glared at him. He knew he'd been caught ogling Gia. He hustled his lanky ass over and asked what we wanted to drink.

"Five shots of Jamo," Cindy replied, smiling brightly. Gia rolled her gorgeous eyes. I hung back to get a better look at their non-verbal dialog between the two girls. Both of them were very obvious in their body language. I read women perfectly. It was clear to me that there was a story behind Cindy's grin and Gia's leer. There was a battle waging—but which of them would win was the question. My money was on Gia. She didn't look like the type of chick to run from a challenge. Her eyes told me more than her voice ever would.

Ender stepped up to help pass out the shots. Shaking his head, Dave looked at me, then at Gia. He knew me well enough to know something was going on. Even if that something wasn't *ever* going to amount to anything. Thick stratus clouds of sexual tension hung heavy between us. *Interesting.*

"Here's to?" Ender began to say.

"I got this, E," Gia piped up, saluting us. "Here's to good friends in hard times, and hard friends in good times."

"Hear hear!" Cindy cheered on with a fist pump. We all shot down the fiery whiskey. The burn was long and steady. My eyes were closed, savoring the sensation. I took a moment to reflect on her toast. While it was sassy and cute, I didn't like the fact that Gia had called Ender "E." The *fuck?*

"Woody and Jake still doing press?" I asked Ender. He looked toward the back of the tent before responding. We always flipped a coin to decide whose sorry ass got to suck ass with the press. The last two times, I was the one the duty fell on—and both times I nearly bit the reporter's head off. Those scumbags always claim it's "off the record." Nothing's off the record—*ever.*

Dave asked the lanky barman for three beers. Instinctively, I turned, looking for Woody and Jake. Sure enough, they were walking over—and they looked none too happy. That made me grin.

"I don't know about you, but after seeing those Ciroc girls, I'm really chubbed up," Woody said, grabbing his dick and laughing. But when Cindy stepped out from behind Ender, his face turned a bright shade of red.

"What's chubbed up?" Cindy asked, addressing no one in particular. We all had a good laugh. Her flushed cheeks matched

Woody's. Then she decided it was time to go to the ladies room to relieve herself, which made us laugh even harder.

"We're all going in the limo. No separate car shit, boys." Dave announced sternly. Sometimes we split up. We all had custom, chromed-out bikes and cars. We loved to ride hard. We were all testosterone-rich, come-filled speed-junkies. Road rash was a battle scar we wore proudly. Even in that we were competitive.

Dave made two phone calls, first to security, and then to the limo driver. Security swiftly ushered us through throngs of screaming fans inching close enough to grab at us. Be it your hair, an arm, your belt buckle, or your cock, they latched on to any part of you they could. It was a vicious sea of opportunists. Thankfully, the driver was standing with the door open to welcome us. I nodded my hello, and let the girls in first. Gia moved to the end of the curved seat. I chose to sit on the back bench, which gave me the strategic advantage of facing forward. After all, I had to see where we were going. And Gia was cock-center— bull's-eye.

The rest of the crew filed in, looking for comfortable places to sit. Not me. I was already fucking comfortable. Jake closed the door and immediately started making cocktails for the crew. I accepted a beer. I decided I would be low-key, chill out, and breeze a few babes; take it nice and easy. The banter was light with heavy eye-fucking going on between Woody and Cindy. Gia seemed to be fascinated by a piece of invisible lint on her dress. Nervously, she wrung her hands. *I* made her nervous. And that made my cock twitch and thicken painfully. *Fuck.* I adjusted myself with no shame. There's no shame in having a big cock. It's just a shame when you don't.

Despite her anxiety, her daring eyes met mine. A playful smile pulled at the corners of her lips—those perfectly heart-shaped lips, lips that would be *Nirvana* wrapped around my cock, killing me sweetly. Gia adjusted her position to face me head-on. Purposefully, she crossed and uncrossed her toned legs, serving me an agonizingly slow glimpse of her pussy. As in "look what I got for you, Abel." *Fuck me.*

I lost my breath for a moment and grabbed the door handle to brace myself. I needed to tether myself to something tangible to keep from fucking losing my shit in my pants. The air-conditioning button was above me. I turned that fucker on high. I never took my eyes off of her, though. Something snapped in me. My blood pushed through my veins with the force of Niagara Falls. I wanted to take her over my knee right then and there for that display. She was being a perfect little brat. The thought of her perfect globes under my hands had my heart pounding. My resolve was to own her—mind, body, and motherfucking soul. I extended my hand to her. She accepted it with a sly smile. There was no smiling for me. My dick fucking *ached.*

I helped her onto my lap, my jeans playing cock-block. Ender was the first to notice. He frowned. Woody, Jake, and Dave's eyes followed, but they each went back to their conversations. I paid them no mind. I had a gorgeous girl perched on my lap who needed schooling. Now *she* had my full attention. I fought it all I could, but I was fucking done with that.

"You like to poke the snake, little girl?" I asked, pulling her hair away from her ear as I nipped at her.

She shuddered under my touch. I placed my commanding hand on her thigh to quiet her. Soon her body would come to know my touch, crave it, and need it. I would be the only nourishment she would need.

"I needed to get your attention somehow, right?" she whispered, leaning into my chest and craning her neck toward my ear. "I'm trying to keep your attention. Tell me how a girl can do that."

She pressed her ass into my already rock-hard dick. *Keep doing that, sweet girl* ... I never make promises, especially if I can't keep them.

Maybe, just maybe, I'd do a casual thing with her—just for the night. What could it hurt?

"Well you've got it, babe. Let's focus on tonight. Tonight you will be mine. I don't like sharing. Are we clear?" I told her straight out how it would be: I didn't fuck around or mince words. When I wanted something, I took it. And I wanted her. Even if it was for only one night.

We arrived at Blue. The line as usual was wrapped around the mansion-styled building. Security was at the door to walk us in, as per Dave's instructions. With Gia at my side, I made my way in amongst the screaming fans. We had a tremendous and loyal following. I made a mental note to thank Jake for heading up our social media. He and Dave constantly tweeted and posted pics on Instagram. Fans loved that shit. Carlo, the club owner, joined us as we walked in.

"Glad to see ya, man." He shook my hand hesitantly. I only nodded. I didn't do that man-hug shit; the other boys did. That was Ender's thing. It was a cultural affirmation for him. Carlo looked past me to see Gia peeking out from behind me.

"Who've you got here, Abel? Sweet thing, isn't she? What's your name, sweetheart?" He grabbed Gia's hand to kiss it. I stepped between them to circumvent it. That prick was not putting his fucking lips on what was mine. And *she* was fucking *mine*.

"Not going to happen, dude. Who she is, is none of your concern. Now, where's our table?" He stepped back. I stepped forward. His face draining of color. With that, I emphatically ended the power play for Gia.

"No disrespect, Abel. Follow me to your table. It's nice and private so you can get to know each other … if you know what I mean." He winked at Gia as I motioned for her to scoot into the booth. This fucker was getting on my nerves. I grabbed for his neck. However, Woody stepped between us.

"Lad, if ye don't stop acting like a cunting maggot you're gonna get your clackers ripped off," Woody told him. Wood's Irish lilt always shined when he was drinking. I had to laugh at the expression on Carlo's face. He didn't have a clue what the man had said, but knew enough to walk away. Woody turned and braced my shoulder with his hand.

"Lad, chill for fuck's sake." He nodded in understanding. I turned to Gia and she smiled, patting the bench beside her. Man, he was right, I needed to chill the fuck out. I nodded to Woody.

"I'm good, bro. Drinks? Let's get the waitress here—in a hurry," I said, impatient to get on with it. The rest of the boys filed in with Ender taking a seat next to Gia. *Motherfucker*. Cindy sat next to Woody, who was clearly fascinated with her tits. The boys were ready to party hard and I wasn't far behind them. A hot, blonde waitress in hot pants and a bra strutted over after winning a fight over who's going to serve our table. We were good tippers. The waitresses weren't only good at serving up quick liquor. They also were quick lickers. They were as totally proficient and mastered in getting a dude off in record time.

"Hey, babe. Haven't seen you in a while. Where you been hiding? I've missed you, baby." The waitress leaned in, squeezing my bicep.

"Haven't been hiding, just not interested," I snapped. "Now, how about those drinks." The bitch shot me a death glare. Fuck it. These chicks were tough as nails. Fan-girling took a certain amount of low self-esteem. These girls bounced back and came at you harder the next time. It didn't mean I enjoyed being a prick. I didn't. It's just if you give an inch you'll have a dick warmer on your hands the whole night. And the only dick warmer I wanted was about to lay claim to me by sitting on my lap for everyone to see.

"Excuse you, babe," Gia said with a smirk. "Well, there really is no excuse for you, is there. Now, be a love and bring the drinks." She and Cindy snorted. Dawn, the waitress, looked stunned. But she recovered quickly, ignoring Gia by smiling and winking at me. *See?* Gia stiffened in my lap. Perhaps she wasn't used to being disrespected. But fan-girls were a different breed of chicks; when it came to celebrity cock, they were fucking ruthless. The table vibrated with the heavy bass of the song. This club primarily played dance music. It wasn't really my scene. But my boys were cool with it and enjoyed hanging out here.

"Babe, you keep wiggling that tight ass of yours, I'll have to fill it with something," I told her, leaning in to smell her hair. Man, she smelled good—too good …

After an hour of straight drinking, the boys wanted to cruise the club. We were standing around the table. Ender was doing his thing on the dance floor, surrounded by scantily clad women pressing against him. Or was he pressing against *them*? Couldn't really get a good look. Woody went off with Cindy. And Jake was at the back bar with Dave. So that left Gia and me—alone. I needed to taste her. God knows she smelled good enough to eat.

"Babe, get that fine ass in the booth," I ordered. Smiling, she scooted in deeper. I moved in to meet her, pressing her back against the butter-soft leather booth cushions. The kiss started out nice and soft, then quickly became heated. Grabbing the back of her neck, I forced her to submit. She had a lot to learn, and that was her first lesson.

"Open for me," I commanded. Looking into her eyes, I slipped my fingers between her thighs. Since she had on thread bare panties, I ripped them off of her in one hard yank. She gasped. I chuckled. After smelling them, I stuck them in my pocket. My hand met with her saturated pussy. *My* pussy. I needed a taste. I pushed my index finger and then my middle finger inside her, curling them, looking for that sweet spot. I finger-fucked her to the heavy beat of the bass. I wanted to see her fall apart in my hands, and watch her face as I brought her there.

"Fuck, Abel. God, don't stop." She pulled me closer, writhing deeply on my fingers. She threw her head back, giving me access to her perfect neck. My tongue, the opportunist, took advantage of it. I licked, sucked, and nipped her column, moving downward toward her gorgeous tits. They were just over a handful and I had a big hand. Umm-hmm. She was flushed and moaning my name. I pumped faster and twisted my fingers as they fought against her contracting pussy walls.

"That's it, baby-girl. I'm gonna take care of you. Come for me, Gia," I growled, nearly busting a nut in my pants. Fuck, what was this chick doing to me? I'm not one for open displays of anything. Down-low was one of my nicknames. With Gia, it was quickly becoming otherwise.

"Fuck, fuck, fuck!" she screamed, losing it all over my hand. *Fuck, yeah.* I waited a moment and kissed her deeply before removing my fingers, locked up tight in that sweet cunt of hers. Her fragrant smell was permeating the air. I slowly vacated her, immediately tasting the goods; her flavors bursting on my tongue.

"Come, were taking a walk," I commanded, extending my hand. With me, there was no asking, only taking. She nodded, smiling with her flushed face looking up at me.

"Wait, let me fix my dress. I'm all fucked-up," she said nervously, looking around. She had just come all over my hand in the middle of the club and she was worried about her dress. *Chicks.* I couldn't keep me fingers from my nose. Her scent was addicting and I was a slave for it. I moved us quickly through the crowd, nodding to Dave and Jake. No words were needed there.

Outside, there was a grotto-like out-cove I walked us into. Lush outdoor furniture decorated the place. Heaters were strategically set around to keep the tropical temperature perfect. It was private and empty. I texted Dave, requesting that he post security outside the entrance. I didn't need people with their phones uploading this shit. I would protect her as much as possible from *that* humiliation.

"We're not going in there … I mean the Jacuzzi, right?" she asked worriedly. The hardness she mostly portrayed was only a thick skin she used to blanket her child-like sweetness. I liked it. I liked feeling needed. The Dom in me relished it.

"Babe, it's completely private here. Security is right outside. Nobody will interrupt us. You hear me?" I grabbed her chin a little too forcefully. I was wound up and needed to bottom out in her sweet cunt. The water from the Jacuzzi cast an ethereal visual display on the walls, giving a nice vibe for the seduction that was going to take place.

"Come to me," I said as I sat on the couch. And she did. I took hold of one of her thighs. They were baby-soft. She looked down at me through her thick lashes.

"Take your dress off, Gia," I instructed her, never taking my eyes off her so there was no misunderstanding. There were some things I needed in order to give her what she needed. Full submission was at the top of the list.

"Slowly. I want to see your beauty," I rasped.

"Okay, Abel," she answered. *That's right, baby, show me what you got.* She pulled her arms free and let the dress pool at her feet. She blushed under my gaze.

"You're gorgeous. Never be embarrassed of your body. You hear me?" I nodded for her to continue. Lastly, her French Chantilly lace bralette hit the floor. She winked, stepping out of her discarded clothing. *There's my girl. My girl?*

"Come sit here, babe." I patted my leg. I wanted her astride my legs. Her ass needed a proper spanking. There was no going slow with her. I couldn't. I wouldn't. She was going to meet the Dom that dwelled within—and serve her Master. She sat on my lap offering me her lips which I willingly accepted. Kissing those full lips was the sweetest agony I've ever experienced. I didn't do sweet. However, with her, I wanted to make love to her lips for hours. I grabbed her neck with both hands to keep her face in place. I couldn't get enough of her. Her tongue. Her taste. Her scent. I didn't want to rush things. However, I was having difficulty reeling it in. And if I didn't, I was sure to scare her.

"Gia," I panted. "Turn over my knee, sweets," I commanded.

"Seriously?" she asked anxiously. There was a fire in the pit of my stomach moving at break-neck speed to my dick, threatening to set me ablaze.

"If you're going to question everything I ask, then let's call it a night. I thought I was clear about what I needed. My needs and wants may be different than you're used to. Nevertheless, you will either submit or walk away. There's no in-between. No other options on the table." I started to stand up, to make my point. I had put it out there in its simplest form—truthfully. It's the only way to be. Her eyes panicked. Then she sighed and relaxed back into me.

"I want this, and I want this with you," she said unequivocally, then turned over on my knee. Her beautiful body draped across my thighs, a decadent confection. Her lush, bitable ass taunted me to spank it. My hand was itching to do it. But I would force myself not to give in to the darkness—not just yet. She yelped as I forcibly fisted her hair before the first in a series of five slaps came down. My cock, hard as granite already, thickened painfully. And her squirming didn't help matters.

"Hold still. You're not going anywhere, babe," I commanded. I wasn't selfish. It was important to give something back in return for her submission. I ordinarily wasn't a soother, but again, it was different with her. I wanted to reassure her.

"Okay, I'm doing my best here." She sounded hesitant, but resolved in her determination to do better. And that made for the perfect partnership between a Dom and a sub, *each giving and taking willingly.*

"And I do appreciate that, love. Really I do," I said, bending to kiss her reddened cheeks. I nuzzled her ass without meaning to. Her softness I could not resist. She moaned. A rumble from deep within my chest pushed forth, hindering my control. Five more slaps came down. Her bottom was cherry-red and she was sobbing. For a moment, I thought I hurt her. I was suddenly ashamed ... until her wetness seeped into my pants. She was drenched—a definite indicator that she liked it. *Thank fuck.*

"See how wet you are, mama?" I offered my fingers as proof. Mewling was all the response I got. It was all I needed. I rose, cradling her as my most cherished gift. It was time to give her something to remember me by—the kind of orgasm she's never experienced. Laying her down gently on the couch, I started disrobing, kicking off my shoes first. My shirt was next, followed by my button-fly jeans. I always went commando. Utterly naked, I kneeled between her legs, spreading them wide apart. The thought of a spreader raced through my mind. But I wasn't home and couldn't get my hands on one.

"Open those legs for me, Gia. I want to see that pussy, babe." I helped her by putting one of her legs over the couch. I could see her clenching, and my tongue was nowhere near her hole yet.

"Look how hot your fucking cunt is for me, babe ... glistening all pretty and shit."

I dove in, lathering my face and growling in her pussy juice. If I could bathe in this shit, fuck, I would! *God help me.* I wanted to live in there—crawl the fuck in there and live and breathe this girl's pussy. I pushed my nose in as far as I could, circling her clit with my lip ring. She was bucking like crazy; oh yeah, she liked me going down on her, liked having her pussy licked. Paying close attention to her nub, I nibbled. She screamed my name. I loved to hear her scream my fucking name over and over again. Loved that *I* did that to her.

As I held her down with one hand, I started pumping my fingers with the other one until I felt her cunt gripping them like a vice. After one more pump, I removed my fingers and sat back in the kneeling position. Gia's hands were still forcefully grip-ripping the couch. She panted heavily. After waiting a beat, I pushed her widened thighs toward her chest in a V. Spitting hard in the other hand, I worked my cock over good. With my head, I moistened the tip with her fresh, creamy orgasm—got it real wet so I could work myself in one ring at a time. It was time she became intimate with Jacob's ladder.

"Hold your thighs real wide, babe. Gonna work my piercings in slowly until your cunt opens nice and wide for me," I growled. Wide-eyed, she didn't say a word. All she could do was nod and blink. That was all I needed. Words only got in the way. I had already moved past them, and was barely holding on to my humanity. Like an animal, I growled and grunted with impending ecstasy. I worked the head of my cock in, making sure my Apadravya was well-coated in her slickness.

"Something's really hot ... feels like it's burning," she said worriedly, without letting go of her thighs.

"It's my piercing. It gets hot when my cock is hot. And babe, my cock is burning up right now—for you. It needs fucking in there, now. Arch your back for me, babe," I gritted through my teeth.

At this point my cock felt like it had its own heartbeat. It was throbbing and twitching with every breath. With cocksure movements, I started to descend on that pussy. She arched fully, and I surged forward. *Fuck,* I was home, buried balls-deep inside her. She needed a moment to adjust before I started rocking. Her pussy walls softened around my cock, which was my cue to start thrusting. Slicking noises filled the grotto. The bluish glow from the water lit up the walls. She closed her eyes, her neck lolling back and forth. I couldn't blame her; it was that fucking good. But still, I wanted her eyes on me.

"Open those pretty eyes, babe," I said mid-surge. Dark chocolate eyes simmered decadently through thick inked lashes. She wasn't overly made up as most girls these days are. She had on just enough to enhance her natural beauty. And she was beautiful. Beautifully flushed and pinned underneath me. *Fuck, yeah.*

"Lock your hands together above your head, babe," I demanded, and she acquiesced. Hooking her leg over my shoulder, I grabbed the arm of the couch with my free hand, surging with full power.

"Oh my fucking God!" she screamed, spurring me on. I ground even harder. Her screams drew a smirk from me; *that's right, honey; I am your fucking orgasm god.*

"Grab hold of my neck and hold on tight, Gia," I instructed in a primal growl. She clung to me tightly, wrapping her one leg around my waist and holding it with her hand. That little maneuver of hers sent me into a pussy rage. I *destroyed* her fucking pussy, pounding with my full weight, burying her into the couch as her pussy walls squeezed my cock. I knew she was close. So I worked my Apadravya against her g-spot until I had her singing my name at the top of her lungs. I reached between us to pinch my tightened sac and pulled back quickly to come, ejecting thick, creamy ropes all over her tits and stomach. I stroked myself a few more times to mark her fucking pussy. *Mine.*

Chapter Seven

Gia

One breath in. One breath out. Was it because this über-hot rock deity had just taught my pussy what it meant to be owned? Or simply because my heart was already breaking at the mere thought of the night ending? If we could live all our lives in one moment, *that* would be my moment. People always talked about meeting the other half of your heart, your soul, your equal—how it completes you. I felt I couldn't get any closer to Heaven on earth if I tried.

But those emotions had me second-guessing my charge at hand. Could I ever hurt the man who had ruined me for all other men? I'd like to think not, but I was the spawn of Eva Mastro, the Medusa—the social-climbing, black-widow, money-hungry, bipolar whore, who always found a way to get her way. She wasn't above pimping out her own daughter to get the deed done. Fuck, this was a train wreck waiting to happen. I felt it coming the way my mother could feel rain coming in her arthritic joints …

Abel and I had just finished having the best sex of my life. He moved to grab some cloth napkins, dipping them in the warm Jacuzzi water to clean me up. No one had ever taken care of me before. To be treated with that kind of care made me feel adored. My own mother had never nursed my wounds. I learned what that felt like from stepfather number two, who took pity on me and treated me like his biological child. But later, when the shit hit the fan and my mother was exposed for the money-grubbing whore she was, I was cast aside—forgotten. It hurt temporarily—until I learned a skill that served me well. The cloak I wore wrapped tightly around me barred anyone from seeing the real me underneath: the rotten human being who was ashamed of being her mother's daughter. And I don't mean by blood. I mean there was a part of me that actually identified with her purpose. I wanted to live a good life. Be adored. Showered with gifts. Treated with respect and equality. So I made up my mind to use whatever means were necessary to reach that state. I was goal-oriented. To be so was the first lesson I learned as a child.

He finished cleaning me. I felt self-conscious and wanted to cover up. If he noticed, he didn't say anything. He chugged a beer he had just opened. Damn, I needed a drink. And as if on cue, he offered me his. Just like that. That one gesture meant the world to me.

"Thank you. I'm so thirsty." I swallowed a mouthful of golden lager. I wasn't much of a beer drinker, but damn if I would complain at that moment.

"We should probably head back before your girlfriend Cindy sends out a search party," he said, and I agreed. I got dressed in record time, remembering I didn't have my bag to refresh my makeup. Cindy and the crew would plainly see that we had fucked. I'd never hear the end of it. Hopefully, she was wasted and hooked up with Woody. As long as he was paying attention to her tonsils, we were good. Combing out my hair with my fingers, I was almost ready. One last adjustment to my dress. Tits check. Hair somewhat tamed. I hoped I didn't look as freshly fucked as I felt. I just remembered I had no panties. They were ripped and in his pocket. Ugh.

"Come." He grabbed my hand and escorted me back into the club. I noticed the security at the entrance keeping a watchful eye, but he never acknowledged them. I walked by them with my head down. I was beyond mortified. Of course, they knew what we had been doing. Hmm, I wondered how often they did that for him. My chest squeezed at that thought. It made me sick to think of him with another woman. Fuck. How many women has he been with? And being the dipshit that I am, I had not used protection. Though, come to think of it, that would be a nice little surprise, wouldn't it? In no way was I ready to become a mother—*but*. Maybe I was, maybe I could do it—if the child were his.

The club was packed with wasted dancers. Billows of smoke from the fog machine clouded my vision, yet added a little mystique to the vibe. Maybe I wouldn't get ribbed too badly, considering how hazy it was in there. Could I possibly be that lucky? Abel walked ahead of me, proudly holding my hand as we made our way back to our friends. It felt nice and made me smile. People parted as we made our way to our table. I wasn't surprised to see Cindy locking lips with Woody, doing a thorough tonsil check. *Get it, girl!*

The giddiness started to take hold. I had to bite my lip to keep from laughing like an idiot. I was elated and possibly cray-cray with the kind of pent-up, girly energy only a man could give a woman. Finally, Cindy and Woody came up for air as we approached. Yeah, Cindy would know for sure any second …

"Well, here comes Abel's boner-garage," Cindy leered, smacking the table and spilling Woody's drink. They all had a good laugh, including Abel. I wanted to die right there. We were all adults, but that was extremely embarrassing. A *boner garage?* Who even says that shit? She was my chick, but her mouth was getting reckless and she was wasted. I decided not to ruin the night with a verbal throw-down, figuring it would be wiser to join in and vault right back at her.

"It wasn't like that, Cindy," I replied coolly. "Abel just gave me a thorough beard ride, that's all." I said that straight-faced while picking my nails. When I looked up, her mouth was shaped like a perfect O. I smiled and we fell apart laughing.

"Atta-girl." She high-fived me. I rolled my eyes and felt like a sixteen-year-old instead of the twenty-four-year-old that I was. But whatever. I just wanted to change the subject quickly, before the rest of the crew got back to the table.

"Drinks please," I said to no one in particular. Woody shimmed out of the booth to stretch his legs. He hailed blond Barbie, the whore waitress. Abel decided to take a trip to the bathroom, so I scooted in next to Cindy and reached for my purse. I needed to refresh my makeup.

"And?" She nudged me, smiling maniacally. She looked like the deranged joker from *Batman*. Anyone could see she was happy for me, even if deep down she was hesitant. She meant well. She just didn't want to see me get my heart broken. Neither did I. Which had me pondering. *Fate.* That word had never entered my mind—ever. Suddenly, it swirled around in my head like a wind-blown leaf. I didn't believe in fate. However, I did believe in happenstance. My plan was an enormous gamble, my royal flush in life. It was all about how to win the top prize—Abel. *Fuck. What was I doing?* I dropped my head hard on the table, feeling defeated already, then proceeded to thump it a few times, thinking, *what the fuck am I doing?*

"Hello? Come in, Tokyo. What the fuck did he do to you, chick?" Cin asked, brushing my hair out of my eyes. Cindy didn't know my plan. Yeah, she was my chick, but she would never be on board with this level of scheming. I needed to throw some chick bull-shit at her quickly. So I plastered a wild smile on my face, as I slowly picked my head up off the table.

"I'm still having an out-of-body experience, Cin. I mean … talk about being worked over. You have no possible fucking idea. True story." I held up my hand, swearing. She looked at me warily for a moment. But she took the bait. *Bingo*.

"Ok. Ok. Ok. Holy fuck." She bounced up and down, fanning herself. "Tell me already," she panted.

"Let me put it simply. With Abel, fucking is not the answer. Fucking is the question. Yes is the answer," I said matter-of-factly.

"What the fucking fuck? English please, not Giabonics. Give it to me straight, chick-slit." She seized my arm, shaking me.

"He's a tatted, pierced god," I said. Which wasn't nearly sufficient at all. I contemplated this for a moment. She pinched my leg under the table.

"Ow! Seriously? Pinching. Really?" I rubbed my leg. Perfect timing. The blond, train-wreck Barbie was back with a bottle of Jameson, a Fireball, and a few pitchers of beer.*Perfect*. I immediately grabbed the bottle I wanted.

"Shots?" I held up the Jamo bottle to Cindy. Yeah, she wanted a glimpse into what I'd like to hope was mere foreplay. I needed more of Abel. It was not the time for girl-dishing. It was party-fucking-time. And I felt as if it were New Year's Eve.

"I'll let it go for now. But you know you're spilling your shit tomorrow morning, right?" Smiling, she grabbed the Fireball bottle. We did a couple of shots, beer-chased. We needed to catch up to the rest of the guys. Abel had fucked me straight, fucked the effects of the alcohol right out of me. If Cindy was any indication, the rest of the boys were probably loaded as well.

Speaking of Abel, where the fuck was he? I was getting itchy and punchy thinking about what he could be up to, or into. Woody walked up behind Cindy, squeezing her waist. She giggled and returned a drunken grin. *Oh, hell*. I decided to go on an expedition and check out the dance floor. *Hmm*. Where was the rest of the boys? The dance floor looked like a mosh-pit.

But there was something going on in back, in one roped-off corner. Lethal Abel's security team was back there in force. What the hell was going on? Nosy, I moved down the marble steps carefully for a closer look. I could see Ender's distinctive tatted arm fist-pumping to Jay Z's "Show Me What You Got" alongside some brunette amazon. She was showing him what she had, too. Huh? Who knew that dude even danced? He was Spanish, though, and Spanish people were a passionate culture. Made perfect sense he had natural rhythm. And Ender seemed to be a very passionate man. From what I could see, security was having a tough time containing the crowd around him. He was doing some form of modern salsa-style break-dancing, which didn't help crowd control. Girls cheered him on. Dudes left the dance floor in defeat. There was no use competing with Ender. There was no contending with *that* boy's moves. *Damn.* The ladies certainly adored him. It didn't surprise me that he was a gifted dancer. He mastered everything he tasked.

People-watching was one pastime Cindy and I enjoyed together—especially when we were drinking. The more trashed people got, the more idiotic they behaved. It was just more goofing material for us. I turned to see if Abel had come back to the table—but he had not. What I did see was a very lip-locked Woody and Cindy. *Good for her.* And I meant it. She was a good girl. A fucking fantastic friend. They started mixing "Clarity" into the song. Before I could turn around to get Cindy, she managed to slam into me. Which sent my drink sailing all over the poor guy next to me.

"Gavin!" Cindy cried, hugging me and screaming drunkenly over the music. "It's totally Gavin and Em's song," she said, leading me on to the dance floor. We always danced to this song.

"OMG. Remember last summer when Gail McHugh's *Pulse* came out? Best summer ever!" Cin squealed.

"Let's pay tribute," I yelled back. We were book nerds. Fucking glammed-up, hot, smutty-book-nerds. We had decided "Clarity" was Gavin and Em's song last year. We were entrapped by that book;

fucking *Gail*. She killed it. It was an awesome action-packed summer. Nostalgia hit me hard. She led the way to the dance floor. I happily followed. We found a small piece of real estate and danced our asses off. Not a care in the world. We were wrapped up in the adoring girl-love we had for each other. My hands were in the air, waving back and forth.

Then, during mid-sway, I felt strong arms wrap around my waist. *Abel*. He pulled me against his hardened cock. *Oh my*. He was insatiable. I loved that. I closed my eyes, relishing the feel of his toned body grinding my ass into his hard-on. I was thrilled he was dancing with me. Thrilled for everyone to see I was his. I went for my signature move, "dropping my eagle." I pulled out the whole fucking repertoire of dance moves. Yep, I was going to show him what he would be getting later. Some say my moves would make a stripper blush. But I could move, and I liked to show it.

The song changed to a slower one. I needed another drink, anyway. That's when I noticed Cindy's wide-eyed expression. *The fuck*. I grabbed Abel's hands to keep them on me while I turned around. Searching the crowd, I saw Abel standing on the steps to the dance floor. My breath caught. My stomach churned in angst. *What in the fuck*. I released the hands I was holding and whirled around to throat-punch the fucker whose hands were on me. It was Ender's face I saw. He caught my fist mid-punch.

"Ah ah ah, little girl. Violence never solves anything. Weren't you taught that?" He winked at me, continuing to dance. It was not a dancing situation. My body stiffly moved on its own accord toward Abel. The expression on his face was a mixture of anger and something else. I picked up my pace, slamming into people to get to him. I needed to explain. I thought it was him. I would never do that. Ever. Ever. Ever.

"Get the fuck out of the way, people!" I shrieked, panicking. *Oh fuck, this was bad*. My legs felt shaky and weak. I was probably going to faint due to my heart pounding so hard it echoed in my ears. *Oh Christ … please, please, please, God. I never asked you for anything. Please let him forgive me, let him at least listen to my explanation.*

However, it was not meant to be. Some fucking stunning motherfucking bimbo twat coiled around him like a snake. My fists balled. She was going to get a fistful of wrath when I got her. I was going to rip her fucking hair out—every last strand. I went to lunge at her when Ender and Cindy thwarted me.

"Don't do it, Gia," Cindy pleaded, yanking me toward the booth. *Oh, fuck.* The room was out of focus. Could you actually see pain—physically see it? Fire pushed through my veins. The air felt thick. I couldn't breathe. My hands gripped my head for fear it would explode. It was too much.

"I need to talk to Abel," I insisted as I stood up, holding my head, ready to pull my hair out. Yep, it was that bad; I felt like I could actually rip my own hair out. God, my neck felt tight and my throat swollen. Ender and Cindy just stared at each other, their gaze heavy with meaning.

"What the fuck?" I screamed. "I'm going to find him." I started off in the direction I had last seen him, looking for that head-turning twat.

"He left, Gia." Cindy said. Ender nodded in confirmation.

I rubbed my eyes with my fingers. They were burning. Or was it the tears? I never cried. I didn't think I could. But I had the living proof running down my face right now. Maybe if I rubbed my face hard enough I'd be a new person—one worthy of Abel. I needed to rub *something*, even if it meant I hurt myself. Fat tears ran down either side of my cheeks in torrents. It was bad … real fucking bad. My body was numb. I couldn't feel or hear anything. I wanted to die. Just die. Anything to get away from the pain …

And that thought only made me cry harder. After all, I was the person who found my twelve-year-old brother hanging from the bathroom shower rod. His jerky movements left an undeniable mark on my psyche. What fourteen-year-old girl would ever be the same again after seeing that? The 911 operator had instructed not to touch him. But over the years, the constant replaying of that event in my head had left me wondering: maybe I could have helped him had they let me cut him down. However, at that very moment, standing inside that club alone, I wanted to trade places with my brother. I wanted to be dead. I was the one who deserved it. Not him. He was innocent. A good boy. I was the doppelganger to my mother, and as such, I deserved this apocalyptic shit. And it was apocalyptic. My world as I knew it was over. Steepling my fingers, I took a deep breath and contemplated my next move. My eyes focused on the swirls in the carpet. Depression was seeping in. I could feel the cold isolation already. All around me was the sound of nothingness. I was scared for the first time of my life. Would I ever feel him again? *Abel.*

"I'm so sorry, babe," Cindy whispered, stroking my hair. *So was I.* "You want to leave?" she asked carefully. She didn't know what to expect; she had never seen me like that.

"Wait a minute!" I exclaimed. "Ender, can't you talk to him? I mean, it's totally your fucking fault." I drove my index finger into his chest. He just smirked. He thought this shit was real fucking funny. Fury was taking hold.

"What the fuck is wrong with you, anyway?" I lashed out. "Why would you pull that shit? Huh?" Raging, I stepped close enough to spit in his face.

"What? I was only dancing with you, mami. Besides, what's the problem, anyway? We're two single adults, right? Why wouldn't we dance, Chicka." He thought his explanation was perfectly reasonable. *Boy, was he a thick one.*

"Don't call me mami! And I was with Abel—Ender!" I screamed furiously. *Did he not get that?* What was with the feigning innocence routine? Cindy grabbed the bottle of Jameson off the table, thrusting it at me. That's exactly what I needed. I tipped the bottle, taking a long swig. The burn actually felt refreshing. I wanted the pain. Pain was what I needed. Physical pain and motherfucking agony.

"First of all," he began. "I didn't know you two hooked up. When was this? Tonight? If so, I wasn't around, remember? I was hooking up myself. Do you think I would honestly do that to my bro? I have more fuckin' pride and self-respect than that. I take that shit seriously. I don't fuck over my dudes for pussy. Sorry, but no. I like to piss Abel off when I can—especially because he's always all cerebral and shit. I can assure you, he's not pissed at *me*," he huffed, rolling his eyes. He grabbed his beer for a long guzzle while turning to cruise the crowd. *Oh hell to the no.*

"Oh, thanks a lot, you selfish, Latin, Lothario prick." I pushed him up against the table. I needed to get out of there quickly before I got arrested for assault.

"Whoa whoa whoa, chick," Cindy interjected. "Maybe giving you the bottle wasn't my best idea. Give it back, Gia. Things are getting out of hand, chick." She motioned with her hand for the bottle.

"Here." I handed her the bottle. I needed to straighten up and be on my game for what I was about to do. I feigned going to the bathroom to freshen up so I could grab one of Abel's bodyguards without those two knowing. The giant dude was kissing some twit against the wall in the hallway. Nice. Real fucking nice.

"Ahem, sorry to intrude. I really am, but I need a favor. Abel told me to meet him at his house. We got separated by fanatical fans and security got him out of here. He's probably worried and my phone is dead. Can you take me to him—please?" I begged, giving him my best puppy dog expression. The skank just rolled her eyes. I rubbed my face with my middle finger and smirked. She glowered. Ha! Fuck her.

"You're Gia, right?" He went to pull out his cell. *Oh, shit.*

"Wait!" I seized his arm while looking seductively up through my lashes. "I'd love to surprise him. I have something … kinda sexy planned. I wouldn't want to ruin the surprise," I purred, winking at him.

He stared at me as he tried to decide what to do. I took action at his moment of indecisiveness. I grabbed his arm, dragging him through the crowd. I needed to take charge. I made sure to sneak around Ender and Cindy. Where the hell was the rest of the crew? Probably hooking up, themselves. There were a few limos out front. The one we had arrived in was gone. I sighed as sadness hit me hard in my gut.

The giant of a security man walked me to a blacked-out, stretch Mercedes, opening the door. I guessed it was one of the Lethal Abel fleet cars. I had no time to ponder such niceties. I needed a plan. I needed to salvage my four-hour relationship that I had spent countless days cultivating. The car started with a purr.

"May I have your cell, please?" I asked the bodyguard. "I just want to text Abel to let him know I'm safe and on my way."

He handed me his phone through the privacy divider. I texted Abel, posing as the bodyguard who was driving me to him: *"Hey, just checking that you're home safely. If you need anything, please let me know."* There, it was done. I waited for the return text while I fixed my makeup. I was a mess. I couldn't face him like that. I made sure my own phone was turned off and waited for what felt like hours …

Then *bing!*—the text popped in.

Abel: Thanks, man. I'm good. Home. Enjoy the rest of your night. Ttyl.

Great. I deleted the message and passed the cell back to the giant. "Thanks a lot." He nodded in the rearview mirror.

I burrowed into the buttery-soft leather seats, with my head resting comfortably against the rest. Dwelling on the emotional trauma of the evening, which had sucker-punched me in the heart, I wondered: did I have a choice? This was Abel—the hottest, sexiest, wealthiest, alpha male I'd ever had the pleasure of knowing.

The limo slowed as we approached an Art Deco building with beautifully lit landscaping. The building was impressive in size and décor. It housed the Who's Who of Colorado's bachelors. As a teenager, I would walk by to daydream, imagining what it would be like to live there, to not have to worry about wealth or social status. If you lived at that address, you had already arrived. It was as simple as that. Your address was your calling card. It spoke volumes of your pedigree. The building was sophisticated with an old-world charm. *Damn.* He had some serious cash—which put him completely out of my league. We weren't even on the same playing field. But if I'd learned anything from my mother, Medusa, it was to stay committed and on task. Set your sights on the prize. Hold on tight, with just enough constriction that eventually your prey will weaken and succumb, leaving you the victor. *To the victor go the spoils.* Yeah, that was it. I smiled. *Game on.*

A salt-and-pepper-haired, older fellow opened the car door for me to exit. He grabbed my hand to escort me safely into the building. *Now what?* I smiled kindly, giving him my most heartwarming smile.

"I'm here by invitation for Mr. Abel Gunner," I said, worrying my hands. Fuck. Shit. Crap. Cock. I kept smiling, hoping he would fancy me enough not to ask me any pertinent questions. I blinked more than usual, hoping to come off as an airhead. *They do that, right?* I didn't even have a clue what floor or apartment number. My panic rose in my throat, tasting vaguely of vomit. *Gross. Or was that the Fireball? Christ Almighty, give me some help, please.*

"Follow me, little darling," he said, winking as he walked me toward a separate elevator bank. He had a slow southern drawl. Funny he didn't look like a southern gentlemen, but his slow gait and comfortable speech made me feel secure. That was a blessing. I didn't think they had girls like me where he was from. A beautiful smile doesn't necessarily guarantee you have a beautiful heart. My heart was black.

When we arrived at the elevator, he inserted a special key and motioned for me to get in. I nodded in thanks.

"One question, sir. How do I know which place is his? I'm embarrassed to say I wasn't paying attention last time." I winked. He nodded, blushing.

"The car will let you out in his penthouse." He smiled knowingly and walked back to his post. The elevator door closed promptly. *Oh my fucking God.* The car rose. So did my bile. I wanted to hide. Somewhere. Anywhere. I needed to think. Needed time to think. Suppose he wasn't alone. Suppose he …

And then the elevator door opened. Of all times to have an efficient elevator. *Why. Why. Why.*

Defcon Two: Fast pace. Next step to nuclear war. Be ready to engage and deploy in less than six minutes.

That's how serious this shit was. And to top it all off, the fucking elevator *dinged loudly*—and kept dinging. Those were possibly the loudest *dings* in the history of *dings*. Christ, my anxiety reached hypertensive levels. If I survived this without going into full cardiac arrest, that would be saying something about Medusa's genes. However, I refused to give up.

The scene set before me was a violent one: a guitar smashed into pieces, a bottle of empty Jack on the area rug next to a Zebra-haired chair, and eclectic artsy pieces, including nude marble sculptures in erotic poses, were strewn around the penthouse. Photos and paintings adorned the walls. But what captured my eye was the huge life-like portrait of Abel hanging above the mantle fireplace; in it, he held a rope in one hand while dangling a red scarf in the other.

My body stiffened. I had seen that face tonight. His was the bellicose, daring, fiery countenance typical of an Alpha. I knew everybody had their own ideas about what constituted an Alpha. To me, a man doesn't have Alpha "tendencies"; he either is an all-out Alpha or he isn't. It's that simple. If you're Alpha, you're balls to the wall, with no pussy mush mixed in. And Abel Gunner was Alpha for sure.

I stood in his living room, taking it all in—his unique taste in home décor, his scent permeating the room, the lush red velvet drapes hanging heavy in the windows. All were phallic symbols of one kind or another, all very representative of him, of his masterful presence. I cracked my knuckles in anticipation. Anxiety zip-lined through my veins. My hands fisted. I was prepared for it all.

I made my way to a corridor off the kitchen, lit with melted candles, and stood there for a minute, straining to listen. I could hear soft lyrical whispers, the kind of whispers that had nausea building inside me now, mounting with the energy of a volcanic eruption. *Oh, fuck.* My legs forced my body forward. This could all end here and now. Passing by the erotic art lining the walls of the hallway, I approached two massive wooden doors with ornately carved underworld scenes. The left door featured a grinning demon holding a human heart. The right had two strangely beautiful horned creatures fornicating. I took the deeper meaning of those beautifully twisted images to be that Abel was a tortured soul. His torture brought light to my heart. Could I be the one to save him, to help him move past his darkness? And in so doing, might I find my own way, my truth? And could I even live in truth? My reality was reprehensible—sickening. Could truth ever be my reality? Could we help one another move beyond a lifetime of hurt to live in the light?

My heart wanted light. It didn't want to be the ugly, dark, broken organ it was. That much I knew. What scared me was the process of getting there—the commitment it would take, and the courage it would take to be truthful. Was I that courageous? Sure, I had the guts to sneak into his apartment. But, could I, would I, be courageous enough to live in the moment of total transparency? That I doubted.

Laying my ear against the door, I gripped the cold steel doorknob and listened. He was humming something—I wasn't quite sure what. I could hear the strumming of his guitar. Was he singing to somebody? Oh God, I hoped not. Gently, I opened the door an inch to take a peek. Abel was perched on the windowsill wearing low-hanging sweatpants, a baseball cap turned backward, and holding his guitar across his lap. His tatted, muscled body in all its magnificence was just sitting there in the window, picture-perfect, for all the world to see. In his gruff voice, he was softly crooning "Stay." As with anything Abel touched, he made it his. And his was the most beautiful, heartbreaking, and gut wrenching version of the song I had ever heard.

> *Ooh the reason I hold on*
> *Ooh 'cause I need this hole gone*
> *Funny you're the broken one but I'm the only one who needed saving*
> *'Cause when you never see the light, it's hard to know which one of*
> *us is caving*
> *Not really sure how to feel about it*
> *Something in the way you move*
> *Makes me feel like I can't live without you*
> *It takes me all the way*
> *I want you to stay … Stay …*
> *I want you to stay, ooh I want you to stay …*

His hair billowed softly in the breeze. The lyrics danced over my skin and embedded themselves into my heart. Hesitantly, I stepped forward, sensing no obvious threats in the form of the stunning bimbo-twat from Blue.

"Abel," I whispered, scared to death. I surely didn't want to scare him, either. But the thought of him throwing me out of there made black spots form around the edges of my vision. He never stopped fingering his guitar. Did he not hear me? I moved a few steps closer, but kept near enough to the door in case I needed to exit quickly.

"Gia, I saw you on the security cam. How do you think you made it this far?" he said, focusing his gaze on the world outside the window. His fingers stopped mid melody. It was deathly quiet in the room.

I spoke to break the awkwardness. "I'm not going to get into why you left the club without letting me give you an explanation. I came here to give one in private. I want to explain what happened. And if you don't accept my explanation, I'll leave." I moved farther into the room to sit in the chair facing him. He wouldn't look at me. Instead, he continued to stare out the window, his hand white-knuckling the neck of his guitar. It was obvious he was pissed. I needed to tread lightly.

"Abel, hand up to God, I thought it was you behind me. Not for one minute did I *ever* think it was anyone else—let alone Ender. *Bible*," I said, with one hand on my heart and the other up to God. His eyes met mine in the window's reflection. I was sure I looked ridiculously childish—until I saw a small smirk pulling on his lips. I wanted to fist-pump. But it was way too premature to celebrate. I wanted to go to him, but I needed to know he accepted my explanation. It was better to let him come to me. So, I waited until, finally, he swung his legs off the ledge and placed his guitar against the wall. He stood up tall and proud and looked me in the eye.

"It's very simple, Gia. If I say something's mine, it's mine—meaning you will only be touched by me. You will only be fucked by me. You will only come for me. You will only dance with me. And I don't dance. Any pleasure you receive will be mine—unless I say otherwise. Are we clear?"

He came toward me. All I could do was stand stock-still; I couldn't even speak. He was now a mere inch away, and we were nose-to-nose, his eagle eyes focused on me, his prey.

"I have something I'd like for you to sign," he said. "If you agree to sign it, then we can move forward. If not, I had an interesting night. The first half, anyway, was very interesting. The second, not so much."

He grabbed my chin, caressing my bottom lip with his fingers. Was I supposed to talk? Was that a question? My brain was still stuck on the thought of being his sexual charge and of him giving me orgasms. *Wake the fuck up, Gia!*

"What do you want me to sign, exactly?" I asked nervously, licking my lips. Fuck, it was hot in there. He leaned in, feathering my lips with his. I wanted more. I wanted his tongue in my mouth. On my body. In my pussy. That wickedly talented tongue. I'd sign anything for that tongue. Lacing his fingers through mine, he led me out of his bedroom suite, his gait self-assured.

We walked a few steps down the hall to his immaculately clean and sparsely adorned office. It didn't look like it got much use—or maybe it spoke of the orderly man he was. A simple cherrywood desk with matching cabinets and two black leather tufted chairs with bronze studs were the prominent furnishings. He motioned for me to take a seat as he sat behind his desk. I felt as if I were at a job interview. Very formal. Crossing my legs, I sat back, hoping to drain my nerves. He fired up his computer, clicking a few times to bring the printer to life. He swiveled to remove the paper from the printer, slipped it into a manila folder, and then handed it to me. He rested his forearms on the top his desk, his eyes burning my body with gleams of confidence.

"Should I read this now? Or wait to read it at home? What's the protocol? I've never done this before," I said, smoothing my hand over the top of the folder, my eyes downcast, afraid to meet his. I sensed he approved of my humility.

"I would prefer if you read it now. This paper doesn't leave this apartment. I will give you a few moments to read it over. It's pretty standard and to the point. I don't fuck around. You will find within the pages of the contract the truth. My truth. My expectation. You will sign if you choose to accept to fully submit." All this he said matter-of-factly, and then business-like, he stood up and left the office.

I sat behind the closed door for I don't know how long before I found my curiosity winning out. With shaky hands, I opened the folder.

D/s Contract

I, *Gia Mastro*, with a free mind and an open heart, do request of *Abel Gunner* that He accept the submission of my will unto His and to take me into His care and guidance, that W/we may grow together in love, trust, and mutual respect. The satisfaction of *His* wants, desires, and whims are consistent with my desire as a submissive to be found pleasing to *Him*. To that end, I offer *Him* use of my time, talents, and abilities. Further, I ask, in sincere humility, that, as my Master, He accepts the keeping of my body for the fulfillment and enhancement of O/our sexual, spiritual, emotional, and intellectual needs. To achieve this, He may have unfettered use of my body any time, any place, to keep, as He will determine.

I ask that He guide me in any sexual, sensual, or scene-related behavior, in such a way as to further my growth as a person.

I request of *Abel Gunner*, as my Master, that he use the power vested in His role to mold and shape me, assisting me to grow in strength, character, confidence, and being; and that He continue to help me to develop my artistic and intellectual abilities.

In return, I agree:

To obey His commands to the best of my ability.

To strive to overcome feelings of guilt or shame, and all inhibitions that interfere with my capability to serve Him and limit my growth as His submissive.

To maintain honest and open communication. *(This could be a problem.)*

To reveal my thoughts, feelings, and desires without hesitation or embarrassment. *(Oh, fuck.)*

To inform Him of my wants and needs, recognizing that He is the sole judge of whether or how these shall be satisfied.

To strive toward maintenance of a positive self-image and development of realistic expectations and goals.

To work with Him to become a happy and self-fulfilled individual. *(I could do that.)*

To work against negative aspects of my ego and my insecurities that would interfere with advancement of my objectives. *(Here's the living in truth part. Could I do this?)*

My surrender as a submissive is done with the knowledge that nothing asked of me will demean me as a person, and will in no way diminish my own responsibilities toward making utmost use of my potential. In recognition of my family obligations, nothing will be required of me that will in any way damage, nor interfere with, the performance of my everyday duties.

This I, *Gia Mastro*, do entreat, with lucidity and the realization of what this means, both stated and implied, in the conviction that this offer will be accepted in the spirit of faith, caring, esteem, and devotion with which it is given.

Should either of U/us find that our aspirations are not being well-served by this agreement, find this commitment too burdensome, or for any other reason wish to cancel, E/either may do so by verbal notification to the O/other, in keeping with the consensual nature of this agreement. W/we both understand that cancellation means a cessation of the control stated and implied within this agreement, not a termination of O/our relationship as friends and lovers. Upon cancellation, each of U/us agrees to offer to the other His or her reasons and to assess our new needs and situation openly and lovingly.

This agreement shall serve as the basis for an extension of O/our relationship, committed to in the spirit of loving and consensual dominance and submission with the intention of furthering self-awareness and exploration, promoting health and happiness, and improving both O/our lives.

I offer my consent to submit to *Abel Gunner* under the terms stated above on this the _12th_ day of _May_ in the year *2014*.

Gia Mastro

Signature of submissive

I offer my acceptance of submission by Gia Mastro under the terms stated above on this the _12th_ day of _May_ in the year _2014_.

Abel Gunner

Signature of Dominant

Swallowing a ball of angst the size of Pluto, I grabbed the gold Montblanc pen purposefully left there for me and signed the contract. Before sandwiching it in the folder, I reread it several times. Although I wanted to submit to Abel, the contract seemed a bit extreme. Then again, I'd never been in a Dominant/submissive relationship. The wording was sterile and devoid of feelings. Maybe this wasn't atypical. I was certain Cindy would have a flippin' fit. Naturally, I couldn't worry about that now. Besides, she didn't know what my end game was: to reach his inner sanctum, where I needed to be to execute my plan. The choice I made a long time ago when I set the wheels in motion. Medusa, of course, was going to be thrilled, to say the least. Folder in hand, contract signed, I made my way through the penthouse looking for him. When I got to the living room, I ran into a preppy-clothed man who fancied soft pinks and blues.

"Hello, you must be Gia," he said with a flip of his hand—not the type of gesture a straight man would use. A warm, genuine smile lit up his boyishly handsome face.

"Hi, your name is?" I said, not wanting to be rude. Who in the hell was he?

"I'm Chance, Abel's personal assistant." He moved to shake my hand. "Sorry, I'm just trying to clean up after his late-night tirade. I figured I would stop by after my date to tell him how great Lethal Abel was. I was there with my date—front row." He beamed. His constant Bieber hair-flipping made me grin. He was a cutie. Too bad he batted for the other team. His dirty-blond hair, grey eyes, and olive skin gave him the good looks that made many a girl cream. I found myself wondering whether he played pitcher or catcher. But I figured I'd wait until I knew him a little better before asking.

"I was backstage. It was a ridiculous show. I loved it. I've never been backstage anywhere, ever. Not even a school play," I babbled, bending to pick up the neck of the broken guitar.

"No, no. I got it. It's no trouble at all. He's waiting for you on the terrace." He motioned for me to relinquish the carnage in my hand. "Come, sweets, I'll show you where he's brooding."

"Wait, if he's brooding, maybe we should leave him be. I don't want to interrupt whatever it is he's brooding over," I whispered.

"He's an *Alpha*, doll. He's always broody and pissed off, even when he's smiling. Nature of the beast and all that jazz. Speaking of jazz. I used to dance. Could you tell? John, my newest boy-toy, said I had a dancer's body. What do you think?" he asked, striking a pose with perfect lines that would make any ballerina sick.

"Why yes, now that you mention it, you do have the perfect dancer's body. I knew there was something about your physique. I just couldn't put words to it." I smiled, winking at him. He jumped up and down, clapping.

"Oh, aren't you just the sweetest doll ever in the history of evers." He hugged me tightly, kissing my cheek. "Let's go have a visit with sex on legs."

Gleaming, he led me to the terrace doors. Abel was drinking scotch, neat, with his feet perched on the edge of the chaise lounge. Chance opened the door and pushed me out. I whirled around and glared at him. He winked back at me, closing the door to give us some privacy.

"Hi," I said, sounding like a total idiot.

"Hi." He smirked at me through his inked lashes.

"I signed it. Now what?" I asked, taking a seat in the chair next to him.

"Now, we fuck. You're mine. I can take you wherever and whenever I please. Like right here in the open for everybody to see. Does that scare you, Gia? Or does it make you really wet?" His voice was dangerously low as he stared at my mouth.

Listen to OLN's version of "Clarity" here: http://www.youtube.com/watch?v=a_JgNNBX2bw
Listen to OLN's version of "Stay" here: https://www.youtube.com/watch?v=8Aufxr0Y0-g

---

Chapter Eight

Abel

Her lips were driving me crazy. I wanted to nibble, lick, kiss, and consume them, along with everything else about this vixen. My self-control would snap if she licked those lips just one more time …

At the moment, I had the world by the balls. My career was taking off. My boys were good. I had my health, money, status—and now Gia. All I had to deal with was the black smudge that was Morgana, who didn't understand the meaning of "no." She had the balls to keep calling, texting, and showing up at venues where I was performing. She was relentless in her pursuit. Good thing I had Carlo escort her out before she really made a scene. She already had the horns out for Gia. She had seen the two of us together, and had witnessed my reaction to the stunt Ender pulled.

Speaking of Ender; that Spic fucker was going to get his ass kicked. The minute I acquainted him of my arrangement with Gia, he'd best step the fuck off. Band or no band, friend or no friend, she was mine. Nobody fucked with my *anything*. He needed to be put in his place. I was getting real tired of him yanking my dick for attention. What I needed to focus on wasn't Ender; it was this little minx in front of me. I needed to fuck her, feed her, and bathe her.

"You see this? This is your new parking space." I patted my lap, and in response she smiled brilliantly. I loved that smile. I didn't want to share that gorgeous smile with anyone else. She approached me carefully. I grabbed her and pulled her down on to me. I wanted that ass on me right that second.

"Someone's happy with my new seating arrangement," she cooed, giggling. Yes, my dick was *real* happy with the new seating arrangement. I was as hard as a lead pipe and couldn't wait to get inside her tight pussy. Before finishing off my scotch, I offered it to her. She downed it.

That right there was why this girl was different. She caught my attention with her blithe, yet brash personality. Her vibe wasn't a superficial one. She was just a real cool chick, a chick I could definitely get into. *For now.* My cock had plans for her. And was screaming for attention.

"Babe, take off your clothes. I want to see what's mine. When you're with me, *alone*, there is no reason for you to have them on."

Before she rose, I grabbed her face to taste her, forcefully plunging my tongue into her mouth. Breathlessly, she disrobed, leaving her clothes piled at her feet. I stood up to eye-ball this beauty from head to toe. My blood pumped, raging to one extremity—my cock. After kissing the palm of her hand, I laid her out on the canopied bed. The chill in the air marbled her nipples, which beckoned me home. Taking my own clothes off in measured movements, I assumed the position between her legs. The Alpha in me wanted to become better acquainted with what was *his*. Her sweet pussy juice drove me wild. I was gluttonous when it came to her pussy. I am a man who loves pussy. I loved the way pussies looked, smelled, tasted, and how I made them feel. Lust, carnality, and eroticism were mere words that could only be used to describe what I felt with this woman. I would pay homage to that pussy. It would be my gift for her submission.

"Beauty, rest your thighs on my shoulders," I commanded. Her thighs squeezed my face into her pussy. My arms gripped her ass from underneath, lifting her to face level. I inhaled deeply, intoxicated by this Aphrodite, my tongue parting her folds to expose her clitoral hood. Her clit was swollen and ready to be sucked. I drew it into my mouth, gently sucking.

The wet sounds of sucking carried in the air. She moaned and screamed. With my face sandwiched between her creamy thighs, the crescendo was building to atomic levels. Her clit pulsed in my mouth, but I had her under my thumb. I didn't want her to come yet. I wanted to be inside her when she came. I wanted her to leave my cock thick with her come.

"Fuck, you give good head!" she shouted. "I'm about to erect a statue in your name." She laughed breathlessly. A wide grin decorated her flushed face. She was perfect. I don't remember the last time someone wanted to erect a statue in my name. Fuck, if that didn't want to make me beat my chest. I scooped her up into my arms and headed to the bedroom. I needed a bed for round two.

"I've got you, Beauty," I said, watching her wrap her delicate arms around my neck. She felt right in my arms. Leaning up, she planted a smoldering kiss on my pussy-juiced lips. She gave me a feeling that I've never felt before. It was undeniable. I sat her on the edge of my bed, grabbing for the fireplace remote. She was the perfect adornment for my bed. What more could a man want than a willing submissive? Especially with the spreader bar lying next to her. Either she didn't notice it or she didn't know what it was. Regardless, I would be using it tonight in our sex play. I had it specially made. It was tufted with supple leather and thickly padded. The cuffs were lined with quilted material so as not to chafe her wrists or ankles. Yes, she would learn quickly what it meant to be properly fucked, maximizing every nook and cranny God created. I would go deeper inside her than she ever believed possible. The thought of that made me harder than steel. My cock was already pointing straight up toward the ceiling. Now it was glistening at the thought of exploring her depths.

"Would you hand me the spreader bar, Beauty?" I asked in a low, commanding tone.

"And what and where would that be?" She laughed as if I were joking, looking around. She was now leaning up against it. Maybe she thought it was a pillow?

"The black roll you're lying on with the cuffs." I motioned toward it with my chin. I had to laugh to myself. I normally didn't do girls who were "*cc's*"—*cute* and *coy*. Rockers don't do cute. Fuck that shit. But Gia had my head all fucked-up. Not in a bad way, but in a *what the fuck am I thinking way*. She pulled it from beneath her, holding it up to me.

"This thing?" she asked. "I actually thought it was a neck roll pillow. I didn't notice the shackles on the end. Nope, I've never seen one of these in my life. But it sure is comfy."

She smiled up at me. *Comfy? Really?* I purchased the foam one with padding as to not chafe that creamy perfect skin of hers. I was just going to have to show her what this bondage restraint was all about.

"Babe, it's for bondage play. I figured I'd ease you in. Now lay back with your arms at your side and knees bent. I'll show you what this is all about. I promise you'll be begging me for it in no time." She inched backward, doing as she was told. That pleased me; no questions, no fucking weird looks or comments—just total compliance.

I placed the spreader between her lush ass and feet, then attached her wrists and ankles. There were no words between us—just the look of curiosity on Gia's face, as if she were taking everything in and filing it away. She tested the restraints by pulling. She was securely fastened in. That made me happy. She was curious. The cuffs were padded as well. I had taken every precaution to avoid marring her flawless body.

Seeing her bound before me, with her unquestioning trust and willingness to please me, spurred me on. Even though she was probably scared shitless right now, she never said a thing, but her eyes were speaking to me. They told me her truth. And her truth was that trust didn't come easy for her. Her supplication therefore made it all the sweeter.

It was time to claim my prize. Her lustful gaze was focused on the pre-come on the head of my cock. Umm, my girl wanted to sample my flavor. Grabbing my cock with my left hand, I squeezed the head, producing more of my juice. Rubbing my thumb over it, I then fed it to her, and slowly and deliberately, she sucked it off, moaning as she did. And then her thighs clenched.

"God, please kill me now. I can finally die here and now," she cried out.

"That's right, Beauty. Pray to your God." Stroking my cock with my hand leisurely, I crawled onto the bed, never letting go of my monster, and never taking my eyes off my beauty's pussy. Her skin was covered in goose bumps as she waited for her Master to bottom out in her sweet cunt. With my cock still fisted, I parted her folds with my fingers and rubbed the head slowly over her clit. She was soaked. Her little pants and sighs were driving me insane. She didn't have a clue. I didn't know what I wanted more: her mouth on me, or my mouth on her—that delicious cunt of hers, or her ass. I decided I would have them all.

I inched forward toward her face. "Open your mouth, Beauty. Let me watch you taste yourself on my cock." I demanded.

Her pink tongue poked out, stabbing for a taste of my slit before opening wide to accommodate all of me. Fuck, her mouth felt good. I straddled her chest, lifting up her face for deeper penetration. Her eyes were wide with tears as she started to gag. I loved when a chick gagged on my cock. I started to feel that tingle in my balls. I was about to blow my load too soon. She had a wickedly talented tongue and worked my loops like a ninja.

"Fuck, Beauty," I huffed. "I'd much rather come in that sweet cunt of yours."

She moaned at my declaration. I got off of her to kneel between her legs. I wasn't going to go slow. "Babe, remember this moment. This pussy is never going to know what rest is. Throbbing and clenching for me is all you will come to know. Begging me for time to recover between climaxing. I'm just going to be living inside of you from now on. Your pussy is my new favorite thing," I said, stroking and smiling.

"You are one cocky motherfucker. I'll give ya that, Abel. Put up or shut up is what I always say," she quipped back, mockingly.

"You have no idea, Beauty, no idea." I winked. I was in awe of the fine piece of ass in front of me. Not that I would ever utter those words out loud. Truth be told, there was something more with her. She had a little something extra the others lacked. I slipped into her hot pussy with a loud groan.

"Everything all right?" she questioned in the crook of my neck. I could hear the smile in her voice.

"Fuck, babe, it's more than all right. You feel fucking perfect," I declared, as I started to slip in and out of her. "Your cunt's got a death grip that I'm lovin' right now."

My hips picked up momentum. Christ on the fucking cross, she was nice and juicy, giving my rings a smooth, effortless ride. Her screams filled the air. Her fingernails ripped the shit out of my thighs. And her clenching cunt gripped my dick like a lifesaver. *Fuck yeah. Nirvana.* I was the deepest I've ever been in my life, hitting places inside her pussy at depths I didn't believe possible. The slapping sounds of our flesh meeting resonated through the air. I barely recognized my own voice as I rutted her good. The fact that she was trying to break free drove me even higher. My hair was a sweaty mess. The bed was saturated with our sweat and fluids. I placed ravenous kisses up and down her neck column, sweeping across her perfect tits. I took one tit in my mouth, and squeezed the other with my hand. I pumped like an Olympian, shooting my load deep into her pussy, pumping a few extra times for good measure. I was still coming. This had to be one of the hottest orgasms ever. Lifting my body off of her, I gently released the shackles and rubbed her limbs that were no doubt aching. She lay limply, exhaustion smothering her. Amazed, I brushed her soaked hair off her face while softly kissing her forehead. She needed to be cleaned up, so I went into the bathroom and grabbed a basin under the sink, filling it with warm soapy water. She trembled under my touch, taking little breaths, as if in pain. My insides squeezed with fear. *Did I hurt her? Oh, fuck, I'm one demented dude. What's wrong with me? I didn't even realize …*

"I'm fine, Abel. Actually, better than fine. That was un-fucking-believable. I actually feel spacey from it. Kinda here, but not? Ya know?" She laced her fingers through mine. My heart stopped for a moment. Yeah, I knew exactly how she felt. But again, I wasn't going there, I wasn't in to sharing.

Chapter Nine

Gia

He rubbed his thumb over my knuckles while his eyes burned into me. A moment was shared between us. But it was gone in a flash and Broody was back, being direct and to-the-point.

"I'm starved," he said, rubbing his thickly corded abs. "Wanna grab a bite?" His stomach growled. How could I ever say no to that man for anything? My eyes roamed over his body; *he was one fine fucking specimen.*

"You keep looking at me like that, Beauty, and we'll never leave." He leaned in, planting a kiss on my lips.

"We should shower. We reek of sex," I said, concerned. "And there's no way in hell I'm putting that club dress back on." I put my hands on my hips. He laughed, a full-on rumbling belly laugh. I didn't think it was funny. I was miffed. What the fuck was so funny about that?

"And that's hysterical to you because …" I shot back, half-annoyed with his outburst. He had a nice laugh, too. Nothing weird or unappealing. It was deep and made me dizzy from swooning just hearing it. I couldn't help but crack a tiny smile. God, it took a lot of effort not to flirt with him.

"I'm laughing because it's just such a typical girl thing to say. Besides, I like smelling like you. And I sure as fuck love you smelling like me." He walked into his closet where I heard a series of electronic beeps being keyed in. *Was that his safe?* I was about to gather my clothes from the terrace. *What time was it, anyway? It had to be 2am. Where could we go at this hour? To dinner?*

With a dimpled smile, he approached me with a neatly folded pair of sweatpants and a Soundgarden tee-shirt—and a handful of cash.

"Wear my clothes. They'll be big on you. But I'd rather see you in my clothes than the tight mini-scraps of a dress you had on tonight. Don't want to get into a fight, because some cocksuckers are looking at you and that fine ass of yours." He wrapped his hands around my waist, his eyes burning with intensity. I decided to put the damn clothes on and not say a fucking word. That had to be one of the hottest possessive edicts I had ever heard. *Damn.* I retreated to the bathroom to freshen up. I popped my head out the door quickly.

"Be right out, baby," I cooed. *Ugh, I was starting to nauseate myself with my mushiness.* His bathroom was adorned with monochromatic tumbled marble and handsome brushed nickel. Did I expect anything less than a bathroom fit for rock royalty? In my lifetime I would never have imagined I would be standing there right then—even with all my daydreaming. I refreshed my makeup, then put on his sweatpants. I had to roll the top down a few times. His clothing didn't have that fresh scent of dryer sheets. No. They smelled of him: a heady, musky, woodsy scent that I wanted to bathe in. All men should smell like him. But he wasn't like all men, was he? No, he wasn't. I rushed out of the bathroom, remembering something very important.

"Abel, we left the spreader on your bed. You should put it away before Chance sees it. I'd be mortified if he saw." A cleft smile graced his face. I wanted to grab it and kiss him to death or ride it hard. Good God, either one would do.

"Babe, who do you think bought it?" he said, walking to the elevator. *No?* He put his key into the elevator, pressing the down arrow. We stood silently for a few minutes, enjoying the nothingness. There was a lot to learn about Abel. But what I *did* know was he had a heart—a big one. He wasn't as impervious as he would have people think. Yes, he was a famous, hot-as-fuck rock-star, but he was also passionate about everything he touched. I could see myself having a great life with him. I would join him on the road, party the night away, shop until I dropped—and get my mother off my back. I would do just about anything short of committing murder to get that bitch off my ass.

We took the limo. Security explained to us that the traffic from the festival would make it a nightmare for us if we took his Harley instead. They wouldn't be able to protect him in all the commotion. And that meant he couldn't protect me. All of a sudden, that seemed to be paramount. After a moment of posturing, Abel readily agreed, saying he didn't want to take any chances with me.

I had never felt this adored in my life. My heart was full, and I wasn't exactly sure how I felt about that. I wanted it … that feeling, but I couldn't help the guilt that crept into the smallest fissures of my being. He sat with his legs gaping wide open, with his fingers threaded through mine. I felt like I was having an out-of-body experience. I was there in my body, but my spirit was floating somewhere above. Heartache seemed to follow me wherever I went. Some of it I caused, but most of it I didn't. I only prayed to God I'd be able to keep this feeling forever. But my mind knew better. My heart already ached for the potential hit it would take. *Fuck it.* I would live in the moment. We weren't guaranteed tomorrow, were we? Today was all we had. I was certainly there with a famous rock god. And I had certainly shared his bed with him. And that was all I knew for sure.

On the way to our late-night snack, he kept mad-texting someone. That had me wondering and insecure. I tried not to focus on the angry faces he was making as he returned the text. However, I couldn't help it. Finally, we arrived at a local Italian restaurant with a gorgeous view of clear, starry skies with snow-capped mountains in the distance. I was introduced to the owner, a family friend. The restaurant catered to the wealthy. Not many of us locals could afford a few hundred dollars for a meal. Apparently, the staff was willing to stay late as a favor for their A-list clients. The owner never refused. He was happy to accommodate. The dining room was draped in baby blues and creams with a ceiling painted akin to the Sistine Chapel. We were shown to our table, set with neatly pressed linens, Noritake china, and Edwardian chairs that looked to be heirlooms. The place had a very Renaissance meets New World feel. It was really quite beautifully elegant, and was definitely the most chic place I had ever graced. The Maître de moved in back of me to pull out my chair until Abel stopped him.

"I've got it. Thank you," he said, pulling out my lushly upholstered chair.

"Of course you do," the thirtyish-year-old handsome man responded. Something passed between them. For the life of me I didn't know what. So I decided to *not* be one of those annoying girls who questioned everything. *Arte de Dello's* restaurant didn't exist for my kind. This certainly wasn't where normal people went for a late night bite. But, then again … this was in no way normal, was it? His gaze never left me. I couldn't help but blush. He was just so intense. I usually played a better game. But with him, I had to work on my game constantly. How in the fuck was I going to swing the momentum back my way?

While I pondered that, the same Maître de poured sparkling water. I thanked him kindly. He licked his lips, his gaze burning into me. Not good. Tension rolled off Abel with hurricane force. My breath came in light pants. I didn't understand, it wasn't like I had done anything wrong. And yet, I felt I had. With a crash of his fist on the table top, Abel stood.

"Where is Frank?" he barked, his face red with fury.

"In his office, sir," Handsome responded. "Would you like for me to get him? He did say he'd be out in a moment. But, again, I can let him know you're asking for him." He was polite but his undertone was slightly sardonic.

"What I do want is someone who's respectful of my girl. Respectful of me. You are not. Now, unless you want that tongue ripped out of your mouth, I'd put it away. But, then again, I don't have a problem doing that, either." Abel leaned into Handsome's personal space. Holy Alpha father of God. Damn, it was fucking tense in there. To distract myself, I drank my water, then grabbed a breadstick, looking everywhere around me but at them. Abel sat back down with a sigh.

"Sorry, babe. I don't normally lose my shit. But, what the fuck? He was undressing you with his eyes. And that's even with my clothes on! Can you imagine if you had that dress on? Christ, I would have kicked that fucker's ass up and down this street." He smiled apologetically. I nodded, smiling back. I really didn't know what to say. So why say anything at all? Abel clearly was sensitive. I just wanted to move on already. Tomato sauce and basil filled the air. I hummed appreciatively. I was suddenly ravenous. I wanted whatever the hell that was. *Now.*

"Beauty, you keep humming like that and I'll take you right here. Clear the fucking place out. Fuck you right in that delicious pussy. On the table. Then on the floor, and up against the wall. And then we'll give it a go in the bathroom—both of them." I sighed. I wouldn't mind doing any of that in the least. I was grinning like an idiot. His possessiveness and sexual appetite was catching.

However, the sound of a man clearing his throat interrupted our eye-fucking. It was a sweet, silver haired older gentleman in a crisp, black suit. He nodded to me, then addressed Abel.

"Nice to see you, Mr. Gunner. It is our honor to have you here. As always, I have everything just about ready. All your favorites. I will personally be waiting on you," the kind, Geppetto-looking man said. His blue, misty eyes reminded me of Frank Sinatra's. Abel reached across the table linking our fingers. Geppetto's eyes followed curiously until meeting mine and then traveled back to Abel's.

"Frank this is Gia, my girl." He winked at me, then turned to Geppetto, who seemed morbidly fascinated by Abel's fingers laced together with mine. I wanted to remove my hand. I had a strange feeling I couldn't quite put my finger on. There was definitely something to it, though. My hackles were raised. Was it me? Was I not good enough, even at 3:00 am? Oh shit, maybe it was the way I was dressed. Of course, that had to be it. I was wearing men's sweatpants and a tee-shirt that hung from my body like a loose-fitting dress. I moved to excuse myself, feeling very self-conscious. Then I thought, fuck this. I belonged there as much as anyone else. If I'm to live in his world, I'd better start getting used to being treated differently—doted on. I moved to excuse myself to wash my hands when Gepetto went to get our food.

"Sit!" Abel commanded sternly. He was abrupt. I couldn't help but flinch at his tone.

"I'm going to wash my hands." I raised them to him. "You know I'm not dressed for this place. There's got to be a dress code. No wonder they are looking at me. I can imagine the models you bring here. They're probably dressed in the latest runway fashions. Then, here I am in sweats and a tee." Jealously reared its ugly head. Who did he bring here? What in the world was I fucking thinking? He grabbed my hand from across the table. I pulled my hand back slightly, only for him to tighten his grip. My eyes tilted upward to catch his fierce, heated look. Something moved behind his eyes. I couldn't read this dude for shit. I was fucked. He pulled my hand around the table for me to sit on his lap.

"While I love sitting on your lap, I don't think this is the time or place. Not to mention, Geppetto will have a stroke." I turned my head until our noses touched. He tilted his head, bringing our lips a hair's breadth apart. Then he licked my lips and bit them lightly. I pulled back, but he didn't let go. I opened my eyes in panic. His eyes were filled with light-heartedness, with just a touch of sex in them. My mouth was starting to water. I tried slurping my spit back before I drooled on him—which got him laughing again.

"Let me hear you say: 'I'd be happy to let you feed me with my ass perfectly perched on your cock,' " he murmured playfully, my bottom lip still in his grasp.

"Seriously?" I murmured back, followed by a slurp. His shoulders shook with laughter. "I'm going to drool in your mouth. And down your face," I said in my most threatening voice.

"I had my tongue deep in your pussy. Do you think I'm worried about spit?" he insisted. Meanwhile, someone was filling our table with what smelled like my favorite Italian dishes. Oh God, it was Geppetto. He was going to think I was an under-dressed hoochie after that.

"Kay… kay." I tried to nod. But still nothing would come out of my lips—except spit.

"Say it," he repeated biting slightly harder.

"I'd be happy to let you feed me with my ass perfectly perched on your cock." There, I said it. Release me please. *Slurp.* He let go of my lip after he gave it a good suck. I melted into him, wanting more than a kiss. I wanted his talented fingers. I was now perched on his perfectly hard, tatted and pierced cock. I sighed. Would I, could I, ever resist this man and go back to being the cool chick I was before him? I was unraveling quickly.

"Stop thinking. Let's eat," he announced as Geppetto served up healthy portions of Mozzarella en Carrozza, Arugula Tomato Salad, Chicken Scarpariello, and fresh Pesto Gnocchi. Umm. Best date ever. Wait until Cindy hears about it.

"This is ridiculous. Look at all this food. There's only two of us. We won't even put a dent in these dishes," I said in total amazement, shaking my head.

"So, you take the leftovers. Problem solved." He stuffed a piece of the freshest fried Mozzarella in breadcrumbs into my mouth. And for the next forty-five minutes, a whole lot of sighing, humming, and belly rubbing went on. Gepetto dutifully packed up our leftovers as I begged Abel not to order dessert. I couldn't eat another stitch. My stomach was just one burp away from vomiting all over Abel. As promised, he dropped me off at my apartment, giving me a swooning kiss to end the night. We got out of the limo as he helped me carry the cartons to the door. I just got my keys out to put into the door, however, the door was nearly ripped from the hinges when Cindy opened it with brute strength. We both jumped.

"Christ, you two. Could you do that licking-kissing-moaning thing any louder? Another minute of that and the whole building will be fucking."

"Yeah, and you have the strength of the unstoppable rebel force. You nearly ripped the door off and scared the fuck out of us," I laughed. She rolled her eyes and Abel watched the dynamic between us. He was clearly entertained.

"Eww, why do you reek of garlic?" she pinched her nose. Of course she would say that. I was going to punch her face in. Abel lifted the cartons up toward her.

"Brought you leftovers, Cin." He handed them to her, and she willingly accepted them. We said a final goodbye with the promise to text and call. Once I was back inside the comfort of my apartment and saw what time it was, exhaustion descended fast.

"Nice outfit, chick." Cindy said packing the fridge with our goodies. I grabbed myself a water before offering her one. I knew that look on her face. She wanted deets.

"Not now, Cin, but tomorrow. I promise I will give you all the details. I swear." I held my hand over my heart. I could barely keep my eyes open. Besides, the sooner I closed them, the sooner I would see him again. I knew he would be running on a loop throughout my dreams.

"Whatever you say, chick. I'm beat anyway." She said goodnight, retreating to her room.

I fell asleep to the All-American Rejects, "It Ends Tonight." What little sleep I got was interrupted by Medusa's ringtone. I had given her the Darth Vader theme song.

"Hello, Medusa. To what do I owe the pleasure of this 8:30am call?" I snapped, annoyed.

"Don't you call me Medusa, you unlovable little bitch! Get your ass over here. I want to know what's going on with the Gunner kid," she roared, hanging up.

My eyes burned with rage. My brain surged past full-function mode to pissed-the-fuck-off wrath. My entire existence had been about her, her needs, her wants and selfish desires. I decided to get this house-call over with. I was determined not to be daunted all day by her wickedness. My limbs screamed in protest as I dragged myself from the comfort of my bed. I took a 3 minute shower, slicking my hair afterward into a ponytail and throwing a cap on with some lip gloss. Then out my bedroom door I went.

Cindy's door was still closed. She wouldn't be up for another few hours with any luck. I didn't want to get into it with her about visiting my mother. Girls from nice homes in nice neighborhoods with nice families didn't understand the incessant need for acceptance. We would argue constantly about my need to please Medusa. "Why don't you kick Broom Hilda to the curb," she would say. It didn't make sense to her. Things had to make sense to Cindy. She just didn't get the abusee/abuser conundrum. People who grew up like I did knew the score. We smelled it on each other: the shame, disappointment, and the lack of courage that change required. I was not only a product of my abuse, I would now become what I knew: the abuser. And that, I hated. The lack of control I had over it unnerved me. I understood it plainly, as all children of abuse do. However, it was changing that was the tricky part. And let's face it: it took too much work. It was easier being who I was than it was to try to be a better person. But that also made me an enabler, as most abused children were. That was all we knew. Medusa was the only one who was always in my corner. She may be hate-filled.

And it might be the darkest corner, but it was something, right? Anything from her was better than nothing.

I opened the refrigerator door and the night before came barreling back. The delicious smell of garlicky take-out from Arte de Dello's restaurant made my stomach growl in hunger. I opened one of the pretty, white containers and ate the Pesto Gnocchi with my fingers. I was in too big a hurry to waste time getting a fork. I needed to feed this sense of shame that was my mother. I shoveled the shit in, hoping to bury the guilt along with it. I ate to forget; I ate to remember. It was psychosis in its rawest form. It was self-mutilation. I hated who I was, hated how I felt. I would do just about anything not to feel. My feelings ran too deep. Superficial ones, I could do. I stayed far enough away from the deep end. However, I was envious of everyone who had courage.

Before I could put the carton down, I purged. I had to force the pasta down the drain with my hand. *Gross*. Robotically, I started rinsing out the sink when all of a sudden a gasp got my attention. *Cindy!* She ripped the squished carton free from my hand.

"What in the fuck, Gia? This again? What's gotten you this upset? That incubus that calls herself mom?" she asked, grabbing her car keys.

"Please. Please don't. You'll only make things worse for me. I'm fine. Really. I promise." I smiled joylessly.

"What? Make things worse? How could they get any worse? Scratch that, stop making promises you don't mean, Gia."

She retreated to her bedroom, slamming the door. *Fuck. Fuck. Fuck.* My day was already going to shit, I didn't need her adding to it. I. Did. Not. Need. It. At. All. I brushed my teeth and brewed coffee from the Keurig. I figured I must have been one of the only people in the world who could puke and drink coffee right after. My stomach was used to the abuse. I was used to the abuse. Cindy was not.

I was standing in front of Medusa's lair with the *Halloween* theme song playing in my head. She was my Michael Myers. The ever-present knot in my gut broke off into multiplied tiny herniated ones. The window curtain moved slightly. *It was time.*

I made my way up the walk of the old Victorian I used to call home, my breath steaming my sunglasses. Fuck, it was a cold day. That home housed many of my demons. And the biggest one would be on the other side of that door. The house was never a home. It was a mausoleum. I was never allowed to touch any of my mother's prized possessions, never allowed to use the living room. I was isolated to my room. She even had control of the color. But as long as I had my shelves full of books, I was fine. My books were my escape. It's a nerdy escape, but an escape, nonetheless. My hand shook as I unlocked the door. I leaned my forehead against the wood for a moment. *One breath in. One breath out.* I opened the door and walked inside. The smell of Tiger Balm hit me hard. To me, I associated that smell with Medusa and pain. And when Medusa was in pain, you were in pain.

"Are you going to come in? Or just stand there like an idiot? Close the damn door, Gia. Unless you're paying my heating bills now." She rolled across the parquet floor in her wheelchair. I winced at the sight of her. She caused me physical and mental pain. It was hard not to dwell on my past. That's why I didn't like to go there. It was easier to just text or phone her. That day, I didn't have the luxury, though. I wouldn't be spared. I closed the door, somberly hoping that if I showed obedience, the visit wouldn't be too bad.

"Is your pain that bad that you're in the wheelchair today? Didn't you take your meds?" I asked, walking over to the one chair I was allowed to sit in while visiting.

"Isn't that a moronic question? To think, I birthed you," she tisked. "Of course, the pain is bad. You're making it worse with your ridiculous questions. Now, tell me what I want to know and leave." She wheeled closer. She was a human lie detector. I couldn't lie to her face.

"I met Abel when he stopped by work. Then was invited to his concert. There was an after party, to which Cindy and I both went. And I um … um … went to his Penthouse for a visit."

I waited for her retort. My palms were sweating, my knees knocking, and my nose running. I was definitely allergic to her. My body reacted strongly to her presence. I was told once by a school counselor that the mind was powerful, that it could make you symptomatic of anything it wanted. Right then, it wanted me safe from her clutches. So much so, my anxiety took on physical form. There was that healthy side that fought her at times. I relished those moments. But I needed to be in the right head space to be able to do so…

"Is he a freak like I read? Did you do everything he asked? Men like him are very particular in their needs. If you give him whatever he wants, whatever it is he wants, he will give you the world—which would put me in a great position." She reached for her bottle of Percocet, shaking a few in her mouth. She chewed them like tick-tacks. Christ, she was a twisted druggie bitch.

"You need a glass of water, Mama? That medicine has to be nasty." I went into the kitchen to get some for her. The dining room table was filled with unopened bills. It was a mess. Returning with some iced water, I handed it to her. She took a sip, gargling with it before she swallowed. I couldn't help but shudder.

"Sit. When will you see him again? You should try to make yourself available whenever he calls without looking needy and pathetic. Can you do that? Not look pathetic?" She scowled at me. Her words carried the weight of mortar. I started twirling my hair—a bad habit I had picked up as a kid, a habit that drove her into a fit. I knew it was unwise, but I couldn't help it.

"How many fucking times, girl." She slapped my hand away from my hair. "How do you expect to get a man to bed and keep you, acting like you do?" she barked. "You like an immature, ill-mannered, little girl. Next, you'll be rocking back and forth, thumb-sucking." She wheeled her chair to the window, peering outside. I wanted to stab her in her fucking eye.

"I'm not immature or ill-mannered… I'm not a little girl, either. And I'm certainly not an idiot. I'm a college graduate. Do you forget that, Mother?" I moved quickly for the door.

"Gia, don't you forget who paid for that diploma. Make sure you pick up the phone when I call. I want updates on your progress. I want to see an announcement in the paper about upcoming nuptials. If it were me, I would have wrapped it up already. But I keep reminding myself you're not as bright as me. Be a good girl and lock the door on your way out." She smirked.

"I'm always a good girl," I said, slamming the door. I wanted to cry—cry and rip my hair out. I needed food. I needed to make this pain go away. I drove to McDonald's, ordering enough food for a college dorm. I parked my car behind the dumpster, and then I shoved Big Macs into my mouth faster than a fox in a forest fire. Four Big Macs, two large fries, and a sundae later, my gut was percolating. My brain was on sensory overload. I couldn't deal with the weight of these feelings, the hatred I had for my mother, the need to prove her wrong. I wanted to prove her wrong, and shut her the fuck up. The time bomb was ticking. I needed release.

So, I opened the car door and puked all over the pavement. My esophagus burned. The acrid juice seared the tender tissue. Fat tears streamed down my face as I stared at my spew. How very representational of my life it was. Shame chilled me to the bone. I needed a warm shower and some wine to rid myself of this … this *thing* I called my life. It was time for change. That night I would try to find the courage to embrace the life I wanted. I'd slip on the mask I wore the night before as Gia the Vixen.

Chapter Ten

Abel

W̶e were on lunch break from our Saturday afternoon jam session. I was journaling some lyrics that danced across my mind, begging to be recorded.

Promise me you'll try to leave it all behind
You … you … you …
The only way is to let my guard down
Stay with me …
This is what we need
This heart, it beats
Beats for you
My heart is your heart
What am I gonna do with you … everything

Now, I just needed Jake to work his magic to make it shine. It was a productive day, despite my lack of sleep. The boys were having a rough go of it. It was hit or miss being hung-over. We either played like shit, or we sounded great.

The boys made their way to our favorite lunch spot while I hung back. They refrained from commenting, but the sideways glances were plain to see. Just as well. I didn't really feel like sharing. It was none of their business. Ender would be the first to argue that point. Anything to do with a member of the band, personal or otherwise, *was* band business. As per *my* rules. Which was why he strutted in there like a peacock that morning. He, Jake, and I had some heated words in the mastering suite. Until I had control of my temper, I couldn't speak to him. Brother or no brother. Band or no band. That was basic fundamentals. She was fucking *mine*. He knew that, and he fucked around regardless. He needed to be kept away from me for the day. I would find my way to him when I was ready. The studio wasn't the place for fighting. However, he and I were going to sort this shit out one way or another before the end of the day. Dave was in the booth keeping a watchful eye. *Feelings:* that word I had true distain for. There was no way around it, though. I was *feeling* something for this chick. She had become my muse. And because of that, I rocked it hard that day. Wrote some great tunes.

"You writing again, dude?" Ender entered the studio sucking a blow-pop. What was it with him and lollipops? Some kind of oral fixation. Chicks dug it, but I thought it was a punk move. I didn't need props to gain attention from the babes. He insisted Dave keep a bag of them around the studio.

"Is that what you really want to ask? Am I writing? Are you going to start this convo insulting my intelligence? Really, bro?" I uncrossed my knee, moving to my feet quickly, my fists balled at my side.

"Yo, dude. Chill the fuck out. I'm not looking to insult you. I was honestly asking. You've been struggling these past few months. I was happy to see you with your journal today. That's all I meant." He was holding his hands up defensively, yet his eyes never wavered. "I want to apologize for last night. I meant no disrespect, bro. Truth." He pounded his chest, his stance pensive.

"And you know damn fucking why I've been blocked. That cunt Morgana playing media games with my life. I can't write when my heads in a bad space. Besides Gia, I haven't had proper time to get my shit off. And you meant no disrespect? What would you call grinding your dick on my girl's ass?" I stepped forward.

"Your girl?" He laughed, stepping forward. "Now she's your girl? Since the fuck when?" We were nose to nose, eye to eye, neither of us wavering.

"Hey! Back the fuck off, both of you," Dave broke in, his cigarette ash hanging long from the side of his mouth. "You break any of this studio-owned equipment and you pay for it. You break each other—you live with it."

"That's right, *esse*. I stuck my cock in her, which makes her *mine*," I said, grabbing my cock.

"Dude, I didn't know you fucked her. I must be on your pay-no-mind list. Did you tell me? How would I possibly know you laid claim to her? Was I hanging with you guys? Did I partake in a threesome I don't recall? No!" he stated flatly, rolling his eyes.

No one moved. Dave's ash still hung long from his cigarette. The smoke was annoying me. The tension was thick. Testosterone had both of us amped up. We didn't distrust each other. However, this fucker was always being an asshole. Though it was funny and shit.

Dude, seriously." He extended his hand. I waited a beat, still staring warily at him.

Finally, I extended my hand. He pulled me into an Ender man-hug, kissing my face. A weight lifted. Forgiveness was a beautiful thing. I didn't easily forgive, but then again, Ender had never given me a reason not to trust him. And I hoped he never would.

Woody and Jake filed in, arguing over what the next single on the album should be. And just like that, we were one again and back to making music. Ender lingered with his arm around my neck a bit longer than necessary. But, that was Ender. Very touchy-feely. Maybe I'd be different if I had grown up in a warm, loving home, full of passion for life. My home was filled with superficialities and false niceties. Being born with a silver spoon in your mouth made for a lonely, isolated existence. Music made me feel alive. Fucking made me feel alive. Eating pussy made me feel alive. I was finally waking up. The beast within me was waking, and needed to be fed. My nourishment was a delicious Italian girl with a pussy that called to me.

"You twats chill?" Woody wrapped one arm around each of us. "Who wants to get pissed?" he asked with a lazy tongue.

"Did you have a liquid lunch, Wood?" I asked, cracking a smile.

"Don't be a chancer, Abel. You two sorted?" A sluggish smile pulled at the corner of his lips. His eyes were glassy. But Woody could hold his liquor just fine. He was enjoying the festival revelries this weekend. He was one big party, most days. An event like the festival was like spring break for Wood.

"We're sorted, *esse.*" Ender kissed Woody's cheek. Only Ender could get away with that shit. Woody was a homophobe.

"You've got some fanny balls, Ender." Woody laughed as he walked back to his kit, twirling his sticks between his fingers. Jake put his guitar strap over his head. The boys were ready to jam.

The studio was our sanctuary from life. We loved expressing ourselves through our music. We spoke to each other through our rifts, vocals, and beats. That night, on the second day of the festival, the massive crowd of fans would be all the high we would need. Fame was a blessing that had been bestowed upon us, and for that, I was grateful. We all were. Most musicians never see the success we had achieved. And it didn't come to us by accident. My name was my cross to bear. I'm sure the guys didn't see it that way, but I sure did. I lived it. I was gifted with the last name Gunner. With that came certain obligations— one of which was to be successful. The other big one was to preserve my father's legacy. His behind-the-scenes string-pulling had landed us a platinum record deal. He was a manipulative, cunning fucker. Transparent as the day is long … at least to me. This kind of shit didn't happen to struggling musicians. Even though we were gifted musicians, we had been given a break. Dave thought he was the goose that laid the golden egg when we were offered such a sweet deal. He beat his chest proudly. Truth be told, the deal was most likely negotiated behind closed doors in my family-owned building. My father didn't want a musical artist for a son. It was bad enough that I was a wild, tatted, and pierced mess. But imagine a Gunner being a struggling one, at that? Made me sick what an un-accepting elitist he was …

I was just starting to warm up my vocals when my phone vibrated in my pocket. Smiling, I dug it out, hoping it was Gia. I wanted to meet up with her before the show that night.

But it was Dad. The text in all caps, *WILL YOU ANSWER YOUR DAMN PHONE, ABEL!*

I'd been ignoring his calls as of late. My father only reached out when he wanted me to do something, or if I had done something that would reflect poorly on the family. In either case, I didn't want to hear it. Ignoring him was really an incredibly bad idea. He would come looking for me. Most likely embarrassing the fuck out of me. At that thought, I stiffened, and not in the way I wanted, either. It was not good. But, I didn't give a fuck. I was tired of his constant tampering in my life. My younger years had been fraught with doubt, insecurity, and self-loathing. Back then, my life meant nothing to me. If I lived or died meant zero. I preferred washing pills down with alcohol over my home life. My friends, of course, didn't get it. To those who didn't have money, having it was the solution for every problem. Death was my solution—legacy be damned. Death would be the final fuck-you to my father. However, it was music that saved me. My boys saved my life. They knew it, too. My frankness about it left them unnerved. Music was everything to me; it was my salvation. I was grateful to have been blessed with these guys. I had so much to live for. I had learned controlled self-reliance. As long as I was in control, I was at peace. The body I had was tuned to perfection. When I had anything heavy to deal with, I did so with carnal desire. I took what was mine. What I'd earned. Simple brute fucking kept my head straight. Being a Dominant—having that control to do whatever I wanted to with my partner, whenever I wanted—got my rocks off like nothing else.

Speaking of getting off, I wanted some play time with Beauty before we went on stage. And then afterward, I would need another fix.

So, I texted Gia: *Beauty, I'll be by at 4:00 to pick you up. Pack a bag for the rest of the weekend.*

Shortly, she replied: *Caveman much? LOL! See you soon. Xx*

I came back: *You haven't touched yourself today, have you? I'm the only one who has that privilege.*

She was ready for me: *I can still feel you. Besides, it feels so much better when you do it. ;) I'm putting together an Abel survival pack.*

I was a bit confused: *?*

She explained: *Ice packs, icy-hot soothing gel, pain killers, Devil's claw, Fireball, Kind bar, and EOS (lips) *giggle**

Now I got it: *LMFAO! Devil's claw and Fireball? Sounds more like a sci-fi flick. I should get a patent on this, stat! See you soon, babe.*

She had the ability to make that hollow feeling in my chest disappear. My world seemed lighter around her. I was looking forward to being with her. She didn't know it yet, but we were all going to eat before the concert at Finns, a local ribs, pulled pork, and brew place we loved to kick back in. It was down-to-earth and chill. Perfect spot to ease her into the chaotic world of touring. A few weeks after the festival, we would be going back out on tour and heading to Europe. I wanted her to go with me. I didn't want to be on the road without her. She would come with me; it was that simple. I was sure my old man would have a few choice words for me. But fuck him. She was mine. No one would take her from me. Especially my old man.

I decided to take my bike. I couldn't live my life in a bubble created by the paps. It was a gorgeous day out. There was a chill in the air, but the sun was shining brightly. Perfect tee-shirt and leather jacket weather. My leathers I wore while riding exuded rock star appeal. And I did enjoy being a rock star. *Fuck, yeah!*

My driver was going to pick up Gia's bags while I was gigging. Right now all I wanted was her delicate arms wrapped around me, her heat against my back. Life sure was a bitch. Why did I feel like some romantic asshole I usually made fun of? That's Karma for you.

I pulled into the Terrace apartment's driveway, expecting to wait for Gia. I was surprised to see her waiting just outside the vestibule, ready to jump on. Her gorgeous full lips begging to be kissed. Not wanting to wait another minute to feel them, I grabbed the back of her neck, drawing her to me. Pushing my tongue deep into her mouth, I could feel her sigh. She relaxed into me, taking everything I had to give.

"Mmm, so fucking good, Beauty," I murmured, almost unintelligibly. Licking and nibbling her lush lips. Which made my cock press painfully against my zipper. I had to withdraw from her embrace to adjust myself.

"Oh my God! You really *are* a caveman." She slapped my hand away from my dick. "Damn, I have neighbors, rock star. I'm sure millions of women would love to see that make the cover of one of the celeb magazines. Abel Gunner adjusting his *anaconda* on his Harley."

We both laughed. That would be pretty epic. Paps had tried to pay many of my paramours for an exclusive picture of my tatted, pierced cock. I don't let chicks take any pictures of me—ever. Let the elusive anaconda stay exclusive to intimate settings.

The helmet I had bought Gia looked fucking hot on her. Her chocolate eyes were wide as saucers with want, and need—for me. The look of adoration she was giving me did nothing to ease my painful hard-on.

"Hop on, Beauty. You keep looking at me we'll never make it out of here." I helped her balance herself as she swung her leg over the seat. I swore under my breath when her hot box pressed up against me as she wrapped her arms around my waist.

"I'm not wearing panties, babe. Aren't I such a good listener?" she whispered.

"*Fuck*, Beauty." I grabbed my dick really hard, trying to strangle it into submission. The fucker had a mind of its own. With no relief in sight, I needed a plan B. I checked the time; we had forty-five minutes until I was scheduled to meet up with the crew. Where could I pull off to for some privacy? Her hands were already underneath my tee-shirt. Christ Almighty, this chick was killing me.

"Hold on, babe." I revved the bike. The exhaust was loud. The chrome screamed sex. I wanted sex. It was a carnal pleasure-seeking motor vehicle. I needed my Gia pussy fix—now. My cock was a heat-seeking motherfucking missile. Her pussy was its target. We weaved between traffic, her nails biting into my stomach. I pressed my hand over hers to calm her.

"Put your goddamned hand on the handle bar, jackass. I'm not trying to become road kill!" she yelled in my ear, nearly losing it.

"I got this, babe. Relax. Not the first time I've ridden a bike, Beauty. You're good with me."

My tone soothed her until she relaxed her weight onto me. Her statement had me laughing really fucking hard. She had fucking balls, talking to me like that. She was comfortable. Normally, that had me running the opposite way. You let a chick get chill with you, and before you know it, you're dealing with incessant nagging and ultimatums. Not my idea of a good time. Fuck that drama.

The state park was off the next exit. I took it, my cock thickening just thinking of her pussy. Forget about the smell of it. I'd blow my load for sure. The park was crowded with Wall-Street-Journal-reading executive geek families. Not my usual haunt. But I was desperate to tear that pussy up. Taking the next left through the parking lot, I drove toward an isolated parking area. *Bingo.* I rode over the grass to park next to a cinder block building. There were chains on the entry doors. That was my cue that it was unoccupied. I turned the bike off and took off my helmet, running my fingers through my sweaty hair. Gia used my shoulders to balance herself while getting off. I turned to help her, when all of a sudden she slapped my arm—hard.

"Are you a crazy, motherfucker? Answer me? If you think I'm getting on that death machine ever again, you can kiss my ass, Abel." She slapped my arm again while yelling. Her face was white as a ghost. Oh shit, she was terrified. I needed to diffuse this shit, now. This was not how I had intended this to turn out.

"Come here, Gia," I called, extending my hand. She stared at it like I had leprosy. I didn't like it. Not one fucking bit.

"Come here, Gia." I nodded for her to take my hand. She took it warily. "Come here, baby girl."

I lifted her from underneath her arms until she was astride me. "Listen here, Beauty. I would never put you in harm's way. I'm sorry I scared you. I can assure you that was not my intention. And yes, I am a crazy motherfucker. Crazy motherfucker for that pussy of yours. That's what's got me all knotted up. Feel this…"

I lifted my tee-shirt so she could see my piercing sticking clear out of my jeans. Now, that was some crazy shit. She moistened her lips, her eyes fascinated on the pre-come beading on the slit of my head. She looked up. Our eyes connected in a silent, heated battle. Her pupils dilated and turned darker.

"Forgiven." She leaned in, kissing me like she owned me. Maybe she did. Maybe for the first time in my life, I wanted to be owned by someone—by her. She melted into me while her thumb swirled, playing with the juice on the head of my cock. My body was fraught with pent-up sexual tension. Explosion was imminent.

"Babe, I'm going to make a big mess of myself if we don't take a walk right the fuck now," I said, helping her off my bike as she giggled. I grabbed a blanket from my saddlebag. I took her hand in mine as we walked. If I could have carried her into the woods running—I would've. But I needed to chill. She had already called me a caveman and a crazy motherfucker. My behavior wasn't exactly screaming *chill*. I was acting like a crazy, caveman motherfucker. Biting my lip to the point of bleeding pain in order to stop the obsessive emotions I was experiencing, I wondered if one of the guys was fucking with my dosage again. After the last meltdown, you'd think not. But they were assholes sometimes—well, most times.

I walked us over to a beautiful, blooming tree. I shook out the blanket, straightening the edges. I turned to Gia to strip her bare ass, but was met by a face filled with pain. Those beautiful brown, bedroom eyes were welling up with tears. What in the fuck? What could I have possibly done now?

"It's not you, it's me. That sounds so cliché. What I mean to say…" She sniffled, wiping her eyes. "What I mean to say is … you're so perfect, Abel. We've only just met. You've showed me more affection than …"

She cleared her throat. I moved to her, grabbing her chin. I wanted to look into those eyes. I needed to look into those eyes.

"What's not to adore, Beauty? Huh? Why the tears? Who did this to you, babe?" I wanted to know, needed to know. I demanded to know.

She shot me an indecisive look as she stiffened. Not a good sign. I knew when someone was keeping a secret. And she was definitely keeping one. She had all the signs. Something or someone was making Gia suffer. That was for fucking sure. I was conflicted. Part of me wanted to know—but part of me didn't. So I did what I do best, what my body was built for. Wiping a stray tear from her cheek with my thumb, I brought it to my lips to taste her. Fuck, even her tears tasted sweet. Staring into her eyes, I ran my fingers through her hair, grabbing a tight handful and tugging her head down. Her nipples hardened. Her pupils were ebony pools. She unbuttoned my pants, hooking her dainty fingers in my waistband, watching me the whole time. She yanked them down. Without hesitation, she bent over and drew the head of my cock into her warm, wet mouth, making tiny lip movements over the piercing on my head.

"*Fuck,* Beauty," I growled. "What are you doing to me?" That was less of a question and more of a plea. Her purring on my cock was going to get her a mouthful of come any second. A shudder rolled up from my toes through the base of my spine. Lacing my fingers through her hair, I started to fuck her mouth.

"Beauty, you keep sucking like that, I'm gonna give you something to swallow real soon." She made a ravenous little slurping sound that set my shit off like Grucci fireworks. I came hard and fast. She swallowed my whole load. *Damn,* if that didn't make me fall just a little bit more. *Fuck me.* She looked up at me with those sinful eyes, licking her lips like my shit was the tastiest shit she had ever had. Yeah, she was *my girl.*

I released her hair, helping her to her feet. I made quick work of my pants and shirt. I wanted to undress her. And so I did. She spoke not a word, just lifted her arms over her head so I could remove her shirt, wiggling her ass to help with her jeans. There, I was proud of the *goddess* that stood before me. Proud she was *mine.* My eyes never left her body. I moved to the blanket, languidly stroking my cock.

"I want you to ride me. I want to see that tight little body move. Show me how my cock makes you feel. Show me everything, Beauty." I laid back, fisting myself. There was no conversation. She straddled me, dropping to her knees in one move. She grabbed my cock out of my hand. With her other hand, she started to stimulate herself with her fingers.*Motherfucker.* If that wasn't the hottest image ever. Short of bleaching my brain, I would never be able to forget it. I'd been with hundreds of beautiful, hot women. But Gia took it to a whole new level. She brought her fingers to her mouth, tasting herself. It was the sweetest torture I had ever experienced. My sack was tight. I squeezed my balls with my free hand. She nudged the head of my cock between her pussy lips with agonizingly slow movements. My vision blurred. It took every ounce of will power not to thrust upward. Finally, she relieved my suffering by impaling herself in one swift move. I usually didn't do the bottom—ever. However, I wanted to watch her get herself off with my cock. I needed to see it as much as I needed air to breath.

"Fuck, baby. You're so goddamned big," she exclaimed. "I feel so deliciously stuffed right now. Your cock feels unreal." She gave herself time to adjust. I twisted my hips, signaling for her to move. This was fucking with me big-time. She responded with a resounding smile, her eyebrow quirking up. She knew she was torturing me.

"Is my Master impatient? Doesn't a Dom pride himself on his patience?" she taunted, lifting herself up and down on my cock. Motherfucker, she was right. In a normal world, I was the pillar of patience. But what was going on here with this woman was far from normal. She picked up the pace, performing a grinding move with her hips. My thoughts were jumbled. I wanted to answer her question, set her straight. But she was right. What was there to say? What was I going to do—make excuses for why I was so impatient with her, admit so early on I was pussy-whipped? Not likely. She played with her tits without me asking her to, pinching her nipples until her buds were rock-hard.

"Oh God, baby, you feel amazing. Your piercing is hitting my g-spot." She lost it, screaming my name for the world to hear. *That was the icing on my motherfucking caveman cake.* That was the vision I would go to sleep to, and take everywhere with me. It was one of those erotic moments a man doesn't forget. In the middle of an ordinary day something extraordinary happens. That was one of those times. Her riding me in daylight in the middle of a state park with no worries, just the two of us together. Life couldn't get any better than that, than it was right then and there, with my hips meeting her sweet hole halfway, and the sounds of her pussy suctioning me out of my fucking mind.

"I'm gonna fuck you, now. *Hard*, Beauty," I said, flipping her over. "On your knees, Gia."

The command in my voice had her purring like a kitten. Nudging her shaking legs apart with my knees, I asked, "You ready, Beauty?" She answered by pushing back onto my cock. I responded with a thrust that almost sent her off the blanket. But my girl held her own.

"Jesus, babe. You're so fuckin' tight and hot. My cock wants to live in this pussy." My hands gained her hip for purchase. I ramped it up, my hips moving like pistons. I reached around to rub her clit. I needed her to come again. I wanted to hear the noises she made when she came. "I'm gonna ruin you, babe. You're mine. Do you hear me, Gia? Fuckin' *mine*." My cock slammed into her heat.

"Oh fuck, oh fuck, I'm gonna come," she crooned, her pussy tightly gloving my cock, draining me. My muscles tightened to the point of spasm. I grabbed her hair, pulling her up to me, my teeth latching on to the meat between her neck and shoulder. My load came hard and swift, filling her sweet cunt until it seeped down the inside of her thighs. I released her shoulder, and sat back on my legs. Both of us were panting furiously. She was in a downward dog position. I laid down, pulling her next to me, face-to-face. I peeled her sweaty hair away from her face. It flushed beautifully. She was stunning. All I could think about was the night ending with her in my bed.

Chapter Eleven

Gia

Abel promised to take it easy on the way back until I got used to the feel of the bike. Between the ridiculously loud exhaust pipes and the weaving through traffic, I thought I was going to lose my shit again. Go figure, after all the abuse I put my body through, at the first thought of dying, I lose my shit.

We spent five minutes outside Finns discussing plans for the night before going in. I have to admit. I was a little embarrassed as to the fiasco of what went down the night before with Ender. My nerves were frayed. After what had happened, the last thing I needed was to see Ender. I wanted to punt-kick him in the balls. So I decided to text Cindy: *Hey, chick, I'm with caveman @ Finns. Get dressed and meet us. Woody's gonna be here. Xx*

Right away she texted back: *Get in here already. We heard you pull up eight minutes ago. What's the problem? Caveman beat the box too hard? LMBO! Xx*

I came back at her: *Har har har. Fuck you very much. CU in 2. :p*

Abel secured our helmets on the back of his sex machine, grabbed my hand firmly, and walked us in. Finns was a local favorite. Its home-style, comfortable vibe provided a down-to-earth atmosphere we relished. The décor was rustic with picnic tables lined up along the walls. Bigger tables were arranged in the middle. Our crew sat with two picnic tables pushed together. And it felt great calling them my crew. It felt like a whole new life. A life I finally wanted. A life I chose. However, we were sure to see people we knew there. Cindy and I spent many football Sundays enjoying comfort-food and drinks in that place—not to mention the hot guys in football jerseys. It should be real interesting when Abel's fans see him there with me. Come to think of it … I wondered why we were able to take his bike out. Security was so dead-set against it last time. I back-burned it until I was able to ask him about it later.

At the hostess desk, the girls fawned over him. And he ate it up, his dimpled smile setting fire to their panties. After posing for a few photos with his groupies, we were escorted to a private table toward the back. Cindy was in her retro *Frankie Says Relax* tee-shirt paired with ripped jeans. She and Woody were talking very closely. Dave was texting someone. Jake was flirting with two cute waitresses. And Ender's eyes never strayed from us.

My stomach twisted nervously. He smiled and winked. *Jackass.* Abel squeezed my hand in affirmation. I stood stock-still, waiting for Cindy to notice we were there. She finally pulled her head out of Woody's face, jumping up to greet us.

" 'Bout time chick." She kissed my cheek and hip-checked Abel. I watched as the paparazzi started setting up outside with their long lens cameras. I was nervous as hell, yet oddly fascinated by it all. I'd always fantasized about being a celebrity. What would it be like to be on *TMZ* or one of those shows? Make the papers? How did it all work? I had seen an entertainment show that explained that some celebrities scheduled the paparazzi—told them where they'd be, that type of shit.

"Cindy." He nodded his hello, then dropped my hand to greet the boys. Hugs, fist-bumps, and shaking of hands went on for ten minutes—real bromance-type stuff. I laughed to myself. Ender did some complicated handshake with Abel that had me spellbound. I guess all was forgiven between the two—which was a relief. Jake poked my side, patting the seat next to him in an effort to get me to sit. I hadn't realized I was standing there gawking at the groupies taking videos with their camera phones. Who lives like this? The table of boys went about their business unruffled. I caught Cindy's eye and she just shrugged. I took Jake's hand, stepping over the bench seat to sit. He poured me beer from one of the pitchers on the table. I wasn't a beer drinker, but when in Rome.

"Thank you, Jake," I said. He nodded. Abel lifted me off the seat only to redeposit me on his lap.

"Ah, that's much better," he crooned, inhaling my hair. "Smells very outdoorsy. Maybe pine?"

I elbowed him in the gut, eliciting a grunt. The table erupted in laughter. The boys all high-fived me. And just like that, my nerves dissipated. I settled into Abel's form, taking full advantage of his perfectly sculpted, hard body. The servers laid a smorgasbord of good eats before us. I think Abel ordered three of everything on the menu. How those boys stayed so fit was a conundrum. I was positivity shocked how high each of them filled their plates. They were sexy hot rockers with tatted arms, pierced brows, and crazy hair—but their demeanor spoke of culture. I didn't know everyone's stories. What I did know was, they fit together. They were of the same breeding. I would have been very surprised if someone told me otherwise. These boys exuded sex appeal like a stripper on a pole. It was just there. Just watching them lick their fingers was like watching a porn.

The boys spoke of their European tour, finalizing last-minute bookings across the continent. My life wasn't that fucking fascinating. Cindy and I fell into an easy conversation as to what we were wearing for the rest of the festival. We lived a boring life compared to the guys. I tried my hardest to ignore Abel's fingers tracing the words *I want to fuck you* on my back continuously. I had to laugh at how persistent he was. I couldn't laugh at how turned on I was. He demanded my attention. He finger-fed me one of the most erotic meals of my life. He didn't give a fuck who was watching or taking pictures. He made his intentions very clear for the world to see. To say it didn't thrill me beyond words would be a lie. He insisted on hand-feeding when we were together. His eyes fixed on my mouth as I took in every delish morsel he fed me. However, he was interested in what Cindy and I were talking about. I loved that. Most men wouldn't give a shit about girl-talk. He was different. Cindy and I made a shopping lunch date at the mall. I needed some new things. I wanted to get some jaw-dropping outfits. Cindy and I had a real eye for that kind of stuff.

"Anything you want, Beauty, just ask," Abel whispered, kissing my neck. My body erupted in goose bumps. A shiver ran down my spine, curling my toes. My nipples were in need of attention. Oh, God. Anyone could see how turned on I was. Looking around to pour another glass of beer, Ender's lusty eyes zeroed in on my nipples. *Shit.* I excused myself, dragging Cindy to the four-stall bathroom.

"Where's the fire, chick-clit?" Cindy asked, digging her lipstick from her jeans to apply.

"Ender's being weird and creepy. I just don't want a repeat. Nor do I want to point it out to Abel. I don't want any drama tonight." I borrowed her lipstick, refreshing mine.

"Ah, that's just Ender. He's a big flirt. He would never act on it." She threw her head upside down, shaking out her hair. Wow, she really must've liked Woody.

"I've been so preoccupied with my own shit. How's yours?" I asked, washing my hands. I was the worst best friend in history—so fucking selfish. I knew she didn't take it personally considering who I was with.

"My shit's good. Real good." We both fell over laughing. Good times. No matter what. We never missed a beat. Our conversations picked up wherever we left off. We were lucky to have each other. I was especially lucky she still embraced me despite the multitude of secrets I was keeping. She knew some of them, but not all. We walked hand-in-hand out of the bathroom, laughing back to the table.

And then I saw her, the gorgeous bimbo-twat from the night before who wrapped herself around Abel like a rash. Instinctively, my fingers tightened, crushing Cindy's.

"Ow!" She frowned shaking out her hand.

"That's the trashy model from last night." I was seething. She had her arms around his neck and was getting right up in his face. Camera bulbs were flashing. We were pushed into the wall, as patrons hurried out of the bathrooms to catch sight of what was going on.

"She's a fucking troll. That's Morgana, his ex. That's the fucking cunt who's blackmailing him to get him back. Nice try, asshole." Cin grabbed me by the arm, storming through the crowd of spectators. *Fuck.* My brain was swirling with thoughts of homicide. Bloody, dismembering homicide. Her hands were massaging his biceps. Security was around them, partially blocking my view. I looked to the table—and all conversation stopped. The whole group held one collective breath. We were bearing witness to intimate dialogue between two former lovers. They had history. That much was clear. It fucking gutted me. She knew him better than I did. Knew what he liked. Knew what he didn't like. My fingers burned with energy as I seethed in anger. I started to feel real fucking punchy. My mind was concocting more scenarios between those two than I could keep up with. I had the need to hurt her. Disfigure her. It was insecure of me, and childish, but I couldn't help it. Her presence reminded me I wasn't part of his world. Didn't grow up in his circle. I wasn't cultured enough to be with him. I wasn't a country clubber. We were social mismatches. But, sure as I was standing there, I was not letting her have him, either. *Mine.* A big-busted server was walking by with shots atop her tray. I reached over and grabbed two.

"Heeeey!" she cried. "What the fuck?"

She looked between Cindy and me. Damn, she had an annoying voice. I downed the first shot. Whatever the fuck it was, it was god-awful. Big-tits was standing there in complete horror, with her mouth gaping open. Did she think I was gonna give them back to her? Cindy was rubbing circles on my back. She knew how insecure I was on any given day. It was just my past fucking with my head. The way this man made me feel—I couldn't lose it. Not now. What would I do if he decided to be with her again? *Fuck.* I needed something quick to defuse my panic. My eyes zoomed in on where she was touching Abel. Big-tits was still yapping about me having to pay for the shots.

"Chick, if you know what's good for you, keep walking," I said, downing the second shot and grabbing a chair for balance. Ew. Worst shots ever. She was still standing there with her hip extended until Cindy threw a twenty on to her tray. *Christ.*

"Pump your brakes, doll." Cindy was worried I was gonna lose it. She was right. I needed to reel it in. I didn't want to be perceived as a loose cannon. I had to handle this properly. I had to show Abel I was the right choice. If he was going to choose, I was going to make sure it was me.

"Yep, just did. It's all good, chick. I got this." I threw my arm around her. I needed that little bit of libation to compose myself. I walked us up to the security surrounding Abel, and tapped one of the guards on the shoulder. He moved a smidge so I could wiggle through. I could hear what Abel was saying. He was facing away from me. But he was speaking in icy, malevolent tones—just the opposite of how he always spoke to me. His posture was stiff. I found a tiny little rainbow in that. Here goes nothing: I walked over to him, putting my arm around his waist.

"Hey, babe. Problem?" I asked, looking up at him. His eyes turned down to my lips and he softened immediately. *Bingo.*

"Not at all. She was just leaving." His tone chilled even me. Her astute, eagle eyes caught my arm around him. With my other hand, I was rubbing his thickly corded abs. I winked. *Mine.* Her face rinsed red with anger. Her fists balled. A repugnant smirk twisted her lips. All of this was unspoken girl-code for *bring it.* Cindy had better give me some kind of medal for my stellar behavior. I was so proud of myself. Losing my mind would have been what the bitch wanted. *Fuck her scrawny ass.*

"And you are?" she asked snidely, eye-balling me. Abel's answer would be interesting. Who was I, exactly, to him? I wanted to hear myself, so I looked to him, and then to her. I was ready to respond for him, but he beat me to it.

"She's my sub. My new sub," he answered, taking the wind out of her sails. She stepped back in horror before stepping forward to touch him. He moved away. I wasn't thrilled that he told her that I was his sub, because I thought I was more than a private agreement. Why couldn't he have just said I was his girlfriend? What was the difference between a submissive and girlfriend? My preference would've been for girlfriend. But I couldn't afford to be picky at this point.

"She's no sub! Look at her. Please. She'll never be able to make you happy, Abel. She can't give you what I can give you. The control you crave." She snarled, turning to me.

"You'll never take my place, hon. Not in his bed. Not in his heart. And definitely not as his submissive. That's for fucking sure. Enjoy it while it lasts. It won't be long. That I can promise you."

She turned away, storming off toward the back door. The crowd parted for the piranha as she made her way there. I won't lie. Her declaration nearly stopped my heart. I was nauseous, even. Abel lifted my hand, kissing the top of it, his eyes glued to mine in a silent affirmation. It was meant to comfort me—but it didn't. Quite the opposite. That piranha bitch got to me. How could I possibly compete with his past? With her? He must have felt it in my stance. I was stiff. Long gone was the relaxed, vivacious, party girl.

"I'm sorry. She's a vengeful bitch who's used to getting what she wants. She's desperate. And it makes her look weak. I hate weak." Well, thank fuck I hadn't gone all Medusa. I had learned a quick, vital lesson. Less is more. I wasn't entirely positive I'd be able to pull it off all the time. I'd try, though. I'd try for him, for us.

"Let's load in," he yelled to the boys. Dave threw a few hundred dollar bills on the table and we were out. A few media trolls followed us out the door, hurling questions at warped speed. Where was Cindy? I couldn't go back in for her. She could've been ahead of me. I needed to make sure Cindy wouldn't be left behind. Christ, where was she?

"She's with Dave." Abel leaned down, speaking directly into my ear. His warm breath sent a thrill of excitement rolling through my body, causing me to tremble. *Holy fuck.* He chuckled at that. Right in the middle of this mass exodus, my pussy was clenching just from the sound of his voice. He had that effect on me. His sex appeal exuded all things Alpha. His Alpha had Alpha. He was walking, talking, breathing, and living sex. I nearly tripped over a reporter who jumped out into our path. Abel pulled me closer to his side.

"Abel, is it true you're getting back with Ms. Morgana after she threatened to expose your lifestyle choice? Can you confirm what lifestyle that is, please? What about the sex clubs?" The questions were intimate and personal. *Morgana. What kind of a fuckin' name is that, anyway? Where'd she come from—Middle Earth? Sex clubs?* The boys flanked his side like sentries, providing a human shield. Well. Well. Well. The stories were true. They really were a band of brothers. That notion warmed me just a little. I had always wanted to be part of something epic like that. Hell, I wanted just to belong. One thing I knew for certain: I wanted him to depend on me for comfort, not some other bitch. The crowd descended, snapping their photos for updated statuses on Facebook and Twitter.

"Jesus fuck, you squirrel-faced cunts." Woody lowered his shoulder to barrel into the paparazzi who were in our way. Blacked-out stretch SUV's screeched to a halt up in front of us. Someone grabbed my head, pushing me down and into the back of the vehicle. Chaos was the only word for it. Was that how they lived? They didn't seem angry, just annoyed and inconvenienced. I slid across the seat to the window. Abel slid in next to me. Dave sat up front riding shotgun. Woody, Cindy, Jake, and Ender got into the other vehicle.

I was in a trance, staring out the window at the hordes of photo-snapping onlookers. Their numbers seemed to have multiplied in fifteen minutes. It quickly turned into a three-ring-circus, I thought, shaking my head. Abel's sigh caught my attention. I turned to him, lifting my chin in a spirited way. He pivoted toward me. My senses were assailed by his scent of beer, salt, and something wild. His eyes were dark and dilated. His thumb brushed against my lower lip.

"You okay?" he asked quietly. Was I okay? Hmm? I really wasn't. It was a lot to take in. But I would never be so foolish as to act like I was anything other than perfectly okay with it. I assumed I'd get used to the paparazzi's influence, as annoying as it was. It was fascinating. That was what I wanted. To be a part of his world. The good, bad, and the ugly. I didn't fully realize the ugly would include Morgana. Now that was some ugly shit, there. I wasn't going to even mention it to him. He didn't need another drama-queen bitching him out.

"I'm great!" I said, pulling his head down for a kiss. He groaned. I grinned in triumph.

"Be careful, sweet girl." His voice had a dark, foreboding edge. I shivered. "Come. You're not in your proper seat, babe." He pulled me onto his lap. I'd be very happy to spend my life perched on his lap like this. Fire washed through my body. I nuzzled his neck, eliciting another groan.

"Look at me, Beauty," he demanded, his voice tense. I turned to straddle him. We were eye-to-eye. I glanced over his shoulder to see if Dave was paying attention. Abel's soft fingers held the back of my neck firm and steady. He didn't want me to pay heed to anyone else—but him. His eyes held me captive, sparking with raw power. I needed to win back some control. This man ate up every ounce I had—or what little I thought I had. He reached over and closed the partition. His features were hard-cut, his erection formidable.

"Take your clothes off and hold on to the back seat." He stretched his neck from left to right. *Motherfucker.* I stripped as quickly as possible. He opened a compartment next to the partition button and removed a set of handcuffs. A trickle of liquid heated the inside of my thighs. I assumed the position facing the back seat. However, not before I could steal another peek of him. I needed to see him. He rolled his shoulders to loosen up, the vein in his neck pulsing. His abdominal muscles clenched, ready to pounce. He was all male. But there was something wild added to the mix, something I hadn't experienced yet. His nostrils flared as he inhaled deeply. "You ready to be fucked?" he asked, his voice low and dangerous. Was that a question? Of course I was ready. "I asked you a question, Beauty. Are you ready to be fucked?" A note of warning sounded in his voice.

"Yes. I'm more than ready to be fucked," I answered assuredly.

"That mouth of yours, Beauty. I love that mouth of yours. Now put your hand behind your back," he said, moving to kneel behind me at my apex. His heartbeat was loud enough for me to hear. I leaned forward on the bench and put my hands behind me. He fastened the cuffs around my wrists. I turned a bit to look and a devilish smile played at his lips. That had me bristling. I had never felt that way before—ever: so wanted, so needed. It was as if he needed me to breathe. He skimmed his fingertips over my pussy, then down my thighs and up to my tits, humming his appreciation while pinching my responsive nipples.

"We don't have long, my beauty. I'm going to take you hard and fast. Your job is to hold this position."

His hand settled on my back, pushing me into the seat cushion as he nudged my thighs farther apart with his knees. This position was extremely awkward. With the vehicle in motion and no use of my arms…I didn't feel very sure I'd hold the position. However, I'd try my hardest to satisfy him. I knew 100% that I was incredibly turned on and wet as fuck. The piercing of his head glided over my clit until his cock was sufficiently lathered in my juices. He entered me none too gently, his hands bruising my hips. I planted my face in the seat as he proceeded to pound the fucking life out of me. My body went soft with surrender. His strokes were long and hard. He growled before lifting both my legs off the carpeted floor. He never stopped pumping. My face rutted in the butter-soft leather. My shoulders were holding me steady. I tried to push back ever so slightly so I could breathe. He wasn't having it. His pace was that of an Olympian. Synapses fired through every cell of my body. Molten fire pushed through my veins. A stirring deep in my womb. My orgasm hit me hard, threatening my vision. White sparks exploded around my peripheral eyesight. I was at war with my body in a way I've never been; he controlled everything— my air, arms, legs, pussy, orgasms, and now my heart. On his knees, with my ass held high up in the air and his balls punishing my pussy mercilessly, he growled wildly, the sounds reverberating throughout the truck. What. In. The. Fuck. I could never face these people again. However, before embarrassment took a firm hold. I needed another orgasm—and I didn't have to wait long for it, either. His sounds alone kept my pussy locked tight around him. His body tensed as he unloaded everything he had inside me.

"You. Are. Mine," he ground out, pumping hard. His thrusts were still controlled, but slower. *Thank fuck.* Eventually, he stopped pumping. I jumped as he grabbed my pussy lips, asking, "What are you doing to me?" I froze. Was he talking to me or my pussy? Maybe I wasn't exactly coherent at that point. I was a sweaty mess. The truck slowed down and he unlocked the handcuffs. His fingers softly rubbing my wrists. *Fuck. Tell me we're here. Kill me now.*

I sat on my heels, taking deep breaths, trying to pull in as much oxygen as I could. I've deprived my brain for God knows how long. I heard him buckling his belt, and then the doors opening and slamming shut. I couldn't go to his concert. I was fucking wrecked. I was about to ask him to please leave me in the car or have the driver take me home when I heard the keys to his iPhone dinging.

"Thank you, Beauty," he whispered, kissing my shoulder and groaning. "I'll never get my fill of you." He kissed the other shoulder. "I'm not going anywhere without you." And then he licked the side of my face.

"Dave, have festival security meet us at the south entrance. I need twenty minutes in the suite," he barked into his cell. "I don't give a fuck. Make it happen or I'm out."

He pocketed his phone. "I've got you, Beauty. I take care of what's mine." He pulled my naked body to his. I believed he really did have me. He was like no other man I'd ever known. His arms caged me, comforting me and making me feel secure. He showered me with tiny wet kisses while nuzzling me; it was pure Paradise. I sat tucked under his thick arms while he stoked my hair and dialed Chance.

"Hey C, do me a solid. Can you get some clothes for Gia to change in to? Yep. Sounds about right. Exactly. Thank you. Meet us in the south-side suite." He sounded relieved. I melted into him while he searched the floor for my clothes. His phone rang, letting us know we were at the south entrance.

"Here, put this on." He handed me his shirt while seizing the rest of my scattered clothes. "We're in front of the south-side door. The suite is 100 feet on the left. Security has the exits blocked. Let's go and get you changed. And keep that sweet ass covered."

He opened the door, grabbing my hand as we made a run for the dressing suite. His strides were much longer than mine, and it was obvious he was trying to keep me out of view. Testosterone thickened the air. His eyes threatened anyone who so much as glanced my way. Security lined the hallway to obscure me from prying eyes. A janitor was polishing the brass name plate on the door: *Abel Gunner, Lethal Abel*. Pride swelled my face into a wide smile. I couldn't help it. I wanted to pinch myself, scream, and act silly. Hell, I felt crazy. It was inconceivable. Never in my wildest fantasies did I ever think this could be my life—that he could be my life. We came to a halt, giving way to the janitor, who looked at anything except us.

Inside his decadent suite, I was struck by how ostentatious it was; it was the total opposite of his office at his penthouse. This was a festival, not an opera house—but you'd never know it by the lush décor. My mouth gaped open as my eyes took in the room: exotic flowers, toile couches, baroque lamps, and hardwoods floors covered with Persian rugs. What. In. The. Fuck.

"Deirdre, my mother. This is what she does. Decorates. This is how she shows love. I'm over it." He frowned, turning his back toward me. *Uh-oh. There's a story there.* Then again, who didn't have one, right? Hands down, Medusa held the record for world's worst mother. So while I felt some sadness for him growing up unloved in the lap of luxury, I was skeptical.

"I'm sorry this is how she chooses to love you. What I've learned in my life is that some people just aren't capable of showing or feeling real love." I rubbed his back, placing kisses across his shoulder blade. "Hey, Mister, you have a concert to do." I patted his plump ass cheeks.

He grabbed my wrist firmly. "Thank you, Gia." I nodded with a smile. God, he was a broody, beautiful mess. A knock sounded at the door, sending him striding powerfully over to open it. Shit, he was intense. He looked like he was going to kill someone. I stepped into the bathroom quickly, pulling out my phone.

I texted Cindy: *Yo? Where you at, chick?*

She replied: *Yo, we're hanging, waiting on you two idiots. WTF? Holy obsessive caveman, chick! Do you have a magical pussy I don't know about, G? LMBO! The guys are getting antsy. What's the holdup?*

I reassured her: *We just got to the suite. I just need to change. See you soon. Xoxo*

Cindy reacted with surprise: *Change? Um, ok, I won't even ask. Xoxo*

I switched my phone off to save the battery. It was then that I noticed both males standing in the doorway, one with a huge electric smile holding a shopping bag. That was Chance. The other still had a frown plastered on his face. That was Abel. Jesus, he really was broody. His eyes sparked when they appraised my naked legs. His tee-shirt just skimmed the tops of my thighs, just below my ass. Chance hurriedly stepped in past me. Abel's eyes burned my flesh with their intensity. I just chewed on my bottom lip. Then all at once, he smiled, leaving the bathroom alcove.

"Fuck, that was intense," Chance chirped. "I've never seen him so intense. I mean I have, but not like that. You guys been having some fun, yeah?"

He greeted me with a kiss, handing over the bag of goodies. "Oh my, Deirdre really must be feeling guilty lately," he said, observing the elaborate décor. He opened up a drawer, pulling out a tortoise brush and placing it in front of me with a quirked eyebrow.

"Subtle, Chance. Real subtle." We laughed as he turned the shower on. Yeah I knew I looked a mess. My hair so knotted I wondered if I'd ever get the knots out.

"In you go," he prompted. "You have ten minutes. Work it." He winked, sashaying across the marble floor and closing the door behind him.

I pulled Abel's shirt off, deeply inhaling his scent; it reeked of salt and spice and everything that was Abel. He was all male. Instant heat shot through my body, pooling between by legs. Shit, I was sore. I could never deny him or myself for that matter. This was what that man did to me. His essence made my blood sing.

I put myself together in under fifteen minutes. That was a record for me. However, when you had a man like Abel waiting, you got a move on it. I couldn't be too careful with that piranha Morgana lurking around. With a quick spritz of perfume, I was ready. Chance had hooked me up with supple, cream-colored leather pants, a black, off-the-shoulder shirt, and a pair of black snakeskin Christian Louboutin's. The clothes had cost a fortune; he had not even bothered to remove the price tags. I made a mental note to thank Chance. Damn, he had to have some awesome connections to pull that kind of outfit together at the last minute. The clothes were a bit conservative for a rock star's taste. But, they reeked of money and class. Not that I thought Abel didn't have either. He did. And plenty. I was just surprised by his choices, that's all.

"Well, well, well," Chance said, as he spun me around. "You look positively edible. If I were hetero, I'd take you here on the floor." He laughed deeply. It was a very manly laugh. I didn't have any gay friends to compare him to. But I could see myself falling in love with his personality. What was there not to love about Chance? He was everything you'd want in a man: gorgeous, built, and loyal.

"Is that Abel?" I could hear his voice streaming through the Bose speakers. I had fully anticipated he would greet us before going onstage.

"Yes, love. He couldn't wait. Dave was worried he wouldn't make it to the stage on time for sound check. You guys got delayed, apparently?" His smile was contagious. He pushed my hair behind my ear and wrapped his arm around me. "Come, enlighten me while we walk. He's expecting you."

He guided me out of the suite. His broad arms settled around my shoulders. The same security sentinels lined the hallways, speaking into their earpieces as we approached.

"What's the deal with all this security? I know the band is über-popular, but the guys seem more relaxed than Abel. He's a bit intense. No?" I was perplexed. One minute we were on his motorcycle and the next we were being mauled by paparazzi. "What I mean to ask is: is this an Abel thing or a Lethal Abel thing?"

Chance blinked a few times before answering. "Both. As of late, with Morgana's threats hanging in the wind, the gossip rag reporters have been vultures. Also, the band just went platinum. So, there's that. Then, there's you." He squeezed me tightly against his hard body. *Then there's me?*

"Me? What would I possibly have to do with this? I don't need security. I'm a frigging secretary," I said nervously, awaiting his answer. But before he could say anything, Dave met us for the handoff. Now, it was Dave who was in charge of directing me to my place.

"Wait, where are you going?" I yelled back at Chance. Christ, the music was so loud.

"My seat, love. Front row. Right over there." He pointed below the stage.

This sucked. While I wanted to hang with Cin, I also wanted to pick Chance's brain. "Just make him happy, Gia," he said, leaning in to kiss my cheek. "He deserves to be happy. He's different with you."

Happy? Me make someone happy? Imagine that? I was thrilled! I was elated with all the possibilities swirling around in my head. I could do this. I wanted to be happy. Hell, I deserved happiness more than most. A burning sensation crept its way up to my nose. Tears gathered in my eyes. I paid no attention to Dave as he escorted me to the side stage just across from the band. I was a total, blubbering idiot. These feelings and sensations were new to me. I didn't know what to do with them. I murmured a thank you to him. It was left unanswered. He was busy with all that was going on. He was the backbone of the band. I didn't envy his job. He smoked like a chimney. And when he was in the zone, he barely said a word. However, he saw to the band's needs and made sure the event ran smoothly.

Wiping my eyes, I took my cell out of my purse to check my messages. Medusa had called several times, leaving no voicemail. Her two texts just said *Call Me.* And therein lay the problem. Abel's voice did nothing to soothe the unease that had taken hold. I powered down my phone and returned it to my purse, my eyes still blurry with tears. I blinked them away, letting them rest on top of my cheeks as a cathartic plea to the universe. Someone, anyone, help me. Help me find the courage to seek my own happiness, releasing me from my mother's torture. She knew my vulnerabilities. She was an expert at tormenting me and using me to do all her dirty work. Only this time it was different. I was different. He was different. I couldn't allow her to ruin this for me. No. I wouldn't.

So, I pulled myself together, wiping the tears from my eyes. Then I noticed Cindy across from me frowning. She mouthed the words, *"What's going on?"* I quickly pulled my happy mask on and smiled. I mouthed back. *"Happy."* I pointed toward my smile, then toward Abel. That would shut her up. She pointed toward Woody, raising her eyebrows suggestively. I laughed. She had a way of making my darkest hours brighter, if only for a few moments. Those moments were everything to me. That's the thing. Children of abuse saw things in moments. Sometimes they were all we had. In those moments, we *lived*. But I had found a way of life that I never wanted to give up. I wanted to live all my moments with *him*…

I was lost in thought when I heard him calling my name. I came to with a jolt. *What. In. The. Fuck.* I looked around me. I saw Dave scrambling toward me. His lips were moving, but nothing registered. He was pointing manically toward the center of the stage where a roadie was placing a chair. *What?* I looked in that direction to see Abel waving me over. I turned around, looking behind me. The stage hands were smiling and pointing. *Where the fuck were they pointing?* Dave finally got to me, all out-of-breath, his cigarette hanging from his lips.

"On stage, doll. Off you go." He pushed me out from behind the massive curtains and onto the stage. I was in full view of thousands of screaming, out-of-their-mind fans. Abel extended his hand, motioning for me to come to him. I went into a Jan Brady catatonic trance. Cheers rose up as he approached me, smiling gently. I managed to smile back. Still, I had no clue what the fuck was going on.

Abel's soft hands gently guided me to a high bar-chair placed next to his microphone. My heart pounded in my ears. I looked for Chance in the front row. I needed to focus on something familiar. His animated smile ignited my numbed brain. The crowd was going wild. Abel continued to taunt them with my presence. Shouts of "Oh My God!" and "Who the fuck is that?" could be heard rising up from the audience. I was getting twitchy sitting there. The lights were hot and blinding. Christ. How did they deal with the heat on stage? I wiped my forehead free of sweat. I turned to find Cindy standing behind the curtain. Woody's drums were the precursor to the next song. Cindy was waving frantically, screaming, "Enjoy, Gia, enjoy!"

Finally, I turned toward Abel. From his Doc Martins to his Lethal Abel tee-shirt, he was the epitome of the Rock God. He owned the stage. His shirt rode up as he fist-pumped the crowd into screaming my name. Ender's guitar licked seductively into the melody. It was Lethal Abel's rock version of "Stay." I crossed my legs to give myself something to do, and anyway, it helped to steady them; they were shaking from nerves. *Breathe in. Breathe out.* Abel grabbed my chin in his signature move. He wanted me to focus on him. And so I did.

Along it was a fever
A cold-sweat hot-headed believer
I threw my hand in the air and said show me something
She said if you dare come a little closer
Round and around and around we go
Ooh, tell me now, tell me now, tell me now, you know
Not really sure how I feel about it … something in the way you
move …
Makes me feel I can't live without you
Yeah, it takes me all the way
I want you to stay …

I relaxed into the song, getting into his rock version of it. I thumped my leg to Woody's beats, thrashing my head to Abel's wicked lyrics. There were no tears left in me to cry; all I could feel was joy. That was the happiest moment of my life. Abel kissed the inside of my wrist before grabbing my face in a smoldering kiss, just as the lights blacked out. The roar of the crowd seemed to intensify the darkness. I was shuffled off backstage, this time to Cindy's side.

"Are you fucking kidding me right now?" She jumped all around me, clapping. "Possession is nine-tenths of the law. And your pussy has possessed that boy right there." She pointed at Abel, who was beaming at me. Her behavior was addicting. Had we been in private, I would've joined her in celebrating. But it was totally un-cool to go all fan-girl in front of the guy I was fucking.

For the rest of their set, we head-banged to their songs. Being backstage made the whole experience much more intimate for us. Music flowed in a circuit from Cindy to me, looping us in its prism. I was feeling high from the energy. I searched the crowd to get a visual on Chance. However, I got something I wasn't expecting. *Her.* Front and center where Chance was no longer sitting. Yes, Morgana had taken his place. What. The. Fuck? Were they operating together against me? What was she doing in *his* seat? Where the fuck was he? My eyes squinted for him in the crowd. Maybe with all the excitement, my brain was manufacturing things. Possible, right? But no such luck. It was the piranha cunt, all right. She was tapping her watch to insinuate I'm on borrowed time. Cindy followed my line of sight.

"You've got to be shitting me!" she raged. I held stock-still, engaging her in a silent war. Her eyes threatened revenge. My eyes answered: *bring it, cunt.* A maniacal smile tugged my lips. Fuck this cunt… She was not getting him, not taking him from me …

I hadn't even realized the set had ended when all of a sudden, Abel joined me and Cindy, lacing his hand through mine while rubbing his thumb on my knuckles. They say your skin is the largest sensory organ in your body, that touching and being touched, or the lack of it, profoundly effects your development from infancy on. Sadly, I hadn't had much experience with that. My mother and I had never really bonded. She had never properly nurtured me, and had given me very little in the way of comfort or security. All she ever gave was callousness and pain. But Abel's caring touch did things to me. His warmth seeped deep into my skin, wrapping me in his strength and courage—neither of which I naturally possessed. I was hoping I could use his to gain some of my own.

"What's up, Beauty?" he asked, kissing my forehead. We cleared the stage so the next band could set up. Lethal Abel was done for the evening. Now it was party-time. Time to celebrate another successful

night for the band. I looked over at Cindy, then over my shoulder. Morgana was nowhere to be seen. The showdown with her had left me feeling rattled and vulnerable. What game was she playing? Cindy squeezed my arm in solidarity. Thank fuck she was at my side. I needed a small army to take the bitch down. Twice in one day was more than enough to make me all twitchy and punchy.

"I want to make you sore," Abel whispered in my ear as he led us through the halls. That statement produced seepage. *Fuck yeah, I wanted to be sore, too.* I'd settle for being locked away with his hot ass for a few weeks. And after all that fucking, I would still want more. He was unforgettable, and most definitely undeniable.

[Listen to OLN's version of "Stay" here: http://www.youtube.com/watch?v=8Aufxr0Y0-g.]

Chapter Twelve

Abel

Two nights down, one to go. Lethal Abel was playing real tight. We sounded fucking great. By the sound of the crowd, they were loving it as well. I left myself out on that stage that night, gave my fans all of me. My heart slammed against my ribs when Gia came out. I offered her my hand. At first, she didn't take it. Instead, she looked at me with a stranger's eyes. My stomach knotted up just thinking about her rejecting me. Forget the obvious—that we were in front of a few hundred thousand fans, and my band. Not to mention, being simulcast around the world. We were also being taped for an HBO special to be aired at the end of our European tour. It would feature a view into the lives of rock stars on the road touring. We had a ton of PR for our new album. Since it went platinum, Dave had been exceedingly busy setting everything up. As always, my old man had his hand in the mix, stirring the pot from wherever he was, making sure the Gunner name lived up to its stock. My eyes had begged her to hear my heart's plea, to take my hand, and trust me to do right by her. That moment felt like an eternity, as if we were locked in a silent battle of hearts and souls. I only wanted to share a song that meant something to me. I wanted her to see it through new eyes—my eyes. I was showing her my hand. That much I knew. I knew my boys would give me hell for being so done-in for a babe. However, we don't really get to choose who we love. *Love?* Was I falling in *love* with Beauty? Did my heart not ache for those few stolen moments at daybreak? Was my mind not constantly drifting to her? Was I not always finding ways to bring her name up in conversation, even if it was just to talk about Cindy? When I showered, did I not oil my fist and fuck my cock thinking of how her tight pussy owned me? Yes, I did. I did all of those things. If I was truthful with myself, the answer was a resounding *yes.*

I couldn't wait to get her firmly under me and sink into her warmth. I could die a happy man inside her pussy. But I wanted her to be happy. I didn't want to be selfish. It wasn't all about me. I wanted it to be about my Beauty. And whatever made my love happy, I'd do.

"I love that smile of yours," I said. And I did, too. It was everything to me. I just wanted to be the only reason it graced her face. Yeah, I was fucked, all right.

"You put it there, Abel. Thank you." She looked up at me with wide eyes, blushing. See, that right there, that was the pureness I loved. It made me want to beat my chest, throw her over my shoulder, slide deep inside her heat, and shower her with enough come to mark her forever—mental shit no dude in my position had business toying with. I was a rock star. I wasn't fucking *Nicholas Sparks.* I didn't do forever. Fuck. It wasn't in my vocabulary.

"Anything you wanna do tonight? Anything? It's yours." The band was gathering for a quick meet-and-greet in the suite. The boys and I usually celebrated hard after concerts. But if Beauty wanted to be alone and make a night of it, who was I to stand in her way?

"Cindy said she was going with the guy to the hookah place. I've never been there before. Can we go for a little while? We have the whole night together. It's still kinda early," she answered, shrugging. Like I had the balls to say no. She had my balls in her fucking purse. She didn't know that. At least I could try to redeem myself by pretending to have some.

"Sure, we could go for a little while. I have some business to attend to. Who says I can't conduct it there." I winked. *Lame.*

I led us back to the suite where the fans were already filtering in. I left her safely with Cindy while I took my position with the band. We had a few giveaway winners, one of which was a picture with a member of the band along with something special from said member. I was signing swag as usual, when Dave announced the night's winner. A drop-dead gorgeous blonde with blue eyes and a pair of double DD's walked up to claim her prize. I silently prayed she wouldn't ask for me. Before Gia, I'd rock out with my cock out. However, I didn't want the complications or the fucking drama. From the looks of this girl, she was a grade-A, slutty fan-girl trouble. She already had her poppy-red, manicured nails running the length of my tee-shirt. *Fuck me sideways.*

Dave came walking over with a jubilant smile on his face. What. The. Fuck. He knew this was some bullshit. He got off on this drama. His famous last words were, "All press was good press." He wasn't even opposed to Morgana outing me to the press and dragging my family's good name though shit for money. I took a step back.

However, Ender stepped up behind me, hip-checking me into her. She dramatized her fall into my arms. She was wobbly enough in those six-inch, fuck-me spikes. So the little bit of exertion had her falling into my arms for the cameras.

"What's the matter, baby, you can't wait?" she cackled. I righted her onto her feet and turned to look for Gia. She was grabbing a drink with our record label VP, Jeremy the snake. Her wine glass fell from her hand as she watched, slack-jawed. Jeremy was there, rubbing her arms from behind before she ran out. Cindy's frown said it all. I looked up at Jeremy to tell him to keep an eye on my girl, when he mouthed the words, "*Epic fail.*" Was he fucking kidding me? I balled my fists.

"Where the fuck is Ender?" I asked Woody, who was standing with his hands in his pockets with a disappointed look on his face. "What? That wasn't my fault? I didn't want that slut!" I yelled.

"Heeey!" The skank cried out. "You want to see a slut?" She grabbed my dick, hanging from it like it was a set of monkey bars. I removed her hands forcefully—but not before a dozen cameras clicked. *Holy fuck. I was so fucked right now.*

"Dave!" I shouted venomously as I turned the skank in his direction. Thankfully, Jake stepped up and grabbed her by the elbow, escorting her and her double DD's to the door. Woody's hands found their way to my shoulders, pulling me into a half bro-hug.

"Yer in a load of fuckin' ballsch." He patted my back. "Let's go get yer girl, mate." He grabbed two shots of JD from Jack. Was he actually going to do one with the skank?

"Heeey," she cried, punching my arm. "What's your fucking problem?" She pouted with her bottom lip protruding out. I eyed Jake crazily. I was on the edge of losing my motherfucking mind. Skank was supposed to have been escorted out.

"Don't you ever put your fucking hands on me again," I snapped, getting in her face. Woody pulled me back. I could have killed her right then and there for pulling that bimbo routine. "If I wanted you, you'd know it, sweetheart. I don't fucking want you. Got that? You show up every so often, trying to bend me. I don't fucking bend. Stay the fuck away from me."

I stalked off, leaving Woody to trail behind me. I was losing it. It's my own fault this shit went down. I allowed this crap to go on backstage, welcomed it. It was just what rock stars did. So why did it feel so fucking wrong? Why did I feel guilty for doing absolutely nothing? It all came back to one word, one name that stuck in my throat: *Gia.*

"Where is she?" I growled as I entered the hallway. "Where's Cindy?" I asked Woody. "Text her please, will you? I need to know Gia's okay."

His phone was already in his hand. I stalked the hallways, opening every door along the way. They were crowded with musicians, with drummers catching beats on the walls, guitarists tuning their guitars at the last minute, lead singers with their personal microphones in hand. The end of the hallway was at the south entrance. There stood Jeremy the snake. He was on his phone talking animatedly to someone. He hurriedly put his phone in his pocket, procuring a white piece of paper. He held it up to my face.

"This is for you," he said. I snatched it out of his hands. Woody was leaning against the wall, feigning indifference. I turned back to Jeremy, only to see the door closing behind him. He left the building. I was holding a note on a napkin. I unfolded it.

Abel,

I don't fit in your world. I'm not strong enough to try. It's easier this way. I'm sorry. You don't know how sorry I am.

Gia

I reread the five short sentences, hoping they would somehow make sense. But they did not. I turned to Woody, who was now standing there with Jake and Dave.

"What the fuck does this mean?" I said to nobody in particular. Dave grabbed the note. The boys stepped over to have a look. I was in a world of hurt. Was this an "I'm jealous and can't deal with it tonight" or a "Later, I'm out"? I fingered for my phone in my pocket, dialing her number. My call went straight to voicemail.

"The trucks are outside. We're going out, dude. You're coming," Dave said, pushing me out the door toward the truck. I was a complete and utter fucking zombie. This girl was gonna fucking kill me. Just before getting in the truck, I heard a woman's cackling. I turned to see Morgana in her white, convertible Jaguar stopped fifty yards down. She unlocked the passenger door for the skank to get in. They drove off laughing.

"That fucking cunt of your ex," Jake said, prompting me to get in the car. "If she wasn't a woman, I'd kick her fucking ass inside out." He closed the door behind him.

Woody grabbed the bottle of JD, passing it to me. I grunted, swigging straight from the bottle.

"Anyone holding?" I asked. They looked at one another. "Don't bogart that shit. I need it." I looked to Jake, whose jaw was working like a marionette.

"Jake, I'm in no fucking mood for games," I said, deadly serious. Jake slipped the Otterbox off his iPhone to hand me the package of white goodness. I hadn't had this shit in years. I gave up partying when I started medication. I didn't give a flying fuck tonight.

"Dude, I don't think it's such a good idea. You know how you get. Let's go grab some dinner. Just us." Dave said, trying to rip the package out of my hand. I thrust my forearm forward to block his efforts.

"Then don't fucking think," I said, pouring two bumps on the back of my hand. I snorted one in each nostril, letting my head fall back on the seat. Another swig of Jack coated my throat. The drug dripped down the back of my throat, numbing everything in its path. *Perfect.* I half listened to their worried conversation about me. Fuck it. Fuck them. Fuck everyone. I'm officially checking the fuck out.

We ended up going to the Hookah lounge. Ender split, getting a ride from the other driver—which was curious in itself. Why wasn't he with his boys? *Whatever.*

Jake shook me before trying to pry the blow out of my hand. "Get your goddamned hands off of me!" I shouted. My fists were flying. Jake, Dave, and Woody sat wide-eyed, looking at me like I had lost my mind. Maybe I had.

"Dude, chill the fuck out. We're here. You sure you want to go in?" Dave asked, concerned about my state of mind. I didn't answer. I just tucked the blow into my jeans, then scooted over the seat, getting out of the truck. Dave must have called ahead, because security was outside waiting for us. The line was wrapped around the building. Yeah, someone tipped off the public. I took my shirt off handing it to the bald fucker, nodding. He grabbed the tee-shirt with one hand, extending the other to shake mine. I walked past him. Fuck that. I wasn't shaking shit tonight. They had better leave me to it. I had to sort my shit out. Speaking of sorting, I dialed Gia's number again. *Nada*. I followed Woody to our table in the corner. We ordered our usual, the pineapple and mint hookah. Since they had taken my bottle of JD away, I ordered another.

"Dude, where's Ender?" I asked, looking around the club. I didn't see him. Were they sure we were meeting him here? "Maybe he split with a chick?" I asked. That was highly probable. The waitress, a pretty, petite ginger, came over to take our order, her eyes feasting on my well-honed chest. She pulled her bottom lip into her mouth with her teeth biting down. She was ogling me, memorizing my body like she didn't want to forget my swells of well-placed muscle. *Damn.*

I sat back on the couch, legs spread wide to relax. She stifled a breath of air.

"Doll, you're getting yourself all worked up over this," I said, pointing at my dick. "This will never be in you. I've felt nirvana—tasted it. That's all he'll crave from now on." I rubbed my cock with my hand. Just talking about Gia's pussy had me ready to bust a nut.

"You're a real asshole, huh?" She glowered at me. Woody laughed, throwing me back my tee-shirt to put on.

"Aye." He agreed with her. The boys had a good laugh. She ignored me, taking everybody else's order. Luckily, Jake ordered a bottle of JD for the table. Thank fuck. I was parched. I need another hit, too. Reaching into my pocket, I grabbed my new source of nirvana—blow. I grabbed my Black American Express card to chop it into manageable lines. This shit was rocky as hell. I poured a good amount on the table, quickly going to work chopping.

"Dude, you need to be chill. The photogs are around. You can't spill that shit out for everybody to see," Jake said, resting his arm across my shoulders. I looked back at his arm and growled. He removed it, frowning. "I'm just looking out for you, Abel. No need to be a prick about it," he said sincerely.

I realized he meant it. I just didn't give a fuck about anything at that point. I needed numbness to find me. I needed to zone out and party for a bit. No harm, no foul. The guys moved to my sides, forming a wall. They didn't like what I was doing, how I was acting, but they didn't want me to completely fuck up our public image, either. Rock and Roll was stigmatized by drugs. We partied hard. However, we kept it on the down-low. Getting drunk was one thing, almost expected. Chopping lines in the middle of a club was another. *Whatever.*

Dave had been busy texting someone for the last 20 minutes—no doubt something to do with getting me out of there. When millions were on the line, people sat up, taking notice. I was the face, the brand name of the band. My dudes were gifted, no doubt. However, I was the one who worked the magic on the crowd. Dave placed his phone carefully on the table, watching me intently. I offered him my straw. He declined, as I knew he would.

I snorted two healthy-sized lines and grabbed the bottle of JD off the table. My phone in hand, I waited, scanning the crowd for her. She knew we were there. Maybe she'd come, and give me a chance to explain. I was playing with my lip ring when all at once, Woody slammed his fist on the table and jumped to his feet. *What in the fuck.* I got up on my feet, too.

"Fuck me!" he roared, pointing to the back bar on the other side. My eyes followed his finger.

"Motherfucker!" I bellowed. Sure enough, Ender was rubbing Gia's back while she was wrapped up tightly in his arms. Cindy was doing a shot with one of Ender's boys from back home that he occasionally flew out. The bouncers moved toward us, looking for signs of trouble. We were roped off in the VIP section.

"What seems to be the problem, Mr. Gunner?" the bald fuck asked.

"The motherfucking problem is, my friend has my girl wrapped up in his arms. Now, he has *me* as a fucking problem!" I yelled, while Dave and Jake tried to hold me back. We were causing a big enough scene that people started to take notice. "How many fucking times do I have to warn this prick? How many?" I asked Woody, then turned to Jake. They said not a word. Their silence told me they acknowledged my rage and agreed that I had a right to it. Ender was asking for it. He not only had Gia, but Cindy, too—which meant he had left the venue with them. My mind was processing those thoughts before my mouth could utter them. When I realized what was up, my rage multiplied tenfold. I cracked my knuckles and neck, ready to kick some motherfucking Spanish Lothario ass.

"Don't call my old man to bail me out. You call Chance. Got it?" I told Dave. He nodded.

"Let's hope it doesn't come it that, dude." He grabbed my arm. "Not that I don't think he deserves some shit for acting like a jerkoff." I got him loud and clear. Kick his ass, but don't kill him, don't break up the band. I was always thinking of the band. This all came down to respect. He was disrespecting me with Gia. He very well knew this girl was under my skin. So what does he do? He fucks with me, through her.

The crowd parted like the Red Sea. That's fucking right: move the fuck out of my way before I run your asses down. I took long, assured strides across the lounge. Cindy's eyes were wide with fear. She tapped Gia's arm. Gia started backing up, with fear in her eyes, too. Ender had his hands in the air trying to deflect my rage. There was no deflecting it. He needed to take it like the scumbag he was. I had warned him.

"It's not what you think, bro," he said, backing up against the bar. Now he was corralled. His friend hurriedly pushed the girls out of the way. At least someone had a brain. He knew Ender was gonna get his ass handed to him. The music stopped. People hushed one another.

This would surely make the papers tomorrow. It always did. *Fuck it.* I had a point to make. It was time to drive the point home.

"Dude, I swear to fuck I didn't lay a hand on her. It's not like that," he pleaded. My first punch had him doubled over, fighting for air. The second punch had his head hitting the bar top. Security, along with my mates, jumped in. Ender was hunched over with one arm wrapped around his stomach, and the other hand massaging his jaw.

"You feel better now?" he huffed. "I'm not going to fucking hit you back. You're my boy. I wouldn't do that shit to you." He straightened his pose, pushing his chest out. There's the Lathario. The motherfucking peacock was going to get all chesty on me. He had a reputation to uphold. There's no fucking way he'd look like a pussy in front of people.

"She. Is. *Mine.* You don't *ever* put your filthy fucking hands on what's *mine.* Ever," I growled in his face. "If I see you do it again, I will fucking kill and dismember you. I swear to fuck, I will." I stepped up to him, driving my point into his thick, Spanish skull. I meant every word I had said. I would fucking kill the bastard—I would kill anyone who dared to lay a finger on her.

"I know, I know," he surrendered. Imagine that: Surrender surrendering. Never thought I'd see the day. Must've been a cold day in hell. His eyes never left mine, never hesitating, never blinking. My mind was contaminated with coke. My senses were heightened. My mind was on overdrive. So when Gia turned to run, I was on her quicker than a hooker could drop her panties.

"I don't think so, Beauty," I said, throwing her over my shoulder. *Fuck that shit.*

"Let me down, you skizzy, pervy caveman!" she bellowed, pounding my back with her fists. Cindy moved in front of me, waving her hands like a crossing guard.

"Cindy, I love you, but I will mow your ass down." I kept walking past her, back to the VIP area. She frowned, moving out of my way.

That was a relief. I didn't need two pissed-off women to deal with. I looked ahead to see Dave wiping the table off with a bar rag. My man! He always had my back. He was always protecting me. I appreciated that, big-time. For that, he deserved a raise. I decided I'd have a talk with him tomorrow about that. Jake stayed with Ender. While Woody, Dave, and the girls were in VIP, I lowered Gia gently to a standing position. She kept spewing venom from her lips. I asked everyone to leave us for a few minutes. I needed to remedy what had happened—or what she thought had happened at the after-party.

"Have you lost your fucking mind? Why would you attack your best friend? Why?" she railed. "You're a fucking brat. If you don't get what you want, you act like an asshole until you do." She pummeled my chest. Was I fucked-up enough to actually be turned *on* by this? Because I was—turned on. God help me, I was. "Well, keep acting like an asshole, buddy. You're not gonna have me. That's for fucking sure." She stood with her arms folded defensively across her chest.

"One, I'm not a fucking brat. Two, if anyone puts their hands on you, friend or not, they will eat my fucking fist. Three, I lost my mind a long time ago. Nothing new there."

I stepped closer, making sure she looked into my eyes. She needed to hear what I was about to say. She needed to understand, really understand, what being mine meant. "You. Are. *Mine*. You understand what that means? Let me break it the fuck down so you're absolutely-for-fucking-sure. When you signed that agreement, which meant you gave me your mind, body, and soul, your mind will be focused on me, always. Your body will be under, on top, or spread wide open for me—always. Your soul is entwined with mine, forming one physical body of unity—always." My breath hitched with that last sentence. What the fuck was I even saying? Yeah, I thought it. But never spoke it aloud. Coke had me spewing my guts for fuck sake.

She wiped a tear away, looking up at me with the saddest eyes I've ever seen—eyes I wanted to see every morning, every night, while I was on this earth. "I will never hurt you, ever. You're more precious to me than you will ever know. Trust, it goes both ways, Beauty. Trust what I'm saying to you. Let these words work themselves into your heart. Familiarize yourself with that feeling. Because you're gonna feel a whole lot more than that."

"What are you saying?" she asked shakily. "How do I know you don't feel this way for every conquest?" Her eyes welled up again at that mere thought.

"I never believed in fate, destiny, or love at first sight before. I can tell you with 100% certainty I've never felt so utterly fucking consumed by a woman in my life. You take the air from my lungs with your smile, leaving me breathless. I feel I'd suffocate without you in my life. I want to bury my secrets in your skin. I cherish your kisses, savoring each one." I wiped the tears that were raining down her cheeks with my thumb, then pressed the gentlest of kisses to her lips.

"God, where did you come from? You're the sweetest nightmare I could ever conjure up," she said, kissing me back. "You do know we're fucked, right? This coupling is fucking dangerous. You make me feel emotions I never thought possible. Never dreamed of feeling. Certainly not while awake. Please don't hurt me, Abel. It would destroy me. Fucking destroy me." She sealed her pleas with a kiss.

"Never." I drew her in to kiss her so solemnly, so thoroughly, and so completely. This girl was going to be the death of me. I swore to God right then and there. I knew, my heart knew it, my mind had always known it. Now she knew it. Soon, the world would know it. I threw caution to the wind. I was that confident—that totally consumed and pathetically pussy-whipped.

And just like that, I was horny. Just thinking of a whip had me done for. I said, "My cock has been craving this tight pussy all night, babe." I leaned in, cupping her pussy with my hand.

She sighed loudly. "You really know how to make a girl feel special, don't you," she joked, and we both laughed heartily for a few minutes. I reckoned I really was a caveman. *Whatever.*

Everyone walked back over, ecstatic that my head was screwed on right again. We clanked our bottles in salute. Gia *was* sanity to me. As long as she was near, I would be able to breathe. We partied the rest of the night, Ender-free. That was to be dealt with at another time. We all threw back some shots, including the girls. Cindy, however, continued to give me the stink-eye. She was worried my humping and dumping ways would return, only to fuck over Gia. I assured her that would never be the case.

Chapter Thirteen

Gia

The past few weeks had been sublime. He's opened me up to a world I hadn't known existed in Colorado. During the days, I continued to work for his father, keeping our relationship low-key. The press had their fun with our hookah lounge fiasco. The attention I had thought I would relish in the beginning turned out not to be so pleasant, after all. My private life was no longer my own. Anything we did made news.

We continued our morning ritual at the local coffee bean. He called it our "Sunrise dates." He spent the rest of his day in the studio producing newly written material for the European leg of the tour. He asked me to come on tour with him. I needed time to volley that proposal. I had a job that paid well. I didn't want to lose that. God forbid things didn't happen between us as we wanted them to. Nothing was a given in life.

My mother continued to leave threatening messages on my voicemail about how I was fucking with the wrong person. She kept saying if I didn't heed her warnings, she'd resort to non-familial help getting what she wanted. Either way, she would get her dues. Reflecting back to a time when I had thought one way about Abel Gunner: in the beginning, I wanted his money, not him. I was coaxed into thinking that a man made you who you were, with his money, his privilege, his social standing. My upbringing taught me to claw my way to the top, to put myself in a position to repay my mother for the luxury of being her child. Medusa's health was declining. I was a means to an end: to preserve her middle-class lifestyle. Perhaps, provide her with a better one. From an early age, I had been groomed to be nothing more than a whore for her. I realized then that I never knew what love was. What it was to feel love, and to feel *loved*. I wanted to feel those feelings now more than I wanted anything else. I wanted to rejoice in the freedom to have them. However, I knew it would come at a price. And going against my mother's will would cost me. I also knew I'd never give up the only man I had ever loved. No way in fucking hell would I do that. He was worth whatever misery she might cause. More than worth it …

Abel's Dungeon

Reality

J was bound, but not gagged, because he loved the sounds I made. He stalked powerfully around me. I was at his mercy—a word I'd become very familiar with. My ass was perched high in the air, the way he liked it. The flogger met my backside, leaving tingles across my body. He had desensitized my body by dragging the flogger slowly across my extremities. It never left my body during play. He alternated flogging me with finger-fucking me. He would gruffly probe me with his fingers, hitting my g-spot, bringing me close to orgasm, only to abate. He taught me where my g-spot was. He taught me how to bring myself to a g-spot orgasm through self-stimulation, rather than through my clitoris. My orgasms reached a whole new level. I had never experienced a g-spot orgasm before Abel. However, that was one of many eye-opening experiences I'd come to know under his tutorship. Withholding my orgasms was a fetish of his. Or was it a Dom thing? I didn't really know. What I did know, was that it was so fucking maddening. The build up to an Abel orgasm was worth the sacrifice. With Abel, I never just had one epic orgasm. He prided himself on giving me several before allowing himself release. He was selfless in that way. He was a beautifully complicated creature—almost otherworldly. He stood formidably in front of my legs, his cock powerfully erect with beads of come leaking from the tip. I couldn't help licking my now dry lips.

"What did I tell you about licking your lips, Beauty?" He moved behind me, snapping the flogger across my ass. I let out a scream—not one of pain, but of erotic pleasure.

"You, you, you, said don't lick my lips unless I want to get fucked." I sighed deeply. "You can't take watching me do that because it drives you crazy," I continued. *God, I hope he is fucking crazy right now.*

"That's right, sweetheart. It drives me fucking feral. My beast is clawing to get at you," he growled as he continued to pace like a panther hunting its prey, his cock proudly taut. "Do you want release, Beauty? Beg me. I want to hear what you want. How you want it."

One hand carried the flogger, the other hand firmly fisting his cock. The flogger came down across the backs of my thighs. I yelped. I was certain that when the scene was over and he bathed me, my behind would be criss-crossed in different shades of red. And he would revel in its beauty. His marks meant he possessed me. I wore them proudly.

"I want your tongue on me, Sir. In me. All over me, Sir." There, I said it. Fire licked my face. I still felt self-conscious about asking for, begging for, or admitting to my desires. It didn't feel wrong that I craved what he did to my body; it just felt unfamiliar. It evoked feelings. With me, feelings were unwelcome. As my Dom, he saw my pain though my actions. He had never asked me about my troubles directly. He had only said, "When you're ready, you'll tell me everything. I'm very much looking forward to getting to know all about you, Gia." We were working on that. I loved that he didn't push or pry into my personal life. Sexually, there was no hiding or withholding anything. Mentally, my walls were beginning to crumble. He reveled in my naïveté. I was new to both his social world as well as the BDSM. It pleased him and he thought it was refreshing.

"Please," I begged.

"First, I'm going to eat out that gorgeous pink pussy. Then I'm going to fuck you so hard you'll feel me inside you for days." He settled between my spread legs, lifting my ass up to his face. He smeared my wetness all over him. This man had a penchant for pussy—my pussy. I had no objections to that at all.

"Umm, so delicious. I've missed you, my Beauty," he said between licks. I was so sensitive from his constant licking and sucking. I couldn't help but squirm, which only fueled him further. He embedded his tongue deep into me, twirling it as he played, nibbling my clit. My whining increased as I struggled against my bindings, chafing my skin. There was no helping it. I was being driven mad by his tongue. He worked my sweet spot until I came on his tongue, screaming as he lapped away all my juices, leaving me clean.

"That's it. So responsive. So fucking perfect. I couldn't have built a better submissive myself. Now, you get my cock in you. I'm going to come deep inside you, leaking out of you for the next few hours." He nudged his thick, pierced head at my entrance. I was limp, having had no time to recover. I was exhausted, both physically and emotionally, exhausted from sensations and arousal. He had wrung every last bit out of me—and he wasn't done yet. He started slapping my clit with his Apadravya, snapping me back to life. The sensation caused my pussy to release fluid. He pushed in so hard I lost my breath. Using the restraints to steady myself meant I could not catch it. I pushed backward, spearing myself onto him as his fingers buried themselves into my hips, pulling me into his thrusts.

"Jesus Christ Al-fucking-mighty, don't stop," I cried out. I was met with silence. I turned to observe him, only to see the pupils of his eyes dilated fully, encompassing the brown; they were large, wild, and dangerous. He was beyond talk. Wildly, he uttered garbled, mangled, hissing expletives. He leaned forward, kneading my breasts, pinching my already sensitive nipples. I screamed his name over and over again, pleas for mercy. Why were my ears ringing? Why did I hear my blood swishing through them? Maybe my screams had broken my ear drums? Whatever the reason was, it was deafening. The sting of pleasure tingled up my spine, signaling yet another orgasm.

"Your cunt chokes my fuckin' cock so good, babe. So help me, I'm going to be buried inside of you every day, all day," he spat, his strokes long and sure. He allowed the head of his cock to come almost completely out before he surged back in, bottoming out. The sounds of his balls slapping my ass sounded like the flogger striking my body. His body jerked, spasming as he emptied himself inside me. It was the best sex of my life, to date. He reached out, tracing my jaw line with his thumb. I leaned into his touch.

Abel's cum leaked out from between my thighs, dripping down my legs. His intensity had taught me true symbiotic adulation. We were perfectly fucked-up in all the worst possible ways. And yet we worked. We both got what we needed—along with a few things we never thought to ask for. I submitted to his skilled mastering of my body daily, recognizing his need for control. I wanted to give him what he needed. He gave me everything I needed with a mere gaze. There was no reluctance on my part, only willing submission. It was the only gift he wanted. Everything else was icing on the cake.

His sweaty hair tousled from his hard mounting, he inspected his handiwork on my bottom, then released my ankles and wrists from the St. Andrew's Cross. He massaged the tender area on my wrists. I was still learning and fought the bindings at times, especially when I was face-down and ass-up. Being unable to have a visual fueled my fear. I had no idea what it was I feared. I knew he wouldn't hurt me. But there was this small side of me that always fought to fully submit from this position. During those times, he'd whisper lovingly in my ear to quell my angst. That night, he had taken me hard. I had given him my all. I was too spent to think about anything or anyone else. My eyes stung from the sweat pouring in them, blurring my vision. All of my senses were shutting down, succumbing ... I closed my eyes peacefully with a sigh. *Abel.*

It was 9am and I had just left Abel at the coffee shop. Even though I had just seen him, my hands already longed to touch him. Would I ever get enough of this man?

At work, I was hyper and could barely sit at my desk when Mr. Gunner buzzed me into his office. I turned to Cindy, who only shrugged. I grabbed my open court files, a yellow legal pad, and off I went.

"Mr. Gunner?" I asked, knocking.

"Come in, Gia. Close the door behind you," he said in a monotone voice. Hmm, usually he was a bit friendlier than that. He wore no smile as he nodded for me to have a seat. "How long have you worked for me?" he asked, folding his hands across his desk.

I absently placed the files on his desk. "A year and eight months or so," I answered, biting my bottom lip. What was he getting at? Pensively, I sat up a little straighter. Had I done something wrong? Was I going to lose my job? Oh God, no.

"When you applied for the position at this firm, did you know who my son was?" he grilled, glaring at me. Oh my God. He knew. Somehow, he fucking knew. I needed to think quickly. I started picking my cuticles nervously and scratching my arms, which suddenly itched. It was a reflex. His tone of voice was familiar—it was the same as Medusa's. And I was allergic to Medusa. Her loveless demands caused my body to break out in hives. My breathing became labored.

"Everybody knows your son, Mr. Gunner," I retorted, a little too quickly. "He's a celebrity, the front man for Lethal Abel." He began thumping his fingers on his desk. I watched him watching me. What. In. The. Fuck.

"Did you apply for this job for the sole reason of meeting my son? Did you use this job as a stepping stone for social advancement?" He continued to thump me, mockingly. One breath in. One breath out. The room started to blur on the outer edges of my vision. I began fanning myself with one of the folders in front of me. I needed air. I needed to get the fuck out of there. However, I really needed to quell the situation.

"Is your mother's name Eva?" he asked abruptly, standing. He walked over to his credenza, pulling out his checkbook. He returned to his desk chair. Please. Please. Please. Let this not be happening. I was robbed of coherent speech. All I could muster was a few lame stammers.

"Mr. Gunner, sir. I'd like to …" I stuttered. He interrupted me mid-answer.

He flipped through the pages of his checkbook until a blank check appeared. "I'm prepared to offer you … let's call it a preemptive settlement." He signed the bottom of the check, then looked up at me.

Everything was in slow-mo: the sweat dripping down my face, my fingernails scratching my arms—even the ticking of his analog wall clock. It felt like my life was spiraling out of control; it was a vein ripped open by my boss, Abel's father, Mr. Gunner … I needed to stop the bleeding before I lost Abel in the hemorrhage. Massaging my throbbing temples, I tried to respond, but he interrupted me again.

"Before you speak, I want to tell you: I'm prepared to give you a handsome sum of money. In return, you will leave my employment and my son." He wrote the check out to cash. Wait a goddamned minute, I thought. I wasn't going to sit there and let him pay me off.

"That's not necessary, Mr. Gunner," I informed him as I rose to my feet and stuck my chin up. "What I mean to say is … I'm in love with your son. There's no amount of money you could offer me that would make me walk away from him. I do not speak to my mother anymore. She's an opportunistic social climber. I am not. I resent that you've muddled the two."

I walked over to the window, taking in the picturesque mountain view. I was on a roll. And it felt good. Damn good. Now, to hammer my point home. Fuck it. "If you feel it necessary to assume the worst about people, that's a character flaw you'll have to deal with. I do not. If my employment's terminated because of a wicked, tactless, abusive parent who wishes me nothing but harm … then I guess you have yourself a lawsuit," I said with a cold, unforgiving edge.

I needed to stand my ground or I'd continue to be stepped on by the likes of the Timothy Gunners of this world. I hadn't thought about what I was going to do about my back-stabbing mother. She'd have to be dealt with. I wanted Abel, I deserved him; I would die without him. No more would I allow my mother to put me on a guilt trip and make me feel obliged to take care of her, at my expense. I realized I owed her nothing.

And so I made my decision right there in that office. It was time to execute it, to find my courage, to live in the moment and stand up to Medusa. I had been ignoring her phone calls, texts, and warnings. I decided I would not live like that anymore. I would fight to the ends of the earth for my love.

He extended his hand. "I want to thank you for that, Ms. Mastro. And I want to apologize. Our family can never be too careful. With what has gone on with Morgana, I felt I had to do something to protect Abel. My sincerest apologies. However, I'm not sure he deserves you. He's a lucky man to have a fierce, beautiful woman in his corner. You may not have the desired pedigree, but sometimes it's not everything. Loyalty is very hard to come by."

He moved to shake my hand, and I responded in kind. My head was still spinning from this turn of events. While I couldn't make any excuses for Mr. Gunner's behavior, I wondered if Abel even knew how much his father loved him and sought to protect him. From the way he had spoken of him, I thought not. I resolved I would tell him what a protective father he had, and how thankful he should be; the alternative was having a parent like Medusa. And that wasn't so much an alternative as it was a cross no child should have to bear.

"Abel would certainly want to know how much you care," I said, picking up my files and pad. "I feel he thinks your feelings are the polar opposite. It might give him great comfort, sir."

"I have to insist this conversation remain between us, Gia. He wouldn't see it that way. I know my son. We do not see eye-to-eye on most things. Can you promise to keep this just between us? I can't afford to lose any more of him," he said, pouring a glass of water and handing it to me.

"I understand. Sometimes secrets are kept because we love the person. In the name of love, I'll agree to keep this between us. However, I do hope this is the end of your little tests."

I swallowed that much-needed water. Christ, I was parched. Placing my glass down on the bar we both agreed this was the last of his trickery. But I was still curious. "By the way, why did you think I was running a game on your son? Why would you think that? Where would you get that idea? I never gave you a reason to distrust me," I insisted, as I made my way to his door.

"Very simply: a file found its way atop my car windshield. It was a folder with all your family's personal information. Your mother's past failed marriages to men with money. Along with their detailed allegations of her intent. It clearly underlined what your intentions were. You've been to see her, leaving none too happy as per the pictures. I'm a lawyer, Gia. It didn't take much effort to put it all together," he stated flatly.

Huh? A file with my personal information? Who would have a file on me? To gain what? He moved to his briefcase, retrieving said file. Then he walked over to the shredder and shredded it. Fuck. I wanted to have a look. Maybe then I could decipher who was behind it.

I stopped, with my hand on the door knob. "Thank you, Mr. Gunner. Abel's very lucky to have you in his corner."

Then I walked out, closing the door behind me. Whew. I walked to my desk and took a few sips of my now cold coffee. But it was all I had left of him from the morning.

"So? What did douchbag want?" Cindy whispered, leaning over her desk and snapping her gum. Fuck, she chewed like a cow. What could I say? The truth? I could trust Cindy, that much I knew. But there were some things she'd be better off not knowing. And this was one of them.

"He just wanted to discuss billing the last case out. Wanted to make sure his hours matched mine." I shrugged, blowing it off. Hopefully, she'd let it go.

"I have his hours." She held up the ledger. It was a quick rebound, I had to give her that.

"Got any more gum? I need to chew. You know when you just need to chew. Well, that's what's going on right now." I shook my head. She smiled, reaching into her purse.

"I sure do," she said, snapping her gum again. "That's exactly how I felt this morning. All this fucking nervous energy. I'm all frustrated and shit. Got to chew it off." Her eyes widened in agreement. Did I know my bestie, or what?

The day went by quickly, with the summer sun turning the sky a fiery orange as it set. I didn't see Mr. Gunner for the rest of the day— which suited me just fine. Cindy was meeting Woody for dinner and drinks. She ran home to change quickly. Abel was picking me up, since he had dropped me off that morning. It was rare that I slept at my apartment anymore. We weren't officially living together, but I mostly stayed with him at his place.

I walked Cindy out to her car and waited under the canopy. I wondered what ride he'd pick me up in. Dark storm clouds rolled in, chilling the air. I stepped further back under the awning once the thunder began to boom in the distance. I loved to experience a good summer storm while indoors—not while outside in the elements. I looked at my Cartier wristwatch, checking the time. I loved and hated my watch. The watch itself was beautifully timeless. But the bearer of said gift had only given it to me so it would look like we had money. We did not have the kind of money to buy this watch outright. It had been purchased on credit—as most everything we owned had been.

The wind picked up, blowing a white paper bag past me. It swirled and tumbled across the pavement weightlessly. That bag hadn't a care in the world. It was so light, so carefree, blowing this way and that … How I envied that bag. It's funny how certain symbols make themselves known to you when you least expect it. A simple, empty, paper bag can hit the deepest, darkest corners of your soul. To spend the day floating, barely touching the ground, was a beautiful dream. I was content on daydreaming until Abel came. So much so, I didn't hear the dark-windowed town-car pull up. I pulled my messenger back in front of me, using it as a shield. The window rolled down as a dark shadow moved toward the light of day. Medusa.

"Still daydreaming, little Gia? How many times do I have to remind you that daydreams don't get you money in the bank? Don't get you into the country clubs—and they certainly don't put diamonds on your neck." She snarled at me, lighting a cigarette and blowing billows of smoke out the window. I stepped back, wide-eyed. Where was Abel? Of all times for him to be late! However, I did not want Medusa meeting him, sticking her arthritic fingers in my business where they didn't belong.

"Mother," I huffed, my chest tightening. "We had an agreement, you wouldn't come to my place of work."

Tears burned my eyes. It always came down to this between us; she reduced me to an adolescent within seconds. "Please leave. I have plans. I can't do this with you now. Please. You'll ruin everything. Is that what you want?" I whined. Maybe if I appealed to her scheming side, she'd agree to go. I'd promise her anything right now.

"Oh, now I'm Mother?" she cackled. "How dare you ask me to leave. I'll leave when I'm goddamned ready to and not a minute sooner. I'm the boss here. You have no power with me. I have the power," she said, drawing a deep drag of smoke into her lungs. Then she let it out in a huff.

I needed to get rid of her. "You're right, Mother. I'm sorry I haven't responded to your calls or texts. Can I swing by tomorrow? I'll bring your favorite wine." I'd say anything to placate her. She reeked of alcohol and was clearly inebriated.

She guffawed, taking another drag of her cigarette. "Swing by?" She flicked her cigarette at me. "You mark my words. If you don't come by tomorrow, Gia, you will be in a world of pain. I promise you that. Remember who you're dealing with. You can't bullshit a bullshitter."

And then the car rolled away. Good God. I palmed my eyeballs, trying to relieve some of the pressure, half-afraid I was going to have a heart attack or a brain aneurysm. And the way I was feeling, that was pretty much wishful thinking on my part.

A beep of a car horn had me jumping out of my skin. Abel! He pulled up in a triple black-on-black, vintage Porsche. He jumped out, grabbing my messenger bag and throwing it in the back seat, before wrapping me in a smoldering kiss.

"Umm, Beauty. I've missed you." His strong arms embraced my nervous energy, settling me right down. I could breathe again. I nestled under his chin, hugging him back. His lips found their way to his favorite spot—my collarbone. I shivered as a chill chased up my spine.

"You cold, babe? Get in; I'll turn on the heat." He opened the car door for me. I was cold without his warmth. But it was so much more than that, so much fucking more …

"It's just the dampness," I said, pointing to the sky. "The storm put a chill into me while I was waiting for you."

He frowned thoughtfully. "My bad, Beauty. I just had this car delivered from L.A. on the transporter. I shipped it for you."

"For me?" I asked, trying to decipher his meaning.

"Yes for you, my Beauty. It's my first car I bought when the band hit it big. I bought it with my own money. So it means something to me. It has more than equitable worth." He beat his chest with his fist. "It means something in here." He smiled. "It's a 1963 Porsche 356B convertible. Whatcha think?"

He beamed over at me. What did I think? It was fucking awesome and suited him perfectly. The car was immaculate. It had to cost more than I made in two or three years, at least maybe more.

"It's all you, baby. All you. This car screams sexy rock star." I laughed, looking around the interior. The car was a cream puff, worthy of its driver.

"I'm glad you approve." He reached for my hand. "I had it shipped for you. I want you to drive it," he said, kissing my hand.

"Wait. What?" I asked, thinking I had heard wrong.

"You heard right, babe. It yours." He chuckled at my stunned expression.

I screamed. "Mine? No fucking way, Abel! You can't go giving classic cars away. Who does that?" I was still confused. Was he serious or was this another test? It wouldn't have surprised me if it was, with the day I'd had.

"I can do whatever the fuck I want, Gia. Now, get in the driver's seat and drive your new car," he said, getting out and opening my door. He walked me around the front of the car, shining the emblem as we passed. His eyebrows furrowed. He was pissed. Fuck. I didn't mean to aggravate him, or to sound ungrateful. However, this was all just too much. I'd never been given anything of this magnitude—certainly not from a boyfriend. I wasn't even sure how to respond. I didn't do feelings. In fact, I couldn't remember a day in my life when I felt joyful and elated apart from Abel. The sides of my stomach and behind my ears itched, it was my anxiety's way of reminding me who owned who. I sat in the driver's seat. He adjusted the seat forward with the back rest reclined slightly, then buckled the seat belt into place. He kissed my forehead, lingering there for a few seconds. I scanned the dashboard, nothing looked familiar to me. This was not my Honda Accord. Although my car was fairly new, this car was older than the both of us, and yet somehow, today's technology paled in comparison. Thank God, I knew how to drive a manual transmission. I didn't want to seem not only ungrateful, but moronic as well.

I released the emergency break and shifted into first gear, slowly making a U-turn out of the parking lot. A silver, Mercedes sedan caught

my eye. The woman in front had binoculars. The gentleman next to her was holding a camera with a huge lens. The driver smirked. Morgana.

Chapter Fourteen

Abel

I was perplexed by Gia's reticent posture when I hugged her. Something was wrong with my girl—and it wasn't just that she was pissed because I was late picking her up. She didn't seem especially enthusiastic about the car, either. Most girls would have jumped for joy, and then gone down on their knees to show my cock their gratitude. Either way, I'd get to the bottom of it. I had my own secrets. Eventually, she'd trust me enough to tell me, or the relationship would just end. I hoped it didn't turn out the latter way. My hope was that she'd take an extended leave from her job—which I fully intended to pressure my father into approving. It was the least he could do to make up for his intrusive, unloving, and cold nature. He would always justify his behavior by saying he was doing it for the family. *Fucking yeah, right.* I had a surprise for my Beauty. We were meeting Woody and Cindy for dinner and drinks at the local bar where our band got our first break. Band Aid Showcase was a meet-and-greet location for up-and-coming bands, frequented by record reps, talent agents, and a whole lot of adoring fans.

I rested my hand on her thigh, rubbing her bare skin. Just being near her and inhaling her intoxicating scent got me hard as fuck—especially when she was turned on like she was at that moment. Her arousal filled the air. Thank God the top was down. If we were in an enclosed space. I'd have to fuck her, no doubt about it. At the light, she leaned over, placing a kiss on my cheek.

"What was that for, Beauty?" I asked, bringing her hand to my lips.

"Just because you're you." She smiled. "You make me happy." And then she beamed. It felt fucking good. It felt *right*.

"Have you given any thought to coming on tour?" I asked, wondering if it was even possible she'd say yes. I was losing my mind thinking about leaving her behind. I'd sweeten the pot any way I could to convince her.

"No. But I will say I'm seriously considering it. I really want to go. I have some savings. It's not much. But I should be okay," she elaborated. My heart rejoiced, but I also felt hurt by the fact that she thought I wouldn't take care of her. She didn't need money. She'd go as my … my what? My *girlfriend*. There, I said it. She'd go as my *girlfriend*. And my girlfriend wouldn't want for a thing.

"Make a right at the light. Then a left into the parking lot of Band Aid's Showcase," I instructed. She side-eyed me with a grin tugging on her lips. Fuck, she was beautiful.

So, I laid it on the line. "Let me be real fucking clear so this convo never comes up again. When you're with me, money is not your worry. If I've invited you on my tour, that means I'm not expecting you to pay for anything. I mean *anything*. If that makes you uncomfortable, get over it. You're not taking my balls from me. Men take care of their women. You're *my* woman," I said emphatically—although I felt like beating my chest. Yep, the fucking caveman wanted this woman over his shoulder where he could protect her and take her any time he pleased.

"Wow, we're going here? The last time I was here, I was a senior in high school. A lifetime ago. Someone's playing here you want to see?" she asked, as she parked the car and pulled the emergency brake.

"Who does the great Abel Gunner want to see in this place? Come on, really," she giggled.

"You've never Googled me?" I asked, finding that unbelievable. That's the first thing chicks always did.

"Nope, never." She continued to laugh, finding humor in the situation. I leaned over the console, tickling her sides, which made her kick at me. We both laughed.

"If you had, you'd know this is where we got our first break," I said proudly, finger-combing my hair before we went in. I climbed out, walking over to the driver's side to open her door. She took my hand, and I guided her up and out, onto her feet. She stood on her toes to reach my lips for a kiss. So many feelings were churning in the pit of my stomach, love being one of them. Her kiss was chaste, because the bouncer met us halfway to shake hands. Wally had been with the bar since it opened. He was an ex-Hell's Angel—bad, tatted, and one intimating fucker. It was nostalgic being back there. The band always came back, paying it forward to other bands. We were still a group of down-to-fucking-earth dudes. I introduced Gia to him. They said their hellos as he escorted us to the table where Cindy and Woody were seated. It was the band's official table with Lethal Abel's name engraved on a silver plated tag and our signatures signed across the top. I escorted her with my hand laid possessively across her lower back. I wanted every fucker in this place to know we were together, that she was *mine*.

Leaning down to her ear, I whispered, "Surprise, Beauty." Woody pulled me into a man-hug. It wasn't hard to miss the excitement in her smile as she embraced Cindy fiercely. I was glad we were hanging with them tonight. She'd miss Cindy on the road, so I wanted her to spend extra time with her now. Cindy had given me her blessing, so long as I promised to send her tickets and fly her out to meet us. Thank fuck. I didn't want my Beauty getting homesick. In fact, I was so concerned about it, I had told Cindy I would speak to Gia's parents, if it would help. She had emphatically stated, "absolutely not," saying her mother was a single parent and not much in the way of a mother, at that. I had disagreed at first, until she had explained a little bit about Gia's past to me. After hearing what kind of home life Gia had growing up, I wanted to protect her all the more. I decided I'd have to investigate the situation with her mother further.

"Thank you, baby," she cooed, pulling me into the booth to take her proper seat on my lap. I leaned in, sticking my nose into her hair, inhaling deeply. Umm, she smelled so fucking good

"Anything for you, Beauty," I reassured her, reaching around to take full advantage of her lips. Her tongue fought for dominance, but quickly submitted to mine. Tasting her mouth was akin to bathing in a vat of peaches and fresh cream: it was fucking delicious.

"For fuck's sake," Woody broke in. "Now that you've properly tasted her tonsils, can we order?" He climbed into the booth next to Cindy, swinging his arm around her. She giggled, leaning into him.

"Yeah, what he said," Cindy chimed in, motioning her thumb toward Woody. "Margaritas. Let's get a pitcher. You guys handle the food. We'll eat anything," she announced, looking toward Gia, who nodded in agreement. That was too easy. Those two were cool chicks.

"We don't do Margaritas. Men drink beer or liquor," I declared, nodding toward Woody, who agreed readily. There was light, Top-40 music playing in the background. The DJ was in a booth next to the stage. The owner, CJ, came over to us, pulling up a chair.

"Boys! How the hell are you? It's been a while." He shook our hands. "Glad you're here tonight. The band that's booked tonight didn't show." He grinned at us, pulling his black hair into a ponytail. Fuck. I knew what that meant—what he wanted us to do.

"So ya lookin' for us to sort ya out?" Woody guessed. Exactly. The girls clapped happily, drawing the attention of CJ. He was a pervert. I knew it was only a matter of time before the girls caught his eye. Normally, we all shared groupies. Didn't give a fuck. He was thoughtful for a moment, as a slow creepy smile dawned on his face.

"You two are pretty, sexy little things, aren't you?" He leaned over to Gia, who was still sitting on my lap.

When he moved to kiss her cheek, I blocked him. "Unless you want to lose your face, friend, I'd advise you not to put your lips on my girlfriend," I said angrily. The air was sucked out of the room, and it seemed that everything came to a complete standstill. Woody looked at me, then at Cindy. Cindy looked at Gia, then at Woody. CJ's eyebrows quirked in amusement. He sat back, lighting a cigarette.

"Is that so?" He blew the smoke out of his nose. Gia's body went stiff in my lap. I curled my arm around her belly, pulling her tight against me.

"That's so." I smirked back.

He slammed his hand on the table, shaking it. The girls jumped. I tightened my hold. Wood, CJ, and I started laughing heartily. I'd never publicly claimed anyone, ever, as my girlfriend—not even Morgana. CJ knew when I staked my claim on Gia, I was in deep with her. *Fuck.* I *was* in deep. Real fucking deep. Balls-deeps. The girls eyed us warily.

"What. In .The. Fuck. Just. Happened?" Cindy asked—which only made us laugh even harder. I whispered to Beauty that I'd tell her later in private.

Cindy simpered. "Oh, it must be a balls thing. If you don't have a pair of balls, you're not supposed to get it, huh? Well, we fucking don't." She frowned. "Drinks anytime now would be delightful." Gia agreed. CJ called the waitress over, ordering the girls a pitcher of Patrón margaritas.

"Seriously, we'll help you out tonight, CJ. Maybe sing a few songs," I said, looking to Woody to see if he was onboard with the idea.

"As long as I'm pissed, fucked, and fed, I'll agree to anything," he said as Cindy pulled his hair, bringing him to her for a kiss. His sudden shortness of breath told me she was most likely playing with his dick under the table. I smiled. Good for him. I was happy for him. He scared most girls off with his constant cursing and Irish lilt. Cindy was enough of a badass chick to balance him out nicely. We ordered dinner for the girls as they drank the pitcher of Margaritas. Then the giggling started.

"They're pissed," Wood said, smiling and pulling Cindy in for a heated kiss. He grabbed her tits, massaging them. She moaned loudly.

"Ahem. Don't mind us. Go right ahead. We'll eat and drink around you," my Beauty teased, smiling brightly. Damn, that smile would be the death of me. I could refuse her nothing when she smiled at me like that. She had a gleam in her eye that added something extra. I pushed my dick into her ass, letting her know what I was thinking. She ground back, answering me. I bit into her shoulder, eliciting a sigh. I needed her under me in the next hour before I exploded in public, embarrassing myself.

"Wood!" I called out, watching CJ move to the stage mic. He was going to introduce us. I wanted to walk to the bar for a quick shot to give my dick a chance to go down before I went onstage. He knew. He had the same fucking problem. He was readjusting himself like a madman. *Fuck, yeah.*

"Two shots of Jack. Two Heinekens please," I ordered from the young bartender. The starry-eyed kid was white as a ghost when we walked up to the bar. It made me smile. I'd been doing a lot of that lately. I could only attribute that to the way I was feeling about a certain Beauty in my life. I was this kid's age once, and because of that, I pulled out my wallet, throwing two one-hundred dollar bills down on the bar. When the kid returned, I made his night by telling him to keep the change. He asked if we'd take a selfie with him, which we were happy to do. CJ walked up, all sorts of pissed-off at the kid for fanning over us. He wanted this place to be the one place where we could hang out as regular dudes. No rock stars with a huge fan following here, just a couple of regular guys. Which suited us just fine. Since going platinum, we almost always had security around us, handling crowds and overzealous fans. For just one night, it was amazing to be able to fly under the radar. I only hoped no one uploaded a picture or video broadcasting our whereabouts. Dave would have a meltdown if he found out, because we didn't run this little outing tonight by him. Fuck it. *I'm my own man.*

Two shots were placed in front of us. "Cheers, mate," Woody said, clinking my glass. Then those two shots went down our throats, followed by beer. CJ waved us over to the stage. Gia blew a lip-glossed kiss at me, waving excitedly. Cindy was less pronounced, opting for a wink at Wood. I thanked CJ for allowing us to come back. We considered him and his place family. I adjusted the microphone to meet my height. Woody took a seat at the house drum-set, counting out his beats.

"Good fucking evening, fine people of Colorado," I said, grabbing the guitar from CJ—the one he kept on hand for my impromptu visits. "Thank you for letting me grace this great stage again. It's been way too long." I tuned the guitar. The crowd whistled and cheered. The young bartender's iPhone kept flashing.

A pixie-haired fan-girl yelled out, "You can grace my stage privately anytime, Abel." She hooted. Gia's face dropped, as Cindy pawed her to keep her in the booth. *Fuck.* Maybe this wasn't such a good idea.

"Anyway, tell me what you want to hear. As you can see, it's just me and Wood. We'll try our best to leave it all on stage." The crowd hooted and fist-pumped.

"Billy Joel's 'Strangers,' " some bald guy yelled out. The crowd pelted him with French fries and wadded-up napkins. Woody and I laughed. The guy wasn't a local. Anyone from town knew we didn't cover Joel.

"Slipknot … 'Snuff,' " some yahoo shouted. "I heard you guys in Toronto. You all were fucking amazing." The crowd clapped, agreeing with the local yahoo. Luckily, that song was mostly guitar.

"Ding, ding, ding. We got a winner. It just so happens we know that song," I replied, laughing as Wood counted out "3... 2... 1 ..." My fingers floated, plucking the chords of one of my favorite songs.

Bury all your secrets in my skin
Come away with innocence, and leave me with my sins
The air around me still feels like a cage
And love is just a camouflage for what resembles rage again
So if you love me, let me go
And run away before I know
My heart is just too dark to care
I can't destroy what isn't there

I sang my song, owning the words. Funny, I felt those words meant something to me, especially with the rocky start Beauty and I had. She was too innocent for me. I stared into her eyes. I jumped off the stage, walking over to her, my fingers pulling at the strings until I felt the pain in my fingertips. I needed to feel something real.

I don't deserve to have you
My smile was taken long ago
If I can change I hope I never know
I couldn't face a life without your light
But all of that was ripped apart when you refused to fight ...

Tears ran down her face. She was moved by the song, by my performance. Chicks loved being sang to. It was a deeply lyrical song. I didn't mean to make her cry. My heart hurt at the sight of those tears, and I didn't want to be the reason for them. I wanted to be the reason she smiled, she danced, she laughed, she came, and she loved. But these feelings were getting so intense, I suddenly felt in need of escape. My brain wasn't used to this much emotion. I craved drugs, something to bring me down, numb me, even me out. I couldn't let her see that, though. She'd think I was a loser. I wasn't a loser. I just needed help coping sometimes. Everybody needed help sometimes. I needed coke. Maybe I could text Jake?

I returned to the stage, grabbing for the fresh beers the kid had left for us. I handed Woody his. I looked to Cindy, asking with my eyes if Gia was okay. She gave me the thumbs-up sign. Great.

Then CJ started charging admission at the door, which meant the word was out we were there. He'd make a few dollars that night. And that was cool with me. He'd never taken any money we had offered him for taking a chance with us. So we owed him. We sang "Dark Horse". Well, our version of it. Cindy and Gia were the first two on the dance floor. Once they broke that seal, others followed. The place got crowded and it got harder to keep an eye on my Gia. We finished our set, signed a few autographs, and moved toward our table. CJ roped it off. He stationed bouncers around the perimeter as a precaution. I thanked him for his hospitality as always and asked him for the key to his office. He threw it to me. I turned to Woody, letting him know I'd be busy for a little while, so he wouldn't leave without us.

"Beauty," I said as I came up behind her and kissed her neck. "Come." Wally escorted us safely to CJ's office door. I gave him a few hundred to show my appreciation. I unlocked the door, looking all around for photogs before pulling her inside.

"Where are we going? What about Wood and Cin?" she asked. Was she serious? I could not give a fuck about Wood and Cin. I needed to be buried deep inside her tight pussy, or else my balls were going to explode.

"Beauty, I need you right now. I need you, like, fucking *yesterday*. I need to taste you. Then I need to pound you."

I pulled her deeper into the office, still kissing her neck. "Then I need to fuck you again." I pulled her shirt up and over her head. The bra came next. Pulling her nipple into my mouth, I sucked, swirling my tongue around her areola, licking and sucking like a man starved. And I *was* starved. I hadn't been inside her since the night before. I had myself an addiction problem with Beauty: I was beautifully addicted to her. Losing myself in her tits, I squatted down, stripping off her jeans—first one leg, then the other.

"Lean against the wall," I demanded, pushing her flat against it. I threw her leg over my shoulder, giving me prime access to her pussy. *Bella.* Fucking work of pussy art. I extended my neck, delving in face-first, then added a finger. I wouldn't be satisfied until she was screaming. I exposed her clitoral hood, getting a good suck on her clit. She screamed, pushing my face away. *What the fuck?*

"Fuck. Shit. Motherfucker. It's too sensitive. I'm gonna die if you touch it," she panted, blocking me from getting at it. I turned, eyeing the desk, then looked back at her.

"What? What's over there?" She looked in that direction, trying to peek over the desk.

"Your life preserver is over there." I pointed toward the desk. "You're going to bend the fuck over the desk and hold on like your life depends on it," I rumbled. I had already started taking off my clothes. She stood there with her jaw on the floor. So I opted to help her along. Over my shoulder she went, kicking and screaming.

"Put me down right now, you fucking-cave-dweller! What's gotten into you?" She punched my back. I righted her onto her belly on top of the desk.

"Don't fucking move," I threatened. I started opening the drawers of CJ's desk. Surely he had something I could use … Fuck, yeah. I found us some trailer ties. They would do.

"Use what?" She looked up. "Who the fuck are you talking to?" Oh shit, I hadn't realized I was talking out loud. I was in such a state, I considered myself rabid. Had to be. The smell of her pussy juice on my face was wafting into my nose, causing my cock to pulse in rhythm with my heart. *That's a first.*

I tied each of her arms to one leg of the desk. Then I wondered if she would behave. Or did I need to tie her legs, too?

"Are you going to be good, Beauty?" I asked. She turned to face me.

"Are you serious right now? What could I possibly do? Get on with it, already," she grinned. My little minx liked being tied up. *Nice.* I left her legs spread, but untied. Fisting my weeping cock, I thumbed the semen over the piercings, getting it nice and lubed. I sucked the residue off my fingers when I was done. I loved to cum. And I loved my own cum. Nothing wrong with that, as far as I was concerned.

"I'm as serious as dick cancer," I answered, preparing to take the plunge. I nudged her opening, smearing my semen and her cum around her hole, and leaned in a bit to push the tip of my head in. *Christ.* Her pussy sucked the head of my cock, swallowing it. With fast, stabbing movements, I ravaged her hole with just half my cock. Her cries permeated the air, along with her pussy scent.

"You like that, Beauty?" I growled. "You want my whole cock in you, don't you? Tell me," I gritted through my teeth.

She was fighting for breath. "Yes, I want that gorgeous, girthy fucking cock to rip me open." She didn't even get the last words out of her naughty mouth before I fell into her, going as deep as I could without losing my balls. Fuck, if I could fit those in there too, I would.

"Fuck. You … fucking … own … me," I jabbered, gripping her hips and lifting them slightly. Over and over again, I took her hard, bouncing off her ass. Animal grunts and pants filled the room. She came so hard her pussy cut the blood flow to my dick. I pumped a few more times for good measure, to make sure I gave her every last drop of my cum. I leaned over her limp body, resting a minute. I kissed the shell of her ear, sucking on her dangling earring.

"Fuck, Abel. You're crushing my lungs. I can barely breathe, babe," she gasped. I stood up, fingering my hair out of my eyes. I was a mess—a sweaty pig of a mess. I untied the ropes and helped her up to a sitting position.

"Water?" I offered.

"Please."

I grabbed a paper cup, filling it up with bottled water from the machine. It was cold, thankfully. I handed it to her. She drank it down in one shot, holding the cup to me for a refill. I gave another cupful. She drank that down, too.

"Holy fuck. I feel like I've been hit with an IED. I don't think I can walk out of here. Now that gives you reason to be a caveman. I may need the day off tomorrow, an IV drip, and pain killers. What's gotten into you?" she asked, trying to pick her clothes up off the floor. I gathered them for her and helped her dress. I had taken her so hard, I felt guilty.

I pulled her to me by the nape of her neck. "I'm so sorry, Beauty. Forgive me." I sucked her lips, offering my apologies.

She winced when I let go of her neck. "What's the matter?" I asked, concerned. I was such an asshole.

"My neck is killing me, I think from holding it up," she said, rubbing it. "I'll be fine. I just need to use the ladies room." She leaned up to kiss me. I insisted on waiting for her.

"Go back to the table. I feel bad. We left them alone so long. We're terrible friends." She pouted. "Please?" she begged. Of course, I agreed, kissing her again. We walked to the ladies room door, where I promised to give her a few minutes.

Chapter Fifteen

Gia

Thankfully, Wally made sure I had some privacy in the bathroom. I had to pee in the worst way. I limped in, squatted ever so carefully. Fuck, my pee burned. Grabbing some toilet paper, I could only dab my sore lips. They were swollen and battered. He really was a fucking caveman. Who even fucks like that? I smiled to myself, thinking about it. Imagine, this is my complaint? Life wasn't that fucking bad, or I should say, that fucking good. I sighed, standing to flush, shimmying my jeans up to button them. I heard the bathroom door fly open, hitting the wall. I zipped my pants and unlocked the door, stepping out. *Morgana.*

"What the fuck are *you* doing here?" I yelled, stepping up to her. Fuck this bitch. I wanted to kill her.

She rushed me with a knife in hand. She grabbed a fist full of my hair with one hand, and holding the knife to my throat with the other.

"You fucking skank. You smell like him," she bellowed, sniffing me. She pressed the knife harder against my throat. "You think you're gonna waltz in here, taking my place? Huh?" She tightened her grip on my hair. "I'm speaking English, bitch; answer me."

She was gritting through her teeth. Fuck. Fuck. Fuck. I closed my eyes, thinking of what I could say to get myself out of this. I didn't struggle. I submitted to her. Maybe appealing to her dominant side would soften her. But she was a sub, right? What the fuck did I know? I'd go with it.

"I didn't know he belonged to someone. Belonged to you, I mean," I whispered. "Tell me how I can make this right?" I let a tear fall. Surely, she had a compassionate side.

"Don't fucking cry to me. I know exactly who and what you are. Had myself a little chat with mommy dearest after the surveillance report came back on you." She pulled my head by my hair, bringing my face up to hers. "You and you mother are *grifters*." She shook her head in disgust. "I knew you weren't in his league, but a fucking con artist? Holy fucking shit. He's going to fall hard when he finds out. Guess who will be there to pick him up?" Then she screamed, "*Guess?*"

I cried, salty tears running into my swollen lips. My heart was breaking in two. I needed to talk to him before this fucking bitch ruined everything. I'd tell him everything. Then I'd go with him on tour. "You? You'll be there to pick him up," I sobbed breathlessly. "Please. Let me tell him. If you've ever cared for him, don't hurt him like this—please." By then, I was hysterical at the thought of losing him.

She lowered the knife, dragging the point down my neck to my collarbone, and along my breasts. She licked her lips greedily. "You have some nice tits. I'll give you that," she said, eyeing them ravenously. *What in the fuck was going on?* "You have one fucking week. That's all I'm giving you. One fucking week to come clean, walk away, and never turn back. Have I been clear enough?"

I nodded rapidly. She folded the switch blade, putting it back in her bag. I stepped over to the mirror to look at my neck, keeping my side vision on her. Fuck. There was a cut across my neck. It was superficial, but noticeable. I turned to grab some paper towels from the wall holder. Facing the mirror, I extended my neck for a closer look.

"He'll hate you. You know that, right?" I turned to her, still shaking. But she was gone. *What the fuck?* I walked to the bathroom door, opening it, looking right and left down the hallway. *Where the fuck did she go?*

Wally was catching a wrap with some girl. He turned around, asking me if everything was okay. I nodded and said I'd be right out. I shut the door behind me, leaning against it heavily. Devastated, I felt as if my heart had been pulverized. I touched my chest. My heart was still pumping. I broke out into a cold sweat. I moved to the sink, splashing water on my face, blotting my mascara under my eyes. I added some hand soap, wiping my raccoon eyes free of the residue. Digging in my jeans, I pulled out my lip gloss and applied it. I hit the hand dryer, flipping my head under it to fluff my hair. I needed to pull myself together. I needed to think, to come up with a plan. *Fuck.* I needed a drink.

I left the bathroom, thanking Wally for guarding the door. He walked me back to our table, leaving the girl he was speaking to in mid-sentence. I saw Abel pouring himself another shot of JD. As I walked through the crowd of picture takers and patrons, I couldn't help but look for Morgana. My anxiety was hemorrhaging throughout my body. I walked up to him, grabbing him by the waist and pulling him in close. He wrapped his arms around me and kissed my forehead while brushing my hair back with his beautifully tatted hand. I allowed his scent to take me to my sweet spot of security and happiness. Would I ever feel this way again? Would this be the last time we would hold each other? I realized Cindy and Woody weren't in the booth.

"Um, where are they?" I pointed to where they had been sitting.

"Actually, they left. Dave texted earlier, but I was a little busy," he smirked, kissing my nose. "He reached out to Woody. He called a meeting at the studio in an hour." He motioned for me to take a seat. I did.

"We got offered a show in Amsterdam," he explained. Yeah so? What's the problem? "It's this weekend. We'd have to leave Friday, Beauty, if we're going to make it. This is a big deal for the band. We have to jump on it. So, we're meeting at the studio to finalize the arrangements."

He gulped another shot down. I was speechless. In two days' time, he'd be gone. I put my head down on the table. I needed a breather. I couldn't take one more fucking surprise today.

"I'm hoping you'll come, Gia." He grabbed my hand, stroking the tops of my fingers. "Look at me, Beauty."

I picked up my head, the tears threatening to fall. "Come with me," he urged. "I want you by my side. I won't leave you here. Please."

He stuck out his bottom lip, giving me a pout. He kissed my hand, then pulled me out of the booth, into his lap. My mind was racing. I felt manic. Could I go? Could I just get the fuck out of the country? When we were out of the States, I could tell him everything. I'd hide nothing then. I'd bare myself to him.

"Yes. Yes, I'll go with you, Abel," I assured him, turning to hug him tightly. His scent warmed the coldest depths of my soul. "Now what?" I asked, releasing him. Looking into his eyes, I felt I could spend a lifetime there without ever getting tired of them.

He grabbed my chin with his finger, kissing me gently. "Now, I drop you off and you pack. Leave my father to me. Besides, he likes you—and he doesn't like anybody." He gave me a few pecks on my lips. I was excited. Fuck everything: my job, my mother, and especially Morgana. She wouldn't win this battle. I would.

He dropped me off, promising to text me after his meeting. I flew in the door, breathless, throwing my keys on the table. "Cin?" I yelled out, walking through the apartment.

"G, is that you? I'm in the shower. Come to the door," she shouted over the spray.

I laughed. She always asked if it was me. Who the fuck else would it be? "Hey, chick!" I opened the door partway, poking my nose in. God, the bathroom was steamed out.

"You're going, aren't you?" she asked, sticking her head out the glass door. "I can hear it in your voice." She continued washing. "I would, too, if I were you. Just saying. He's totally in love with you, girl. Anyone with a set of eyes can see that," she said, washing her hair.

"You think? I mean, I'm head over heels for him. But I'm scared," I whimpered. And that was the truth—and it was with good reason that I felt that way. "I'm kinda freaking out, Cin. What about us?" I started to get choked up. She shut the shower off, and stepped out, wrapping a towel around her.

"You're fucking joking, right? I'm not going anywhere. The apartment will still be here when you come back. And your boyfriend's flying me out to catch some shows. I did request a private flight. I won't do commercial anymore," she said, beaming.

I hugged her tightly. "There will always be a you and me, sweetie," she reassured me, patting my back. "Besides, I'm kinda dating his best friend. So either way, we will be hanging." We jumped around the bathroom like idiots. I couldn't have planned it better. Once I told him everything, it would all be behind us. I'd have the rest of forever to make it up to him.

"He really said he'd fly you out?" I asked. Boy, he was full of surprises, wasn't he? "Did you happen to see the sweet Porsche in the parking lot?" I asked, smiling. She was going to lose her shit.

She nodded. "Abel's? I figured. It fits him." She busied herself with towel-drying her hair.

"Nope. Not Abel's. Mine! As in, he gave it to me." I jumped up and down. She dropped the towel on the floor.

"Get the fuck out!" She was stunned into momentary silence. "Holy fuck, that boy's got it bad," she murmured to herself. "Don't get me wrong; you deserve everything and then some, but dayum…" She whistled low.

"He took it home to park it in his garage. If I'm going with him, there's no sense leaving it in our parking lot. Right?" I asked. She agreed. I didn't want to worry about the car on top of everything else. God forbid my mother found out; she'd look to sell it for cash.

Cin and I chit-chatted for a bit before going downstairs to the storage basement for my luggage. It wasn't great luggage, but at least it matched. Shit. I was even worried about what my luggage looked like. There was a bigger problem looming—two of them, actually: Medusa and Morgana. They sounded more like *Game of Thrones* characters then two people trying to destroy me. I really wanted to go to my mother's and tell her the fuck off. However, if those two were talking, that was a really bad idea. Hopefully, we'd get on the plane in the morning without incident. I'd hang in there until then, staying low. And then I'd pack my clothes and get the fuck out of there.

"Chinese?" I asked Cindy, who was folding my clothes suitably for packing. She insisted she was an expert packer. Whatever made her happy!

"Sounds delish," she chirped, giving me her order. I called it in. An hour later I noticed it was after midnight. And I still hadn't heard from Abel.

So I texted him: *Hey! xx*

He didn't respond for ten whole minutes, which tied my stomach in knots with worry. I couldn't relax with Morgana roaming around, and my mother cruising the town in her car.

Finally Abel replied: *Jammed up at the moment. Decided to get in a practice. I'll send a car for you in the am. The driver will bring you right to the tarmac. No more commercial flights for my girl. ;) See you 2moro, Beauty. Xx*

I was overjoyed: *OMFG!! Really? I've never flown in a private plane. The car isn't necessary. I'll ask Cin or take a cab. Xx*

Abel came right back: *Abso-fucking-lutely not! The car will be there at 9am. Be ready. Dress sexy. Gotta go. Xx*

He won. I returned to my room to help pack the rest of my hair products. One whole bag was for makeup, hair, and shoes. I had never packed a bag for more than an extended weekend. Cindy helped me gather together several really sexy-ass outfits. We fell asleep on my bed until sunup. It was a true sleepover. Sometimes you just needed your best-girlfriend. That night I had needed Cindy. I had wanted to purge my soul clean, to tell her everything—starting with my mother's obsession with wealthy men. I knew she had her suspicions. However, I was positive she'd never suspected how deep the well ran. I was determined to figure out a way to make it right. Luck had never really been on my side. But truth? Even if it was late in coming, truth would not let me down. Abel loved me. That was the truth. I knew it. I felt it in my heart. I felt it in his kisses, in the tender way he brushed my hair out of my eyes. I saw it in his smile. And especially knew it when he took me. There was something more than attraction at work between us. Much more. I would tell him the second I saw him. I would tell him how in love with him I was.

enough of a badass chick to balance him out nicely. We ordered dinner for the girls as they drank the pitcher of Margaritas. Then the giggling started.

"They're pissed," Wood said, smiling and pulling Cindy in for a heated kiss. He grabbed her tits, massaging them. She moaned loudly.

"Ahem. Don't mind us. Go right ahead. We'll eat and drink around you," my Beauty teased, smiling brightly. Damn, that smile would be the death of me. I could refuse her nothing when she smiled at me like that. She had a gleam in her eye that added something extra. I pushed my dick into her ass, letting her know what I was thinking. She ground back, answering me. I bit into her shoulder, eliciting a sigh. I needed her under me in the next hour before I exploded in public, embarrassing myself.

"Wood!" I called out, watching CJ move to the stage mic. He was going to introduce us. I wanted to walk to the bar for a quick shot to give my dick a chance to go down before I went onstage. He knew. He had the same fucking problem. He was readjusting himself like a madman. *Fuck, yeah.*

"Two shots of Jack. Two Heinekens please," I ordered from the young bartender. The starry-eyed kid was white as a ghost when we walked up to the bar. It made me smile. I'd been doing a lot of that lately. I could only attribute that to the way I was feeling about a certain Beauty in my life. I was this kid's age once, and because of that, I pulled out my wallet, throwing two one-hundred dollar bills down on the bar. When the kid returned, I made his night by telling him to keep the change. He asked if we'd take a selfie with him, which we were happy to do. CJ walked up, all sorts of pissed-off at the kid for fanning over us. He wanted this place to be the one place where we could hang out as regular dudes. No rock stars with a huge fan following here, just a couple of regular guys. Which suited us just fine. Since going platinum, we almost always had security around us, handling crowds and overzealous fans. For just one night, it was amazing to be able to fly under the radar. I only hoped no one uploaded a picture or video broadcasting our whereabouts. Dave would have a meltdown if he found out, because we didn't run this little outing tonight by him. Fuck it. *I'm my own man.*

Two shots were placed in front of us. "Cheers, mate," Woody said, clinking my glass. Then those two shots went down our throats, followed by beer. CJ waved us over to the stage. Gia blew a lip-glossed kiss at me, waving excitedly. Cindy was less pronounced, opting for a wink at Wood. I thanked CJ for allowing us to come back. We considered him and his place family. I adjusted the microphone to meet my height. Woody took a seat at the house drum-set, counting out his beats.

"Good fucking evening, fine people of Colorado," I said, grabbing the guitar from CJ—the one he kept on hand for my impromptu visits. "Thank you for letting me grace this great stage again. It's been way too long." I tuned the guitar. The crowd whistled and cheered. The young bartender's iPhone kept flashing.

A pixie-haired fan-girl yelled out, "You can grace my stage privately anytime, Abel." She hooted. Gia's face dropped, as Cindy pawed her to keep her in the booth. *Fuck.* Maybe this wasn't such a good idea.

"Anyway, tell me what you want to hear. As you can see, it's just me and Wood. We'll try our best to leave it all on stage." The crowd hooted and fist-pumped.

"Billy Joel's 'Strangers,' " some bald guy yelled out. The crowd pelted him with French fries and wadded-up napkins. Woody and I laughed. The guy wasn't a local. Anyone from town knew we didn't cover Joel.

"Slipknot … 'Snuff,' " some yahoo shouted. "I heard you guys in Toronto. You all were fucking amazing." The crowd clapped, agreeing with the local yahoo. Luckily, that song was mostly guitar.

Chapter Sixteen

Abel

I was full-on in love with Gia Mastro. Denial, my best friend who usually hitched a ride, couldn't even refute that. The moments with her took my breath away. Her very presence was a light shining brightly on my badly damaged soul. I needed to feel her warmth, her pureness, to be fulfilled.

I'd never looked to anyone for comfort. However, I looked to her for it. She calmed me. Her soul spoke to mine. My muse gave me all of herself, expecting nothing in return. This was unfamiliar to me. Someone always wanted something from me. And I felt things when I was with her. She had awakened my heart, and now it beat only for her. That's an experience I've never had. It was earth-shattering, rocking me to my core.

With my guitar resting on my knee, I was scribbling lyrics to a song asking Gia for her hand. Yes, I planned to ask her to marry me during the tour, to make her Mrs. Abel Gunner, my perfect other half, my better half. She was everything to me. Without her, I couldn't breathe. Yes, it was premature. However, my mind was made up. I knew I'd never feel like that again. I didn't want to lose it. Everything with us was emotional. As hard as I took her during sex, I never felt like I was fucking her. She owned *me*. Owned my dick. Owned my cum.

Owned my soul. I made love to her. As soon as I put that ring her finger, I'd get her under me slowly, showing her how very much she meant to me. She'd feel the difference in my slow strides. Fuck, even my heart beat differently. Yes, it still pushed blood through my veins, but now it fortified me with love, nurturing my being. Gia Mastro had brought me back to life.

Motherfucker, if this bitch didn't stop texting me, saying she needed to talk to me. Morgana always needed to talk, was always looking for an excuse to take her clothes off, to submit to me. I would never fall into that trap again.

So I let her have it: *I'm changing my number. It's fucking pathetic: you just don't stop. I will never be with you again. What aren't you getting?*

Morgana shot back: *What if I told you, you were being played out by someone close to you? True story.*

I wasn't about to fall for that one: *I'd say you're full of fucking shit and desperate.*

But the bitch persisted: *1 minute of your time = finding out who's fucking you to your face. Really, is Abel Gunner gonna get played the fuck out!*

Abel Gunner gave an inch: *10 seconds, that's all. Colorado airport, our usual gate.*

Morgana took it: *Ok.*

Fuck me! Why did I even agree to that? She was full of fucking shit as always. However, I had a weird feeling there was some truth to it. I prayed I was wrong. So help me God, if one of the boys was fucking us out of money, I'd end up in lockup before lunch.

The driver let me off, transferring my bags to the plane. The psycho walked down to the tarmac in six-inch heels with her pussy peeking out. *Fucking whore.* She opened the door, closing it behind her. I moved to the other side of the limo, not wanting to be on the same seat as her. *What the fuck was she up to?*

"Hi, babe." She reached for my knee. I moved it away.

"Speak! You're not here for any other reason," I said. I was real fucking tired of this game with her. It was getting old. "I've got a plane to catch," I said, sickened. How I had ever even fucked her was beyond me. Her beauty was eaten up by the ugliness that dwelled within her.

"Your little sub isn't who you think she is." She lowered the window.

"Get out! Get the fuck out right now, you sick bitch." I hit the intercom.

"Yell all you want. Call me names. I don't fucking care. But she's a grifter. Her and her mother. They go after wealthy men for money. Not love. Never love. Just fame and fortune."

"What the fuck are you going on about now? You can't handle it because I'm with someone else. You have to ruin it. You ruin everything. You are so fucking ugly to me right now. How in the fuck did I allow myself to get involved with you? How?" I hollered. I was done. Of course, she'd attack Gia.

"I swear to God, Abel. You can call me whatever names you want to make yourself feel better. But facts are facts. Ask her. I had a chat with her yesterday at Band Aid's. Did she tell you?" she asked. No, I had to admit; she had not told me.

"She promised to tell you within a week. Or, I told her I'd tell you. But the little bitch thought she would run off on tour with you before I could get to you." She smirked. She loved this, loved seeing me in pain.

"*Get out now! Don't you ever contact me again!*" I screamed. I was pissed, about to lose my shit. The screaming drew attention. Ender knocked on the window. I rolled it down.

"Oh, fuck," he said, walking away.

"Ender," I called out. He turned around. "Escort this piece of shit off the tarmac, please." I closed the window. Morgana frowned. *Fuck her.*

Ender hauled her away—but not before she tried to profess her undying love for me, one more time. If she were a dude, I would have killed her then and there. My stomach was sick, my brain confused. Was it true? Was it even possible? I took in as much oxygen as I could. I felt dizzy—lightheaded. I exited the limo, forcing myself upright despite my stomach cramps. I walked to the gate. I needed to talk to Gia. She'd tell me all this was just a ruse Morgana had made up to come between us. The boys boarded Lethal Abel's jet. I waited, leaning against the brick wall for her to come down the ramp. I heard the wheels of a suitcase squeaking along as it rolled. She rounded the corner and jumped.

"Fuck, you scared me!" she shouted, then relaxed into her usual, bright smile. She walked over to kiss me. I put my hand up, halting her. Her eyes widened. A frowned played with her face. She looked down to the ground.

"Tell me it's not fucking true," I boomed, walking over to her. She backed up against the wall. She closed her eyes. *Fuck me.* My heart exploded into a million tiny pieces.

"You know. I can explain. It's complicated. But once I explain it, I hope you'll understand, and you'll forgive me." She stepped forward with tears in her eyes. I closed mine, running my fingers through my hair. I didn't know what to do with them. Finally, they came to rest, balled up at my sides.

"Please." She reached out to me, grabbing my hand. I winced at her touch.

"Don't you dare fucking touch me," I huffed, backing her up into the wall.

"Please, Abel. Let me explain. Give me—" She couldn't even get the words out before my hands were on her throat, my thumb pressing on her larynx.

"Do it. Hurt me. I deserve it," she cried, sobbing, her voice barely audible. Oh, I thought about it; I wanted to choke that bitch to death. I hated her. I wanted to crush her lying throat in my hands. I moved away from her, staring into her tear-filled eyes.

And then I moved in real close, so there would be no misunderstanding. "You. Are. Dead. To. Me," I gritted through my teeth.

"No! *Please*, Abel—*please*. Oh God, please don't do this. Please. I *beg* you." The spasms rocked her body. She fell to her knees in front of me, reaching for my legs. I stepped back. I turned and walked away, boarded the plane—and never looked back.

Enormous Shout Out and Thanks to Our Last Night

This band was my lyrical voice for Abel Gunner.

With their permission, I used this band not only as a muse for Saving Abel, but for their stance on anti-bullying. You will find hyperlinks to the band's YouTube videos throughout the storyline. If you love them (as much as I do), please show your support by liking their video and or purchasing their music on ITunes.

To buy Oak Island EP on iTunes: http://full.sc/1hsXn4d

Join us and The Bully Project to help end the bullying problem. Our collaborative tee shirt is available at: http://www.teespring.com/olntbp

100% of the proceeds will go straight to The Bully Project to continue their efforts to end bullying and make this world a kinder place. Also, please watch their powerful award winning documentary called Bully, available on Netflix and on their website!

http://www.thebullyproject.com/

https://www.facebook.com/bullymovie

Acknowledgements

My biggest thanks is to my PA/PR chick LadyAmber aka Amber aka biatch. You hit the ground running with me every day. Tediously, you listen, read, reread, pimp, promo, blitz, blog, make teasers, and support me continuously support me. For that there are no words only actions. I think you know how much I appreciate and adore you. You're my shoulder to lean on, an ear, and all heart. This has allowed me to muck my way through the murky waters of fictional publishing. Thank you!

The mother of all thanks to BookChick BlogReviews. You are master Yoda. You're ridiculously talented (I'm not going to say patient...lol), lent me an ear when needed. Gave me great advice, and many laughs. Also, hands down the best teasers and trailer's known to man. I am in awe.

An enormous thanks to Elizabeth Llewellyn a talented author with editing skills of a Jedi. Email: Suicide.Ride@live.co.uk or check out her blog: http://ellewellyn.blogspot.co.uk/

A shout out to Regina Wamba at Mae I designs for my beautiful cover.

Huge hugs & kisses to Deena Rae of E-BookBuilders you're epic chic.

Heartfelt thanks to my NY AITC Chicks. You guys are there every morning, afternoon and night. We have a great support system that just works. You truly are my sisters of smut.

Video Playlist

Video1 "Dark Horse" written by Max, Martin / Gottwald, Lukasz / Perry, Katy / Walter, Henry Russell / Hudson, Sarah / Houston, Jordan

Listen to OLN's version of "Dark Horse" here: http://www.youtube.com/watch?v=cKVknRFEhpc

Video2 Clarity written by Robinson, Porter / Bair, Matthew / Zaslavski, Anton / Hafferman, Holly

Listen to OLN's version of "Clarity" here: https://www.youtube.com/watch?v=a_JgNNBX2bw

Video3 Stay written by written by Parker, Justin / Ekko, Mikky

Listen to OLN's version of "Stay" here: http://www.youtube.com/watch?v=8Aufxr0Y0-g

About Gina

She's published six novels so far. Blood Ties(PNR), Beautiful Lies, Saving Abel, Forgiving Gia, Luca, and Avenging Us(Rocker 3). When she's not writing, you can find her with friends and family. She resides in Massapequa, NY with her two beautiful boys. Reading has always been a passion and obsession of hers. You can usually find her typing furiously while shouting obscenities over her latest WIP. Her guilty pleasures are: a good laugh, being snarky, espresso, Pistachio ice-cream, alternative music, sunflower seeds, I.P.A's, Twizzlers, and above all steamy swooning angst filled novels. She's pathologically obsessed with anything to do with royals, Games of Thrones, White Queen, Vampire Diaries, Homeland, SOA, The Vikings and The Originals. If you'd like to chat, hit her up on Facebook or Twitter.

Contact Gina

Facebook: facebook.com/ginawhitneyauthor
and
facebook.com/Gmwhitney1
Blog: authorginawhitney.blogspot.com/
Twitter: @GinaMWhitney
Goodreads goodreads.com/author/show/7093718.Gina_Whitney